I0622384

Spells in Secret

Mary Catelli

Published by Wizard's Wood Press, 2020.

This is a work of fiction. Similarities to real people, places, or events are entirely coincidental.

SPELLS IN SECRET

First edition. November 18, 2020.

Copyright © 2020 Mary Catelli.

Written by Mary Catelli.

Chapter 1—Arrivals

A prefect needed to be timely, and arrive at the school early enough to settle in before meeting the returning scholars. All the more in that before the term began, both masters and scholars would use magics they would never dare while classes ran, but a prefect still had the duty to keep order.

Kenneth hefted his chest to the foot of his bed and looked out the octagonal window. This early in the spring, the tree branches had a haze of tiny yellow leaves, but he could see the maze clearly, and the scholars pouring through the gates. No time to unpack. Or to so much as look about the room.

He yanked on his granite-gray robes and hurried down the stairs. He glanced in the mirror just above the last stairway. At least he did not look so flustered as he felt, heading down the last flight.

The doors were not open. Elgiva, also in her gray robes, was delicate, golden-haired, and patient beside them. Perfectly elegant. And, he told himself firmly, as he walked down the last steps, it was his imagination that she looked smug. No one else was in the room except a gray gargoyle, of enormous dog-like nose, asleep on the side table.

"You look as dignified as the prefects when first we came through the maze," said Elgiva. He felt the heat rising in his face. "I never dreamed of being one of them one day—"

"Yeah, yeah, yeah," said the gargoyle. Kenneth blinked in surprise. It opened its mouth, but not its eyes. "Wavy brown hair, good looks, broad shoulders—all that the silliest sort of sentimental writer would gush—"

Kenneth rolled his eyes.

"You have my sympathies," said Elgiva, sounding almost curious. "It left me alone."

The gargoyle did not twitch. "Ah, glowing golden maiden! As graceful as a lily bending in the wind! Radiant as the dawn in her loveliness!"

Elgiva laughed, turned her back on the gargoyle, and walked to the door.

"I'd say insipid, colorless, savorless—"

Elgiva put her hand to the door. "Why is it supposed to be a honor when a gargoyle—*deigns* to speak with you?"

Kenneth walked over. "Because it is easier to call it an honor than to drive the nuisances out of Graytowers."

The gargoyle hooted and lifted its head. "You just don't like to face it, that your tower choses prefects for their pretty faces. If your scholars weren't so perfectly pallid and spiritless, you'd be a disaster." Its lip curled. "Every other form of wizardry is more interesting."

"Yet," said Kenneth, "there's not a single tower here that was not built with our magic, rather than their own."

He put his hand to the other door. He and Elgiva pushed them open together to the nippy air. The Opening to Spring, they called it. Though he had never seen a rite with so little ceremony before.

The Tower of Clouds had its doors open, and the Tower of Light, but no others of the great circle of towers—and those two were the closest to the gates. Not so late as to shame them, then. A breeze pulled at him.

The maze in the middle, all boxwood hedges, spread below them. From its exits, steps led up to the tower doors. The statues and the patches of dirt that would be flower gardens by summer were set here and there among the hedges, but the pool in the center held no colorful fish-enchantments.

"No new scholars, then," he said. It was, after all, the middle of the year. "At least not today."

The Tower of Fire opened, and then the Tower of Gold.

Elgiva raised her eyebrows. "What? You don't want our fair school graced with more scholars?"

The Tower of Winds opened.

"I don't want to have to give the little history lesson."

"What?" said the gargoyle. "Rattle off how it's stone magic, and the oldest tower? Truly this tower suffers for the way it attracts you goodies. Your prefects are chosen for not so much wits as looks—like your pathetic scholars—"

That was enough of that honor. Kenneth raised a hand and said a word.

The gargoyle sputtered noiselessly and glared at him.

"That's a quieting spell?" said Elgiva.

"Oh, yes," said Kenneth. "Gives things the properties of stone. Or more of them." He looked at the rough gray of the gargoyle. "The natural properties of stone, not those sometimes enchanted into stone."

"Like speech." She smiled and tilted her head to one side.

Though they tried to burst from his mouth, he had no time to detail much of its limits. He managed, "It won't last long," and then scholars ran up the stairs. Aidan, as bright-eyed with excitement as if he were an utterly new scholar and that at younger than the ordinary fourteen, instead of returning for his third term, reached them first.

"Did you see them?" The words burst out of him. "I saw them! They were just behind me!"

"There are many scholars behind you," said Kenneth.

Then a red-head came about a corner in the maze. Moments later, his companions, a boy with nut-brown hair, and a girl with black, followed. His heart seemed to freeze. He hardly needed Aidan's jutting hand and proclamation of, "Them!"

"Aidan, it's not nice to point," said Elgiva, sounding more shaken than severe.

Aidan scowled, but said, "I wonder if they will break the confounding spell."

Kenneth said, firmly, "If you so much as try, you will be expelled. It's too dangerous."

Aidan scowled the more and went in. A gargoyle's voice rose in the hall, commenting on unkempt hair. Kenneth glanced back, and said, to Elgiva, in a low voice, "It's a new gargoyle, with ears like wings. The other one seems to have actually gone to sleep."

"They have been plentiful," she said, and turned to welcome two seventh year scholars, older than both of them.

Kenneth greeted other scholars despite the new gargoyle's heckling, until the three—red-haired Jamie, nut-brown Rob, and Diamond, black haired and pale of face like her sister Pearl, though not so graceful or lovely—left the maze and trooped up the stairs.

Grimly, he thought, or perhaps imagined. They looked neither confounded nor as if they had seen Jamie's parents murdered before them, and by Jamie's own uncle, his mother's brother, at that. Confounding spell, Kenneth reminded himself. Master wizards, and many of them, must have expended their utmost to try to free the three and concluded they could only fail, for them to be here and not subjected to still more disenchantments.

He blinked. He had not thought to feel odd and uneasy at the notion of their presence here. The wizards who confounded them might be truly confident in their spell—but they might decide to make sure.

Then, he told himself stoutly, it was a good thing that the three were in the protections of the Tower of Stone; few places had better in all the land. Elgiva already smiled in her greetings, without a hint of misgiving—perhaps she felt none. He joined her.

As the three went in, he even managed to not look back, and watch them go.

"She looks more like Pearl every month," said Elgiva.

Kenneth let his breath out. "Still not close. She will need to grow taller and less gangling, to match her." To match the lovely Pearl, who had concluded her basic studies just as Diamond had begun hers, and decided to repair elsewhere, for tutoring instead of the basic course of advanced studies.

As any scholar had the right to, he reminded himself, firmly, and turned to the next scholars.

#

Perhaps prefects had their own rooms to hide their embarrassments. Kenneth lay on his bed, without having unpacked. An octagonal room of gray stone, with octagonal windows, a rag rug, his bed and chest, and a fireplace that looked like no one had lit a fire there for a century or two. But privacy for when he felt a fool.

Dinner would be soon. He sighed and stood. They were only a handful of scholars at this point, but they would see him rushing without dignity if he did not move with all due haste this time.

Outside the door, a gargoyle squatted on the table, under the mirror, its eyes closed, its ears as long as tails betraying it was not one of those that had lurked by the door. Kenneth gave it a wary glance before walking on.

"It's a liminal time, you know," said the gargoyle, its voice exactly like that of the other two. "Hard though you stone-workers find to deal with it. It means the solid spells break down faster than usual."

Elgiva appeared ahead of him. He walked on, past closed doors.

"Any of the other prefects returned?" she asked, with careful casualness.

He shook his head. "Maude told me that the older prefects don't return until the very last. They try to do that always if they do not do the Opening, but for this one—they try the hardest."

To leave us on our own, he thought dryly.

She rolled her eyes.

"At least it's before term, with fewer scholars. And there's a certain looseness to it." He thought back. Twelve scholars in all.

#

It felt odd to usher in so small a group. Still odder to walk into a hall where other scholars were as few for other towers.

"Come up, come up." Master Gregory, a teacher with salt-and-pepper hair and beard, smiled upon them. "Term has not commenced, we still stand in the liminal time when Graytowers is open—and not open. All can sit at the high table when all rules are in disorder!"

Master Bonaventure, the regal head master, bald but with a snow white beard, nodded and smiled, with more dignity. Aidan cheerfully led the way up, to where the high table itself held less than half the seats it could.

"Such shining faces," said Master Gregor. "And so many of you are new to this liminal time—more than the transition between terms—the transition from that time to the term itself. Suitable to youngsters themselves, transitioning from one time to the other."

Kenneth smiled a little as he sat, but he thought—the point of it is to grow up.

"The gargoyles are about," said a younger girl, in the misty blue of the Tower of Clouds. People looked over, and she blushed.

"Well, yes," said Master Gregor, faltering. He regained his voice and cheer. "A time of topsy-turvy and wonders—many more wondrous than the gargoyles. I have set magical gates about the schools and all sorts of place. They will appear and disappear, and the first one through each one will find out where it goes." He smiled. "Anyone with boldness and spirit can make it through one."

"All sorts of things will happen," said Rufus, from the Tower of Fire, and while he might have imagined the malice in his smile, Kenneth knew there would be malice in the acts.

Master Gregor still smiled on him. "All sorts of things get turned about!" He raised his hands in the air.

Kenneth reached for his wand almost before he recognized the spell. Unleashing pixy lights and animating dishes could keep them from eating for hours. But no sooner had Master Gregor made his first gesture than he stiffened as the gargoyle had.

"For instance," said Kenneth gravely, "the scholars enchant masters."

Laughter burst out, from childish giggles to the laughter of the full grown scholars. Even Master Bonaventure smiled. Master Gregor's face worked as he lowered his arms, but he managed to nod to Kenneth, as if graciously acknowledging his spellcraft.

"Ha," said a stony, flat voice from the doorway. "Ha. Ha. Ha."

It quelled the laughter, and drew every gaze toward the frog-like gargoyle perched on the doorframe, looking in.

"Ha. Ha. Ha."

The soup tureens started their path down the table, and Kenneth reached to ladle out his. At least the noise helped muffle the gargoyle's laugh.

#

The twilight was bright enough to see the way back from the hall.

"They shouldn't have let them back," said a querulous young voice ahead—a dark and unidentifiable shape.

Kenneth walked more swiftly and hoped the scholar was not up to trouble.

Someone mumbled something unclear, and the voice went on.

"Even if they weren't witched. Didn't you hear? David Servant went and killed Jack and Rosa Howell, and she was his own sister!—and that friend of theirs, Piers Lawrence, too. Who's to say he won't come after Jamie? Or even Rob or Diamond?"

Kenneth ran. The speakers fled like startled sparrows. He got only enough of a glimpse to guess, by their height, that they were old enough to know better, and to know that some of their robes were the flaming red of the Tower of Fire, and others were either smoke or shadow gray, of the Tower of Shadows, or the Tower of Doors, or perhaps the Tower of Winds.

He let out his breath. Not that any of those three towers were above making trouble for the Tower of Stone.

#

It was midnight, the moon near zenith and bone white, and he was not sleepy.

Kenneth walked down still corridors and stairs of the tower, careful to keep quiet. Even the gargoyles slept, it seemed. Finally, he walked out the door, and turned left.

The garden had patches of snow still hiding like little ghosts in odd corners. He hurried through the chill air and up the stairs into the halls.

The automaton was silent, of course. There was no sign of it until he walked through an arched doorway onto a balcony, and could look down at the Celestial Clock.

Metal and enamel, it spread beneath, filling the room. The golden sun could not be seen, but the silvery moon could, and the stars and planets glowed as they inched onward by their clockwork. Beneath them, the year's enamelwork spread. Tiny peasants industriously trimmed the tiny enamel grapevines, still brown and lifeless with early spring.

A resonant voice came over the balcony. "Unusual to find you here, Kenneth. Already invoking your prerogatives?"

Master Bonaventure himself—he emerged from another doorway, nodding.

"Things are topsy-turvy," Kenneth said as gravely as he could.

Master Bonaventure's mouth twitched.

"Odder than usual. The gargoyles never seemed this lively before to me, but I never before came this early before term." Kenneth glanced down. "Is that cyclic? How they act?"

"Who could tell? I know they have been here all the time you have, but they came after my years as a scholar, and before I became a teacher. They were inflicted on us by one Carrigiana about thirty years ago. So a long cycle, if so. They are indeed lively, but they commonly are as the term opens. No one has tracked them, to know."

"Oh." After a minute, Kenneth said, "The three—Jamie, Rob, Diamond—they seem clear-headed for being under a confounding spell."

Master Bonaventure looked grave. "Remember that the House of Justice rules in such matters."

Kenneth opened his mouth and shut it again. Asking Master Bonaventure to elaborate would only make him look childish.

The stars inched onward below them.

"I spoke with Master Gregor." Master Bonaventure smiled benignly. "The doors he cast will only lead to other places within Graytowers. He seemed quite indignant that I ensured it."

#

In the moonlight, returning, he saw no strange door, but heard the giggle before he saw the scholars. It was enough to alert him, and let him pick out the shadows that were out of place, and not misshapen enough to be gargoyles.

He drew his wand and softly cast a spell. A moment later, the whispers sounded in his ear: is he sure to come this way? he has to come back—this is the way.

Kenneth wavered for a moment. He could not recognize the pranksters, they might be from the Tower of Doors—but other scholars could learn such path-finding spells—but he could still them as he had Master Gregor.

He frowned. Then, they had seen him cast that spell. They might have already laid a trap, and since they had not seen him coming—he smiled—he could baffle them utterly.

It did not take him long to circle about. Still less to listen, and be sure they still waited, and complained of the cold.

#

It was not until he returned to his bed that Kenneth remembered that Jamie, Rob, and Diamond had all, in their confounded state, accused Piers Lawrence of murdering Jamie's parents.

He lay on his back a minute, contemplating whether it had been wise to let them return to Graytowers, before he sighed, told himself that no one would listen to the judgment of a scholar not even of age yet, and turned his face to the pillows.

Chapter 2—Discoveries

As the scholars gathered for breakfast, most of them yawning in the gray morning, Kenneth said, briskly, "Today, we are starting lessons."

The young scholars groaned, and the older ones scowled. Even Elgiva eyed him sideways.

"And the lessons are in, how to make a prankster look like a fool by evading his spells, or stopping them altogether."

Sudden interest stirred in the faces turned toward him. Jamie, Rob, and Diamond looked avid enough to disconcert him. Perhaps he ought to remind them—or have Elgiva remind them—that launching such spells when your memory was confounded might prove imprudent, or perilous. They would be judged as if they had listened to the warnings about what they thought they knew.

But that was no reason to let them fall victim to pranks.

Aidan looked bright-eyed. "Are you going to teach us how to turn people to stone, like you did Master Gregor?"

"No. That is an advanced spell and can go wrong. Badly."

"The simplest is a binding spell," said Elgiva. "It's even a variant of one most of you know already, to conjure ribbons at a festivity, and so we should be able to teach you it within in an hour."

"Those fall apart," said Sally.

"Not before you get away," said Elgiva. "Because when dealing with a prankster, presence of mind is good, but absence of body is better."

When the laughter died away, Kenneth said, "After you master that, I'll teach you a wind-raising spell. In case they decide that a rainstorm is a suitable prank."

"It could blow away some other things, too," said Diamond gravely.

"Breakfast first," said Elgiva. "It will help you concentrate."

\#

All being in the Tower of Stone, they soon were all hard at their work. Even if Aidan laughed uproariously at the lime green ribbons he bound up Olivia in—not well, because she burst out and bound him up in dainty pastels, ten times as many.

"You see," said Kenneth, as the other scholars smirked, "you have to do it well enough to make your escape."

But some did, and so he started to teach them the wind-raising spell while Elgiva instructed the others.

Minutes later—"The stick-in-the-muds of the Tower of Stone," said a gargoyle voice by the door. "Already studying when school has not started."

Kenneth did not turn to look at it. Some scholars stared, some glanced over, some, like him, did not look, and all of them returned to the practice.

When he, moving about to check their work, saw the door, the gargoyle had left.

"O look!" called Nina. Kenneth glanced over. A doorway, faintly silver, with an arched top, hung against the wall. It showed not a hint of what stood behind. Nina ran full speed into it, and it vanished. So did she.

All the scholars gawked. Elgiva and Kenneth glanced at each other.

"Enough practice for the day," said Kenneth. "You'll get tired and make mistakes. And you might have the chance to find a door of your own."

Elgiva smiled and did not say that they had to find Nina. When, finally, the others had left, she said, her voice low, "Master Bonaventure told me she had to be within the grounds."

Kenneth nodded.

"Yes!" came a shriek outside. Nina bounded down the stairs, babbling about how she had gone to the Celestial Clock.

Elgiva sighed.

"Have you arrived early at the towers before?" he said, his voice low.

She nodded.

"Is it always this—topsy-turvy?"

She considered for a moment, but declared, however delicately, "No."

His mouth tightened into a line. "I'd be glad, for what it promises for future term, but—if it's odd, we can not know it will end when term begins."

She winced. "That should be the sphere of the headmaster, and the masters. Prefects do much, but not that."

#

They pushed open the tower door again. "A light day," said Elgiva, looking across the maze at the tiny clump of scholars.

"But a new scholar in there," said Kenneth, looking at the pool. A fish swam about.

One scholar ran down the maze and bent over the pool. The fish swam into his hands. He picked it up, and ran down the path to the Tower of Clouds, where the maze would always deliver him henceforth.

Elgiva shook her head. "I wonder who came up with the notion of sorting by fish."

"Perhaps it's in the library," said Kenneth. "To be looked up when term settles down."

A silvery door popped up by the Tower of Clouds, and the scholar stopped running to stare.

"And not a moment earlier," Kenneth muttered.

#

A young man, in the pale gray of the Tower of Winds, walked
through the garden. His fellows from that tower ran to meet him,
and he talked of how he had ended up in the conservatory.

"Mistress Susan was furious! You'd think I smashed all the flower
pots! And some gargoyle came out and jeered at her, and you'd think
I had carried it in, from the way she carried on!"

Kenneth shook his head and walked on. All the day was marked
with pranks and doors. He had heard of dozens before they gathered
for dinner, going to the high table for the last time. With the students this day had added, the table was filled to bursting. The air
burst with tales—indignant, of being caught in animated briars and
scratched to pieces; cheerful, of a prankster whose dye had blown
back into her face on an enchanted breeze and turned her an ugly
shade of purple; ludicrous, claiming to have seen gargoyles waltzing
in a garden where they would have left footprints were it true; and
wondering, at how a gate from the dining had led to the heart of the
maze, right by the pool, or from the top of the balcony to the bottom, and how two doors, even opening in the same places, seldom
went to the same place, but two far distant ones might.

Diamond conceded that she had gone from the main room of
the Tower of the Stone to the conservatory. "And there were frost and
fire lilies—blooming *now*—so herbology is going to study the virtues
of forced flowers."

"Like you ever have to study anything," muttered Rufus.

Then a girl from the Tower of Clouds leapt up and ran across
the floor. Kenneth only had time to notice the glowing door before
she threw herself into it. Half a dozen more appeared, and dinner
dissolved into squeals and disappearances, some of two students at
once, by dint of joining hands, or linking arms, or just walking with
great care side by side.

Many scholars still at table were scornful, and revealed they had already gone through one or another. Elgiva, mildly, said that it was likely they were watching the moon rise in beauty, it was quite lovely from the Blue Hall's balcony.

"Did you?"

She nodded. "Interesting to get back from there—but I went back, on foot, to watch the sunrise."

The doors ceased after a minute, but a gargoyle, almost spherical in shape, ambled in and started to heckle the children, saying they would turn as fat as pigs, or as thin as rails, sparing no one and apparently paying little heed to how much each scholar actually ate.

Kenneth sighed, and rose to more easily silence it.

"Such a killjoy you are," called a scholar. "Imposing the law and order of term already. What prigs the Tower of Stone has."

Kenneth suppressed the urge to silence her as well.

#

The gray afternoon, threatening rain, had Kenneth hurrying back from the library. Elgiva awaited him by the tower's doorway. She nodded toward the inside, still darker than the afternoon.

"I think we should both handle this."

He picked out the knot of scholars before a door, on the fourth floor. He knew which door it was. He nodded, and they marched up the stairs together. Some of the weaker souls saw them coming and scurried off. Kenneth only noted their faces and looked at the rest. Some looked frightened, without leaving, but others were so intent on the door they did not realize that Kenneth and Elgiva had arrived until Kenneth said, crisply, "What is the meaning of this?"

One student—Martine, older than them both—whirled on them to demand, "How can they allow this?"

Kenneth raised an eyebrow.

Martine drew herself up to her full height. "I'm astounded that you're so ignorant. About those three."

Kenneth's voice was clipped. "Of what? That between last term and now, his parents and a friend of the family were murdered by his uncle? And? What is the problem?"

"He left those three," said the ferret-like Walter.

"For shame!" said Elgiva. "To not be glad that they live!"

"He just couldn't take all that deathly magic at once!" said Martine. "What happens when he comes after them here? We're all in the danger!"

Kenneth sighed, loudly. "Don't be such a fool. If he's so intent on *them*, why would *you* be in danger?"

"They wouldn't be enough!" said Martine.

"I see," said Elgiva, "that you need to attend a session with Master Vincent about the spellcraft on this school. All of you!" She looked about. "If he needs the power that badly, he would hardly waste it on getting in!"

"If he wanted them dead—"

"So!" Kenneth took a step forward. "He couldn't kill them before because it would take too much magic, but now he will have some need to use superfluous magic, and that *after* breaking through the spells of Graytowers to get in."

He swept them all with a glance. They still looked begrudging.

"You should study and not gossip. Even those of you who are first years have been here for two terms, and you should have learned better in your first. As for you older ones—"

Some looked down, or away, to avoid his gaze, but he knew he had not stopped the rumors. He let his breath out. To think he had looked forward to having leave to read more books from the library, between his advancing studies and his post as prefect. It was hardly worth looking the books up if he had to do this instead of study.

#

Scholars increased over the next days. So did the doors.

When Kenneth walked down the stairs from the tower, three days later—with a sunny sky but a breeze making it chilly—one appeared ahead, on the retaining wall. Behind the wall, a circle of scholars, led by Rufus, surrounded Rob. For a moment, he wondered where Jamie and Diamond were, but Rufus's sneering tone, if not his words, came clear. Kenneth walked past the door.

"You ought to tell the truth," said Rufus, full of mock sanctimony. "Be rid of so wicked a friend."

Rob's gaze flickered about, seeking escape.

Rufus's lip curled. "You're good at stories. You should be ashamed of yourself."

"Betcha," said one boy, small for his age, rat-faced, "that he knows that Jamie *did* it." At the sidelong glances, he quickly added, "Helped David Servant."

Then one boy's eyes widened, looking at Kenneth. They fled like dried leaves before a wintry blast. He stopped next to Rob. Their towers' prefects would not think this worth punishment.

He sighed. "Let me know if they give you more trouble."

Rob nodded to him, and hurried off.

Kenneth turned back. The door had, of course, vanished to someone more prompt than he was.

It would only lead somewhere else in the towers, he told himself. For all he knew, somewhere he would only want to leave at once.

The breeze blew by him, with a few of last autumn's leaves, bleached as white as snow over the winter.

#

When they gathered for dinner—having returned the high table to the teachers and each tower to its own, lower table—Aidan boasted of having gone through two doors.

"Where did the second one take you?" said Petra.

"Uh, the library."

Jeers followed.

Elgiva said mildly, "You will all return to the library soon enough for your studies."

#

Moonlight shone through the library windows, with the little lamps adding light here and there. Kenneth walked among the stacks. Then he stopped and blinked at the sight of Jamie. Studies would start the day after tomorrow, the other prefects had started to arrive, but he would not have taken Jamie as one to start early. Diamond, of course, would, but—

Confounding, he thought.

He walked closer. To his relief, the boy's book was one about transformations.

"Hullo, Jamie. What brings you here?"

Jamie blinked. "Not one of the doors. I haven't been through one." He sighed and slipped the book into one of the carts, where the librarians would reshelf it.

Kenneth made a mental note to remember Jamie in case of mysterious transformations, but he could hardly rebuke him for studying. "Neither have I," he said.

Jamie blinked. "They said you walked by one like you didn't care."

Kenneth let his breath out and spread his hands. "A prefect's duty is never done. Came here for prefect spells. How else can we track down you malefactors and bring you to book?"

Jamie laughed, merrily. Not, thought Kenneth, realizing it was the simple truth. Then he blinked.

A door appeared behind Jamie. Glowing. It could be seen far more clearly here than all the other, brightly lit places of before, though still nothing could be seen through it.

"Perhaps a door came to bear one of us back to the Tower."

Jamie gave him a curious glance before looking back. He took a step forward, and stopped. "It must have come for you. Besides, you're a prefect. If they whisper about you that you're too much of a coward to take a door—"

Kenneth snorted. "You know as well as I do that the doors can take two." He walked up. Faint iridescence ran through the light. "Unless you don't want to—are your studies here done for tonight?"

Jamie shook his head and came up beside him.

"On the count of three then—one, two, three—"

They both stepped forward at once.

Darkness engulfed them.

Silence, as well, and both were absolute. Not so much as a hint of starlight or a whisper of breeze. Damp cold air smelled of stone. For a moment, Kenneth stood still. He could not imagine where in Graytowers they were. Others had gone through the doors by twos; the spell could not have broken from the strain.

He reached for his wand. A luminous spell showed Jamie's face so pale that the freckles were vivid against it. He suspected he looked rather ghostly himself.

Ahead of them stood a corridor of dark stone, turning after a few strides. Behind was only a wall of the same stone. Great hewn blocks of dark stone, unpolished, drinking down the light. They rose up so high that the ceiling was unseen, even with his light.

His frantic thoughts could not persuade him that it was any section of the school allowed to scholars—he had been in them all, over the years—and a forbidden section would be just as bad. He swallowed. The doors had never carried anyone past the bounds of Graytowers before, but he knew enough of the stonework that had built it to know that these stones could not be found in any part of the school.

"This is not Graytowers," said Jamie, his voice even.

"Yes," said Kenneth. "The spell might have broken down. This close to the ending—Master Gregor did say it turned on liminal time."

Jamie looked fierce. "Or it might be malice." He met Kenneth's gaze. "Master Gregor is a sound wizard, and Master Bonaventure would not let him cast, even before term, a spell that might—*break* like that."

Kenneth grimaced. How true. This might even have something to do with his parents' death, and vindicate the fearful students. Still—that was not his first consideration.

"Whether it is or is not—wands out. Mere pranksters could be dangerous, since they tend to be fools."

"Not enough." Jamie's expression looked wolfish. "Wands out, and spells first, as soon as we see anyone. Questions come after."

Kenneth hesitated.

"Isn't that what you taught us those spells for? So we could use them to protect ourselves?"

"First we try to find out where we are."

"Waste of time and magic." Jamie turned his head to look down the corridor. The light cast stark shadows across his face. "And too dangerous."

"More dangerous than stumbling around? In an unknown place, with a light to betray us? When we might have been sent here in malice, and bewitched so we can not find our way out?" Kenneth drew in his breath. He might manage to alleviate that, but— "It could be a storehouse for some evil, set with traps."

Jamie's eyes narrowed, and his mouth set in sullen lines.

"The only way we would not need to find out is if I was right with my first thought—it's just a mistake of the spell. Then we should be wary of cursing the hapless folk we meet. If you think that it was malice—" Kenneth hesitated. If Jamie knew more about his parents' murders than he told, it might matter here. He plowed on. "—wisest to learn where we are."

Jamie looked at the flagstones.

"Cast the luminous spell," said Kenneth. "I need to cast a different one."

Jamie's eyes closed. Kenneth tried to rally more words for his argument, but Jamie started to cast. A moment later, blinking, Kenneth quenched his own, and delicately cast a locating spell. A small one.

The moment the last word finished, his hand stung. He gasped and barely managed to hold onto the wand.

"So, it *is* bewitched against that." He shook his hand. "I suppose anyone would want that on a labyrinth."

Jamie laughed, shortly.

"Other bewitchments we shall have to find by hand. Quench your spell."

Jamie raised an eyebrow and did. In the darkness, Kenneth cast his again. Then he spread it out through the air, like a mist. It was dimmer, but though the ceiling was still invisible, they could see farther.

"It makes it harder to see us at a glance," said Jamie.

"That, too," said Kenneth. "But it's mostly for us to see farther."

They inched forward.

About the corner, a corridor ran ahead for a stride or two, and turned again, doubling back on the old one. The turn at the end was only a little farther along.

Kenneth sighed. "If we come to a choice, we take the rightmost one. It does not always work, if there are loops, but it is better than rambling at random."

They walked. Ahead, something glowed red. Jamie looked a little less pale, and Kenneth hoped it was not only the glow.

Another turn showed a window of stained glass, glowing as if lit by full sunlight. It depicted a burning house—a vast brown house, set with porches and windows of every shape, and towers and balconies as well, and elaborate gingerbread adorning all with leaves and curlicues. Flames leapt from more than half of it—unchanging, steady without a flicker, but so fierce they looked ready to consume the house within minutes.

Low before it, small in proportion, leaden dark, stood figures in robes. Hoods hid their faces—as if they could see faces clearly in so small a scale.

The corridor stretched away to the right, and other windows could be seen down it.

Kenneth drew a deep breath. "First we see if this window opens."

"I don't see any opening," said Jamie. "And how long should we waste?"

"A minute or two will do us no harm," said Kenneth.

"The light—it might be dangerous."

How full of caution Jamie had turned. "And not looking might be dangerous. It doesn't matter if the labyrinth is impenetrable, we probably want to avoid the center anyway. It does matter if it's inextricable. When I was a first year, Master Oliver used the labyrinth as an example of a signature. They may never find us if we do not extricate ourselves."

Jamie stared at his wand, without so much as a glance up, but his shoulders were set.

"Unless you have reasons to offer why trying this window would be particularly dangerous."

Jamie did not move. Kenneth rolled his eyes.

"Do you recognize the house?" A house that extravagant would be known in its neighborhood. If it was real—

Jamie looked up, defiant. "Those figures there—they killed my parents."

A thousand words fought for his throat—that Jamie had been confounded, that the getup was the natural one for any criminal—but he swallowed them.

"All the more reason to look for a way out." He checked the seams. His breath hissed out. There was not lead between the panes. The panes were set in solid stone, and—they were stone themselves. He stared for a moment without seeing. If he remembered his lesson right, they were not even colored by mundane skill or magic.

"This is the Labyrinth of Thought." He turned back to Jamie. "This window doesn't even have to represent a real fire, only what someone thought of."

If he remembered the class well enough, it was impossible that it had taken the figures and nothing more from Jamie's memory. Someone else had thought of the whole scene. He wished that the class had taught him how long these images could last after the one who thought them left the labyrinth.

At least, the class had taught that trying to break out that way was futile.

"Come."

He set a brisk pace. Jamie made no objections, did not even try to study the passing windows. Kenneth supposed he noted them: a scholar in his study with an orrery and a falcon perched on it; a circle flaming with bone-white and poison-green flames; a philosophical mechanica as intricate as the Celestial Clock but only half-built; one man carrying another, who bled dark crimson blood, through a stony doorway, where both sides were outdoors but not the same place.

Jamie faltered at that scene and its gate: flowery meadow beneath a blazing sun and the barren rock with drifting snow.

"It won't be possible to pry that one open, either," said Kenneth. Jamie flushed.

"It might not have happened," said Kenneth.

"It probably did," said Jamie. "Memories are better than pure imagination." But he walked on.

Soon, between accumulating weariness and lack of any explanation, it would have taken unearthly curiosity to study the windows. They trudged on, and they could not even have counted how many showed mechanica being assembled, or theft of rare and precious ingredients from the storerooms of wizards, or hooded figures about some rituals, which made Jamie pale again, but not speak.

Some scholars in the history class had claimed that the only way out of the Labyrinth of Thought was as magical as going in. Kenneth tried to ignore the thought, and told himself that they might happen on a window that would show them how to escape.

A window showed the hooded figures smashing coffins and hauling out the corpses of small children. Kenneth looked away and hoped that, however improbable it was, that was a thought and not a memory. Then he ran a hand through his hair and wished he had some kind of timepiece. Even if the labyrinth had twisted time as well as their path, it might have given him some notion of how long their journey lasted. The windows they passed appeared too irregularly in the twistings and turnings of the corridor to form any real standard. It had to be hours, for him to grow this tired, he thought.

He waked on. And then, after many more windows—hundreds?—he oddly enough felt less tired.

Jamie said, abruptly, "The Labyrinth of Thought takes the thoughts of those in it."

"Yes."

"None of ours, yet." He raised his head and looked about. "There must be a lot of people about."

"Or one with a lot on his mind. And little of it pleasant. Curse first and question second."

Jamie smiled a little.

"Nothing too dangerous. There are people whose duty it is to think about these things. And we do have questions."

They had not taken ten steps after that when a voice wound down the way toward them, more sweet than honey, more melodious than birdsong, calling, calling.

"Come, come, come, my little one—"

Kenneth shook his head. How the honeyed words drew. Jamie took a step forward, faltered, and stepped again.

"—come my boy, come my sweet child—"

Kenneth lifted his wand and cast his quieting spell. Silence fell, and he gasped for breath. Some corner of his mind dryly noted that he had been able to move when the voice spoke of one boy alone. He thought if it called for two, they both would have walked, charmed and dazed, into the trap. And they had been lucky that a spell he had learned to quell pranksters had been strong enough to face this menace.

Jamie was white as bone again. Prudent boy.

He could hear his own gasps. The quieting spell had been cast off by their enemy.

They couldn't speak anyway. He nodded to Jamie, raising his wand. Jamie nodded grimly, and they crept forward. Their footfalls made soft noises, and he could only wonder that the song had not returned, to try again.

The voice came, clear, light, free of bewitchments. "Such a prudent boy. I feared you would panic. I see I misjudged you, and should merely have spoken. Forgive me."

Footsteps came toward them, and they needed no words to stop together.

Kenneth stared down the corridor, awaiting the moment when their foe would appear. In his softest voice, he said, "Know that voice?"

Jamie shook his head.

"Best to catch, and question," said Kenneth. He cast the quieting spell again, but only on their feet. They padded silently forward.

A window stood about the corner. It showed a moonlit scene, where someone dug up some root by a crescent moon, and shed little light on the stones.

The corridor turned again. Ahead stood cloaked figures, as in the window, their hoods leaving them faceless.

Breath hissed out. "Two? Should have got the younger, only—get rid—"

They shouted spells together. Kenneth shouted the stoning spell, following with entangling and confounding, and only after clearly realized that Jamie had cast as well. He could not even guess at the spells, down to how many Jamie had cast. He had heard a bit, but enough, of what was cast at them. Or, rather, at him.

In the silence after, with the two they faced as still as statues, they did not move for a moment. Kenneth lowered his wand and hoped that Jamie did not realize what the two had intended.

Abruptly, Jamie lunged, casting spells of weakening and blinding.

Kenneth grabbed his arm. "That's enough." And he had been wrong to think Jamie pale before. "The spells you can cast like that are not enough to bind them long. The spells against pranksters are better because they can."

Jamie breathed hard for a moment and whirled on Kenneth. "They tried to kill you, didn't they?"

So. Jamie had heard the spell. "Yes." He shivered, and then shivered again. To actually hear the words—

"Let's see who it is," said Jamie, fiercely, and ran forward.

Kenneth cast a luminous spell and brightened it. They would just have to risk there being more foes than those they had brought down. The two before them, at least, were unmoving and sprawled on the floor.

"Look!" Jamie, triumphant, lifting the head of one. "Look with *care*. Like it was one of Master Oliver's tests on signatures. You'll need to testify."

Kenneth scowled at this strangeness. The confounding spell could produce odd results. He came to look. A commonplace face, looking a bit like a weasel's. He would need even more attention to detail than Master Oliver's tests demanded to remember him among many others.

"That's Piers Lawrence. That's the man they said that my uncle murdered. That's the man who made my parents vanish and probably murdered them—and cursed my uncle and put a confounding spell on me and Diamond and Rob." He hesitated. "He had some help."

Kenneth let his breath out slowly. "And the woman with him?"

Jamie shook his head. After a moment, he added, "She wasn't one of them. With him. They wore the hoods, but they were not careful about the faces."

The way the light shone cast odd shadows across his face. Kenneth could not read his expression.

Still, their path was clear. "The first thing is to get out of here. Or we will testify to nothing. It is best if we can take our prisoners, but escape is first. But—" Kenneth looked over them. "They were waiting for you. They came under their own power, and they expected to leave the same way. Quite possibly a charm of some kind."

Jamie nodded and turned to Piers. Kenneth went to the woman and pushed back her hood. A chain lay about her throat, and a moment pulling it off revealed a labyrinth charm hanging on it. He smiled.

"They had no wish to be trapped here."

Jamie looked at it with a dreadful hope in his eyes. "Can we use it to escape?"

"It's the simplest of charms, once it's made properly. *And*—it will take us back where we came from. The prisoners—" His thoughts ran for a moment. "I'll need both hands. But if we push the two of them close enough together, you can grab them both with one hand. And put the other hand on my shoulder." He paused. "I'll have to kneel."

It was an awkward pose even so, with Jamie trying to keep both their hands linked in his, and his other hand heavier than was needed on his shoulder. Kenneth tried to ignore it as he studied the charm to be sure of it, and then traced the pattern with his finger.

And the floor was not the same. He blinked. It had been easier than walking through the door—

Cautiously, he looked up. The windows still showed a dark sky outside. Robed figures stood in the library, dimly lit by stray light—and wearing no hoods. One stared at them.

Another, mid-grumble, still complained that they had done everything they could, it was clear that the boys were not in the library, for all they knew the spell had falsely reported their vanishing—

Jamie leapt up. "Master Bonaventure! Master Bonaventure! Come *quick*! You have to see so you can swear to it!"

Chapter 3—Departure

The first glimmerings of day showed outside, just starting to dissolve the stars, when Master Bonaventure led the two of them down a corridor and up a stair. Kenneth felt less tired and more dazed and hoarse from having to tell his story twenty-one times.

At least, they were not still testing if he and Jamie could be induced to contradict each other, not if they let them back together.

At an old-fashioned door, carved with roses, made of oak and bound with iron, Master Bonaventure paused.

"If you must sleep, sleep. But, odd though it may seem, you will be better off if you stay awake the day and only go to sleep at your bedtime."

He pulled open the door. A spare room stood behind, with beds and chairs and three arched windows showing the darkest twilight. Candles were set in lanterns, but not lit. Master Bonaventure ushered them in.

"They told me that Mistress Rosemary saw you?" he said.

Kenneth nodded.

Jamie said, "She had us drink this thing of honey and herbs."

"Medicine," said Master Bonaventure. "You will have fewer nightmares from this that way." He looked about the room. "You will be as safe here as magic can make you in the towers. And you can clap on the lights as usual—once the door is shut." He hesitated again. "You will have some company soon, that will put out the lights, and you will need the door shut to light them again."

Kenneth nodded. The towers had many enchantments with stranger needs.

Master Bonaventure sighed, and left. The door shut silently, and plunged the room into colorless gloom. Jamie caught Kenneth's arm.

"Don't. Please. I want to look outside, and the light would blind me."

The twilight would do a fair hand at blinding him, too, thought Kenneth, but did not clap.

But as, in the darkness, Jamie walked over to the window, he said, "You do realize that Piers being alive does not mean the rest of your memories are right. They did, after all, trace deadly magic on your uncle."

Jamie glanced back, his eyes a brief glint in the gloom, and his voice was warm with pleasure. "Oh no. It's not his being alive that does that."

The door opened, but Jamie went on, "It's that they took the confounding spell off. While they were questioning us."

Kenneth blinked.

"And us, too," said Rob, his voice vivid with excitement. He pulled the door shut behind himself and Diamond.

"You know how confounding spells work," said Diamond, calmly as if answering a question in class. "They can't break it unless they know, by and large, what the true memories would be."

Rob turned toward Jamie. "How *did* you persuade them?"

"Piers is alive," said Jamie. "And prisoner."

In shocked silence, Rob and Diamond stared at him, despite the gloom. Then Diamond shifted her eyes toward Kenneth, as if it had just dawned on her that he would be there for a reason.

"First, is this room really safe?" said Jamie. "I would have said the library was, but Kenneth and I were abducted from there. And they tried to kill Kenneth."

Diamond gasped. Kenneth wondered what their faces looked like, but he kept his voice measured.

"With the door shut, yes—you saw the roses. The guarding spell that quenches the light is powerful."

"But the windows are open," said Jamie.

"The similarity wouldn't work," said Rob.

Diamond walked over to the nearest window and looked out. "Roses on the tower. Dried now, but still thorny. They must be part of the spell." She turned back. "Now, what happened?"

With a flutter of wings, a raven settled on the window, gloomy black even in the faint lighting. Its eye glinted.

"Oh," said Jamie, softly. "That's all right, then."

"Do you still want to look out the window?" said Kenneth. The faster they told their story, the sooner he could get theirs, but the room was dark.

"Oh, no," said Jamie.

Kenneth clapped his hands. A few of the candles lit. Then, they would go out again as the dawn advanced. For now—

Rob and Diamond were almost as pale as Jamie had been in the labyrinth. The raven, shifting its weight a little, was just as black as the gloom had made it.

Jamie recounted their tale, truthfully enough, ignoring Rob's starts, Diamond's gasps, and the raven's fidgets. Which, Kenneth noted, were like the other two's, when they heard of the moments of peril. Though all three—even the raven—looked pleased when he recounted their escape.

"That was a big spell," said Diamond. "Whatever trapped you—when we came over, the gargoyles were not moving about, anywhere."

Kenneth blinked and felt pleased. At least, that would help them track down the wizard responsible.

"And *now*," said Jamie, "we get to tell Kenneth the truth!"

"Telling *them* six times was not enough?" said Diamond, and rubbed her eyes.

"No." Rob turned to Kenneth. The sky outside showed dusky red and yellow along the horizon. Within, a candle winked out, Rob paying it no more heed than the dawn. "We will tell all the world! If we must tell it a thousand times! But you first since you were—" He spread his hands. "Diamond and I were at Jamie's parents' for a fort-night. One night, something woke us up."

"A noise," said Diamond. "Or a noise that had been made and suddenly stopped." Jamie nodded.

Said Rob, "We went out on the balcony. There were three hood-ed men, and Piers, holding Jamie's uncle. Another hooded man cast a spell on him. It turned him into a raven."

"There's your deathly magic," said Jamie, triumphantly.

Kenneth looked at Jamie. Then to Diamond and Rob. Finally, he turned his gaze to the raven, and there he did not turn aside.

Jamie laughed, with only a trace of frenzy to it. "We should—you should—show him that you trust him. He's trustworthy."

"If you can," said Diamond, her voice measured. "We haven't for-gotten—"

The raven raised its wings and sprang into the room. After an odd, warped moment, a squarely built man, dressed in black, stood there. Pale as salt—Kenneth let out his breath—not so freckled as his nephew, with dark brown hair—

David Servant crossed the room in three steps and fiercely hugged his nephew—for a few moments, before he put him back and looked him up and down, as if he could not believe that Mistress Rosemary had checked him carefully enough for injuries.

Kenneth swallowed and turned to the other two. "With *that* much deathly magic about—is it sure that his parents are dead?"

David Servant turned from his nephew, though keeping an arm about his shoulders. His voice was deep. "Neither these three, nor I, saw them dead. Or being killed."

"Though," said Diamond, her voice brittle, "we have not let our hopes get too high. The easiest way to get the power to transform *him* would have been their deaths."

Jamie turned his face toward her. "And Piers was a weak-willed ninny. The Labyrinth of Thought didn't show a single thing he saw. We couldn't tell from there."

"It didn't show anything we saw, either," said Kenneth dryly.

Jamie blinked. "We were just there a few hours—"

"Exactly. The two might have been there for minutes, nothing more."

The door started to open. Rob and Diamond looked over, appalled; Jamie started, as if to push his uncle into hiding; David raised his hands as if to become a raven again and fly off.

Master Bonaventure glanced in, raised an eyebrow, closed the door behind him, and surveyed the room in silence. Finally, his gaze settled on David. His voice was dry.

"I see you have lost little time in taking advantage of your known innocence."

David flushed. "I came in when Rob and Diamond came through the door."

Master Bonaventure inclined his head. "At least it spares my having to track you down with the news."

Kenneth felt a sick weight in his stomach. The news was bad. The other four had gone as still as stone, it was that obvious.

"Piers has escaped."

"Escaped?" Scorn filled Jamie's face. "The most bumbling jailor that ever was could not have let him escape. Kenneth and I bound him—them—with so many spells—and we're not even done with our studies! Any master could have kept him in place with new spells."

"Apparently, however, one cast the spell to dispel, instead." After a magisterial moment, Master Bonaventure added, "They had help."

"She escaped, too?" said Kenneth.

"Yes," said Master Bonaventure, "but Lucinda, while belonging to the Web, is not the proof of David's innocence."

Jamie said, sturdily, "She tried to murder Kenneth."

"Like any murderer, she will be pursued—as, alas, David is likely to be."

"I saw him," said Kenneth. "I could testify."

"To what? That Jamie told you who he was? But Jamie was still confounded then."

Jamie's eyes narrowed, and he looked to burst into flame from fury.

"The magistrate observed that there's every reason to think the woman belongs to the Web. You might have been subjected to a new spell. They are always devising such things, that being the purpose—the outward purpose—of the Web."

Master Bonaventure drew a deep breath.

"At that, there is the question of your living to testify. You are all in grave danger. I do not think that the magistrate himself was responsible, Edgar Grayson does not seem the type, but someone in his office was. Nor is the school safe. You were stolen from the very library."

"How," said David harshly, "could you have permitted something like that? Randomly opening magical portals? It sounds like the obvious recourse for evil."

Master Bonaventure bowed his head. After a moment, his voice was heavy. "Master Gregor has cast them for years without evil consequence. Though not at the opening of every quarter. Magistrate Grayson had taken charge of him to question him, but we have found more than the gargoyles are involved."

"That could have been a side consequence of the spellwork," said Diamond.

"No, we have established that the gargoyles brought it in and affected the spell." His mouth drew into a line. "When they stopped so abruptly, that was our first sign that something was wrong. But—" He glanced out the window. The sky was pastel, and the scene clear.

Kenneth blinked, and realized the last candles had winked out as the dawn advanced, and their light was greater.

"We haven't much time," said Master Bonaventure.

"What about our friends?" said Kenneth. He felt a prick of conscience. "Our families? Will they think we have just vanished? That we ran away to escape our studies?"

Master Bonaventure raised his hand and swept the air as if to brush his words aside. "We will acquaint them with your danger, and with your safety." He hesitated. "It may be possible, in a little time, for you to write to them, if you do not tell them where you are." More briskly, he said, "Have you heard of the Order of the Labyrinth?"

"All our parents belonged," said Jamie, shortly.

Rob and Diamond nodded.

Feeling ignorant, Kenneth said, "Wizards. They guard sites for the Crown. Like—Graytowers."

"Guard and use," said Master Bonaventure. "Since Graytowers is not enough—your things have already been packed for you. Fortunately, one of those sites will keep such mischief as the gates and gargoyles from you. It is not allowed."

His face grew stern, and he looked from one face to the next. "Including from you. They take you on from generosity. It ill-behooves anyone to harm the valley in return for their hospitality—even if you did not consider that such mischief may give an avenue of attack on you."

All three nodded. Master Bonaventure eyed Kenneth as well, and Kenneth nodded, quickly. It was one thing to be a prefect at Graytowers, but here—he let out his breath.

"With nothing but the clothes on our backs?" said Rob, and tilted his head to one side.

"Your possessions will be sent after. When we can assure their safety for you."

Master Bonaventure turned to David Servant. "I sent word about the Order about your innocence. They will all be aware. It's a good thing you are here, if—" He sounded more hesitant. "—you could lead them through the Boneyard."

Kenneth's breath came light and shallow. The Boneyard. They said that Graytowers was a place of wizardry, but the towers were nothing next to the Boneyard. Though meant as nothing more than a magical no-place, accessible from about the world for travel, it had, through unforeseen effects of magic, become a sort of lure for all manner of things lost and long dead—

It would, he had to concede, let them leave here. He forced his breath out and in, as deeply as he could. Arriving safely would be another matter.

David Servant gave a faint snort. "What were you going to do if I hadn't been here?"

"Gone myself," said Master Bonaventure. "I have already cast the preparation, but your nephew told me why the deathly magic." His gaze flickered to the window for a moment. "If it does not make the Boneyard utterly unsafe for you, I would think it made it a place where you were master."

David twitched. "Master? No, not at all." He turned his head. "But I hid there much of the time since that night."

Master Bonaventure blinked.

"I must spend two-third of my time as a raven. A good hiding place for one enchanted as I am. The danger is less—and I could learn some things there."

Master Bonaventure smiled. "Then you are the best guide they could possibly have. I will set a sleeping spell along the way, so that early risers will not disturb you."

Chapter 4—Passage

The sky was still filled with many colors, but the scene was as clear as day when they left the building. The maze lay before them, but—Kenneth looked at the hedges—these stairs led to an opening he had never seen before. Then, it would not lead to a tower.

"Follow me," said David. Without a glance back, he led them through the hedges of the maze—not toward the pool—down paths of chipped stone about turns and corners that seemed painfully reminiscent of the Labyrinth of Thought, all the more in the lack of forks. The sun rose, but was hidden by the towers. Golden light came from behind them, and the sky was blue.

Kenneth had not known that any path through the maze could take this long. Diamond's eyes narrowed as if she were already calculating the route and its possibilities.

Abruptly, around a corner that looked like every other, the path widened into a way. It ended at a grassy tumulus taller than a man. A plain oaken door, with wrought iron hardware, stood in it.

David stopped. "That is the entrance to the Boneyard." He turned to face them. "I will bring up the rear, so you will have to lead, Kenneth."

He braced himself and nodded. He was the prefect, and he did not want to bring up the end. It might be no worse than the Labyrinth of Thought by itself.

The door bore no lock and opened in easy silence. Behind it were walls as gray as the towers and steps leading down. Steep steps, but the stairwell could not fit in the narrow tumulus. He started down.

Light shone from the doorway, but cast their shadows over the steps. Wand in hand, he conjured up a luminous spell.

"All of you cast that." David pulled the door shut behind himself. Their shadows all loomed up on the wall from his spell, and David looked almost inhuman from the bright and dark on his face. "The

Boneyard is—interesting enough without making it less distinct than need be."

Obedient lights shone, and their shadows leapt up, paler on every wall. Kenneth did not move.

"We need to pick you out by your light, too," he said to David.

David raised an eyebrow, but cast the spell, and Kenneth turned back and went down the next step. For all the light, the shadows still hid the bottom. He descended, and descended, and finally, the light found a floor, and he reached the bottom.

Irregular but enormous flagstones spread before him. The walls turned off to the right and left, leaving him no guide. The combined lights cast a medley of shadows but showed nothing but more flagstones.

"Walk straight ahead," said David. His deep voice did not echo.

Easy to say. The flagstones would serve as no good guide. But he stepped forward. The doorway would be in sight for some time, he told himself.

His footsteps sounded but did not echo. Moments after, he was followed, his shadows dancing before him. The light found neither another wall nor any roof to the Boneyard.

When he nerved himself to glance back, the door was little more than a suggestion in the wall, but David Servant's face was implacable.

Kenneth took another step forward, and made out something in the gloom ahead. A few more, and he made out blockish shapes of enormous, free-standing shelves. The things on them were still vague from distance, but the shelves themselves were clearly laid out in straight lines and order.

Every step made them larger. A man would need a ladder to reach the shelves only a tenth of the way up. Kenneth fixed his gaze on the gap between two racks, and did not look aside, though he could see that the nearest shelves were laden with bones, in neat stacks: leg bones, skulls, rib cages. As they walked between shelves, they reached where wing bones were stacked, and others that had to be the bones of beasts, and still others where they could not tell. Broken wood lay on the shelves past it; sometimes clearly a boat or a clock or a chest, sometimes shattered until only fit for firewood. Broken glass in colorless or green or brown—some in blue or a swirl of color. He thought he saw amethyst purple, and forced his gaze back to the path.

A rack appeared ahead of them, cutting off the way so that the path turned left. And there were no openings. The only escape would be to wriggle between the heaped up piles. If that were even possible, with all those bones and broken things.

He took the turn. The glass there was purple, or swirls of rose, peach, and violet, and gave way swiftly to metal oddments whose purpose he could not judge.

Another turn appeared ahead. Pottery, most shattered or chipped or cracked—from the crudest in dull red, to delicate plates painted with roses and firebirds. And past that, another turn. He let his breath out. The third labyrinth in a day. Master Oliver had been right about the value of its signature. No doubt, the calculations were already being done in Diamond's thoughts—

"What does this look like from overhead?" said Diamond.

He rolled his eyes.

"No one knows," said David Servant. "It's impossible to get a full view from above." He sounded as if he were trying to smile. "Even if you can fly."

Kenneth glanced up. Their spells did not illuminate the topmost shelves, wherever they were.

"And mapping," said Rob, "would require many a wizard to spend many a year here. Unsafe, unwise." Pottery gave way to broken metal as they walked. After a moment he added, "Didn't stop their trying more than once. They thought the pattern didn't stay in place. But they couldn't be sure."

"True," said David.

"Look on the bright side," said Jamie. "No one could have a charm like the one they used in the Labyrinth of Thought. To bring them to us. We're safe from them at any rate."

Silence fell, for a moment.

"Why isn't it all rusted?" said Rob. "All that iron—and some shows rust, but not much. And the others. No tarnish, no corrosion, no—"

"The air is dead," said David. "Nothing rots down here. The iron that rusted did so before the Boneyard claimed it."

Kenneth walked more quickly. The things on the shelves, like the images in the windows, could be ignored. A right turn, and a long path, a left turn, a short corridor, a right turn and—he blinked—open flagstones before them. He walked straight out from the racks, and three strides later, could see the doorway.

This time the stairs went steeply up through ruddy brown rock, unlike the gray stairs down, or—Kenneth frowned. What color *had* the flagstones been? Their spells had cast enough light for him to see it, but it eluded him, like some unnatural color found only there.

The stones were not the same color as the racks, he thought, but he could not name that color, either.

His mouth set, Kenneth bent his attention to the stairs, until the door appeared. This one, also, had no lock. He pushed it open. Fresh air gushed in, bright with morning, still dew-laden and cool, but smelling of greenery and faintly of flowers.

The valley beyond was fresh with spring sprouts, on steep slopes, sometimes with cliff-faces. The trees were ruddy with the buds of new leaves, except where evergreens stood like narrow sentinels.

He walked forward. The path here was made of ruddy-brown flagstones and curved about a leafless thicket, with branches thick enough to hide what lay behind. Inside it, a low wall held a pool under a clay cliff-face. From halfway down the cliff, water splashed down into it, sparkling in the morning. A woman filled a pitcher there, and a little girl leaned against the wall and giggled. Both were black-haired, with even brown skin, and wore flowing, foreign clothes of green and blue and violet, the colors melding into each other.

The girl jumped up. "They're here, they're here—"

The woman lifted an eyebrow, shifted her weight a little, and went on filling her pitcher as the others followed. All of them, even David Servant, looked pale and wan. A moment later, she put her pitcher down before circling around the pool to offer them a grave smile and a welcome to the Vale of Tranquility.

"Or Quiet Valley, if you prefer." Her mouth quirked a little.

For a moment, Rob seemed to stir at the mention of the two names, but then he withdrew into the wan exhaustion again.

Kenneth drew in a deep breath. All the life and brightness, and colors he could put a name to, seemed only to underscore how strange and unearthly the Boneyard had been.

David nodded to her. "So you are the one to welcome us?"

She nodded coolly. "A surprise, to find ourselves charged with five in need of sanctuary, but that is one role of the valley and has been for centuries—"

"So, you can take charge of four scholars?"

With the faintest hint of bewilderment and more than a touch of anger, she nodded.

He breathed out a sigh, and with a burst of feathers, become a raven again.

She looked at the bird, her eyes narrowed, and she nodded sharply. "An unsurprising effect from so much of the Boneyard's magic."

"Oh," said Diamond, and sat, with a thud, on the flagstones, where she blinked like an owlet at noon.

The woman's hand flew up. A spell surged from her lips—a falling one, he realized—but blotches of black were appearing in his field of vision. He blinked. They did not vanish; they spread and joined up.

Chapter 5—Arrival

He lay flat on his back on the grass. The girl leaned over him. Rob was starting to sit, and the other two stirred where they lay.

The girl sat back on her heels. "He's awake."

The woman nodded. "A perfect normal and even more typical response to the Boneyard." But her gaze flitted between them.

The three did not look well. Kenneth pushed himself up. His arms shook only a little.

The girl said, brightly, "She's Kyra. I'm Anike."

"Kenneth," he said. The others managed to give their names, but like him, got no further than sitting up. He rested. Prudent, he supposed. Lying down might be more prudent.

"There's breakfast up the hill," said Mistress Kyra, "but do not hurry yourselves. I might not catch you in time, if you fall again."

The raven stretched its wings again, and David Servant stood there. He looked faintly embarrassed. "I will help with the falls. But rest, first."

#

Marching uphill was not perhaps the best route after that journey, but at least the way wound back and forth. If it took ten times the distance of the straight route, still it rose only slowly.

Kenneth still glanced back often.

Finally, they reached the low, broad building, made of flint, its roof mossy and its windows round. Anike knocked on the door and introduced the man who opened it—middle-aged, squarely built, with blond hair so pale as to be almost white—as Master Florian. He eyed David but greeted him civilly enough as Anike skipped by.

The room behind was a large kitchen with scores of long tables and benches. Only one was occupied, with a girl about his age, her black hair severely tied back, eating her breakfast. Then she looked up.

"Diamond!" said Pearl. "Whatever are you doing here?" She looked them over. "Any of you! I would have thought Kenneth the last to leave Graytowers in search of greater knowledge—and you three can't! You still must—Diamond, our parents will be *furious*—"

"We had no choice," said Jamie.

Mistress Kyra, still holding her pitcher, followed David in, and closed the door.

"And," said Master Florian, "there's going to be an uproar until we settle them in."

Pearl's face twisted, but smoothed out within a moment. "I'll let Imogene know they are here, then." She took up her bowl and slid deeper into the room. With only a moment to drop the bowl in a basin, she slipped out a back door—the—third of seven. The room was larger than it looked from the outside, thought Kenneth.

"I'll cook you breakfast," said Master Florian. "Anike, show them where to wash their hands."

The girl nodded. Kenneth saw how David stopped to speak with Master Florian and Mistress Kyra, but followed the younger scholars out.

The building had been built into the slope, which explained how it hid its size, but a path lined with pink tulips led them to its end, where a spring bubbled up, edged with yellow tulips and cream-colored daffodils.

"What's the difference in the springs?" said Diamond. "From the one Mistress Kyra carried up?"

Anike giggled. "It's *complicated*."

"How many springs does the valley have?" said Kenneth, plunging his hands into the cold water.

Anike put a finger to her mouth. "Twelve—I think."

Rob snorted. "Bet you it was a place for water before quiet."

Jamie shook his hands in the air, throwing about water drops. "It would help with being a place of sanctuary. It's not easy to cut them off from water."

Diamond started to eye the slope, looking for signs of springs no doubt. Jamie looked farther out, as if guessing when this place had been attacked.

"Breakfast first," said Kenneth. He hoped the dishes hot; his hand still felt numbed by the cold. "Then, perhaps, we can insist on classes in the history and geography of Quiet Valley on full stomachs."

Anike giggled. "They won't make you take lessons today." She skipped off.

And, he thought, would probably find their wishing to study a far-fetched claim. He followed her toward the food.

Back in the dimness of the room, though Master Florian stirred a pot on the stove, David Servant, Mistress Kyra, and Master Florian were deep in conversation. Kenneth caught no more than mention of a meeting that night before David looked up.

"Just as well that term has not actually begun," he said. "The valley can not instruct you as Graytowers can."

"Neither the books nor the instructors," said Master Florian.

"And you can't leave the valley to get them," said Mistress Kyra. "Or anything else. You can't even go to church of a Sunday."

Master Florian dished up the porridge into bowls.

Diamond took her bowl but did not even move toward the table. "Is there a library?"

"A small one," said Mistress Kyra. "And specialized."

A woman's voice boomed over the room. "My! I have never seen scholars so eager to study." A solidly built woman with a broad, ruddy face, and pale hair severely drawn back, beamed upon them.

"Someone," said Kenneth, "did try to kill me last night."

The smile vanished. The woman's mouth opened, and then shut again.

"We need to learn how to defend ourselves from our enemies," said Jamie.

Mistress Kyra laughed. "What do you think you did, bringing you here?"

"Trapped us?" said Rob.

"Forever?" said Diamond. "Or until we learn enough to defend ourselves?"

Anike, looking from face to face, piped up. "Some people do stay. There's a hermitage up there—" She waved uphill, looked at their faces, and fell silent.

Into the silence, Kenneth said, "We did not—we two—account ourselves that badly last night. But that was because we had learned spellcraft enough to deal with what we faced."

Master Florian pulled out a jug of honey and put it on the table. "I trust this means their rooms are ready, Imogene."

"Oh, yes," said Mistress Imogene, faintly, as if from far off. "Oh yes." She drew a deep breath. "Master Bonaventure sent news soon enough for arrangements."

Kenneth took up his spoon, ladled on the honey, and passed the jar. They could not, in fact, leave the valley. It gave them little leverage.

Pearl emerged from behind Imogene. "He could join in my studies."

"If he wanted to join them," said Master Florian, sitting down to his bowl, "he could have done so two terms ago, instead of staying at Graytowers for the standard course." He picked up his spoon. "Besides, even if Kenneth changed his mind, the other three still need the standard course to prepare them for it."

"It's not that urgent," said David, dryly. "At least today they need their rest instead. At Graytowers, they would not be in class yet."

"They should stay up all day until evening, if they can," said Master Florian.

"Still, today they should not study." David faced the four of them. "Ramble over the valley as if you like. Just stay inside the rose hedges, they mark the boundaries. Tomorrow—tomorrow you can start with history lessons on the Web."

"I can show you your rooms," said Mistress Kyra. She faced Mistress Imogene. "If you want to get on with Pearl's lessons."

"Of course," said Mistress Imogene. "Come along, Pearl."

Kenneth hoped it meant that the conservation was ending, not that they were being shuffled aside to avoid hearing the discussion of their fate.

Still, as Mistress Kyra ushered them to a door with stairs behind it, he noted that the doorframe had authority marks on it.

#

Their rooms looked uncommonly like those at the Tower of Stone. The wood was lighter in color, and less carved, but the exact furnishings stood in the same place.

Kenneth walked over to the chest beneath the window, and threw it open. It had his clothing, not even shifted from how he arranged it at the Tower. He looked up.

"A transferring spell," said Mistress Kyra. "Not easy, and not cheap, but making it hard for the Web to track you. I trust you will not defeat its purpose by leaving the valley."

The other three ran off to their rooms—there was this difference from Graytowers at least, that each of them had a room. He sat on the chest, and was glad he liked long walks. It looked like there was little else to amuse. At least, none of them was immensely fond of any of the team sports at Graytowers.

Mistress Kyra went to inspect the other three. Kenneth rose, checked the door for authority marks, and muttered a spell. They glowed, briefly, acknowledging his authority as prefect.

Mistress Kyra came back and nodded to him before leaving. Down the corridor, Diamond whispered to the other two. Something about Kenneth's not getting it.

As if he had not heard, Kenneth said, "Shall we ramble? We aren't going to go swiftly, so we had best go soon."

"Lead on once more, o fearless prefect," said Rob, grinning, "and we shall follow forever more!"

Kenneth cocked an eyebrow.

Down the steps—the room was empty now, no one eating and the fire dead—and out the door to a brilliant and unseasonably warm day. The weave of paths downhill could be made out, more or less, though trees obscured it in places. It would be harder to make out when the trees had more leaves, but they could learn it now.

"Let's go down there," said Kenneth—that path would take them near but not to the doorway to the Boneyard. "Then we can swing around and go up the other side, and come back down here in the last part." He lowered his arm. "We'll be glad to come downhill for the last, if this is as large as it looks."

The three nodded agreeably enough.

Thickets of pale, bright green leaves rose to either hand. Birds cheeped and twittered, hidden from sight. Within a minute, the path turned to steps, and one thicket ended. Instead, beside the path, a stream babbled over tumbled rocks, and formed pools. There, willows were yellow with new leaves, further fledged than any other tree. When another stream flowed into it, a bridge arched over, and where the streams joined, tulips thronged about it like a sunrise in pinks and yellows and pale orange. Diamond guessed that it flowed from the spring where Mistress Kyra had filled her jug, and Jamie stopped to trace the banks back.

Perhaps it was his imagination, as he walked into the violet-filled meadow on the other side, that they eyed him as if hoping to lose him, but then—

He cast the spell quickly. He thought none of them noticed.

"There's another bridge," he said. "I'm not sure it leads farther on the trail. Could just be to reach the marshy land there, and gather whatever plants it has." He glanced them over. "I'll check."

He strode over without a glance back, and was fairly sure they did not follow—and not because they were inspecting violets, or that plant with feathery leaves and purple flowers like small stars, which probably had no magical virtues, because he had not learned it in herbology.

The marshy ground was thick with irises, all sprouting leaves and not so much as buds yet. He kept his back to them, to hide his hand gestures.

". . . it's for his sake, too," said Diamond. "They tried to *kill* him, Rob."

"If we had acted more boldly," said Jamie, "they might not have had a chance. We could have cleared my uncle earlier, but that would have required knowledge, and that would have required us to *learn it.*"

"If they keep us in the dark," said Diamond, "we must shed some light."

Kenneth lowered his hands, turned and walked back. Rob had a sullen look on his face, as if he had no arguments but would not yield. He was the first to blink and look over at Kenneth, and the others looked over slowly. From their expressions, they did not realize.

"Which one of us did they actually try to kill?" said Kenneth. "And has the most interest in what *they*—" He waved his hand at the building. "—plan?"

Rob started. Jamie blushed. Diamond paled, drew herself up to her full height, and said, "You—"

"If you keep me in the dark," said Kenneth, "I must shed some light."

Diamond looked away.

More gently, Kenneth said, "I am still the prefect and responsible for you three."

"We can't spy," said Rob, shoving his hands into his pockets. Breeze ruffled his red hair, and birds sang sweetly. "If they find out, they won't trust us with anything."

Kenneth's hand swept the air in dismissal. "First, we see if we can find out openly. Then we will know if they will trust us with anything now. Gather your questions for dinner tonight."

"And when they don't?" said Jamie sourly.

Kenneth thought of reminding him that the three of them had visibly been under a spell that would make what they said untrustworthy. Then he said, "Why then—" He surveyed the slope. "We do most of our walk. The hermitage up there will be a good place to sleep. I know a charm that will keep that sleep from throwing off how we sleep and wake. And then—"

He looked about. "How *were* you planning on spying on them?"

Diamond blushed. The silence was enough for them to hear bees buzzing from flower to flower.

"We—we hadn't gotten that far," said Jamie.

"Rob wouldn't agree," said Diamond fiercely.

"Wise, if you had no plan to offer him."

"Have *you* got a plan?" said Rob.

"You of all people? To spy?" said Jamie

Kenneth let out his breath. The wind blew down the hillside. He could hardly be a corrupting influence after all they had gone through, and what they knew now.

"How else can a prefect catch troublemakers before they burn down the towers?" He looked them in the face. "Consider that fair warning."

"They'll catch you," said Diamond.

"The authority marks recognize me as a prefect, so—not unless they have new spells. And whatever the plan, that is something we have to risk. We'll listen to them as I listened to you."

Silence fell.

"And that's all?" said Jamie

"And that's all," said Kenneth. "It's not like we didn't take out two murderers with a spell I taught you last week. Sometimes simplicity itself works." He shrugged. "We might as well enjoy the rest of the walk, to while away the time. There's irises over the bridge, but they haven't bloomed yet."

"We'll probably be here to see the flowers," said Rob.

Diamond sighed. "There are worse fates," she said, as drearily as if she could think of few.

"At least I'm sure we'll be able to find out *all* about the flowers for the asking," said Jamie. "If we even have to ask."

The three rang with laughter, and Kenneth smiled. It was not until they walked on that he wondered whether they meant Mistress Imogene or Pearl.

The trail looped about a stand of sprouts that Diamond pronounced to be snapdragons, and they walked onward.

The stream meandered madly about the valley's bottom. Willows in yellow leaves hung over the waters, and ducks paddled about in pools between stand of rushes still yellow and dry, with green sprouts starting to rise among them. Paths led off to places indistinguishable from the rest, and they could only guess at what grew there, or if some other enchantment picked that place out.

Despite the rambles, by midday, they were climbing. Pines that shaded the path were few and far between, with their needles amber

on the ground below them. A few trees were flowering—cherries radiant in white; apples where a few boughs had open, pale pink flowers, and all the rest were decked with fiercely pink buds still furled;
crab apples with their deep pink flowers, and still deeper pink buds,
and their dark, impossible red-green leaves—

It was enough to ease the memories of the night before. But not
the lack of sleep. For all the ease of their pace, he was ready to yawn
at the path's height.

There, he noted, the trees were still leafless, and the crocuses still
bloomed in delicate blue and cream.

The hermitage stood there, and they walked through the
rooms—one for prayer, and they paused before the crucifix; one for
eating; and one to sleep. Where there was no bed any more.

Jamie ran a hand through his hair. "We could go back to our
rooms," he said tentatively. "It's not that far."

"It would tell them we slept," said Kenneth. "It's not like we
would go there to study, and I do not want them to think of using
new spells on us."

"Grass isn't that bad," said Rob. "And it's warm enough."

"All right." Diamond turned her face on Kenneth. "Show us the
spell."

#

Scurrying down the slope by another stream, with the sky starting to
turn as colorful as the flowers, and the air cooling by the minute, got
them to the building in time to hear Mistress Imogene, standing before it, telling Pearl that she ought to find them. She scanned the valley below, anxiously.

"We should have watched them, they don't know where the borders are, and they don't know what sorts of spells can been affected
by the valley—"

Pearl looked belligerent.

"There they are," called David Servant, cheerfully, lounging by the door. "Took your time?"

Mistress Imogene looked delighted, and Pearl as well, at that. Kenneth felt glad that they had checked for grass stains first, and known how to remove them.

"There's a lot to see," said Jamie, mildly, "and Kenneth insisted that we not walk too fast."

"Until the last," said Rob, grinning, and gesturing at the slope.

"You shouldn't have pushed yourself," said Mistress Imogene. "However hungry you are. And you will have time to see more."

"And you should take the chance," said Pearl, her black hair swinging free. She smiled at Kenneth. "As long as you're here, you can learn some of the magic."

David snorted. "You may have to. Just to make yourself at home."

Kenneth opened his mouth and shut it again. They did not even seem aware that they reminded the four of them of their captivity.

The air was growing colder still, and the sunset was turning to darker shades.

Pearl turned to Kenneth. "You said," she said softly, "that you had just chosen the Tower of Stone out of the pool—that it had not been a passion. . . ."

It still wasn't, thought Kenneth, but it was a good course, which would teach him to support himself.

"Come in, come in," said Mistress Imogene. David Servant pushed off the wall and ushered them inside. Half a dozen wizards were gathered around the table. From her seat, Anike grinned.

Mistress Imogene said, "These are Kenneth Mornington, Jamie Fitton, Rob Oldcastle, Diamond Dombrey, and David Servant."

The wizards looked more or less uneasy at that last, a couple of them glancing sidelong at him, but David did not blink. They had known, but Kenneth wondered whether any of them did not believe.

As serenely as if she did not notice, Mistress Imogene went on. "You have met the rest, but these are Master Thomas, Mistress Henrietta, and Master Giles."

Master Giles nodded, his gaze on Diamond, and said, "Diamond Dombrey—two Dombreys?"

"Sisters," said Mistress Imogene.

Master Giles snorted. "Is there a Ruby or Esmeralda about? Or at least a Zaffire?"

Pearl said, circumspectly, "We were named for our grandmothers."

Master Giles shrugged and spread his hand toward the dishes. They all sat as they were served up.

Soup and bread and cheese—Pearl took hers and said, "I told them they should learn the valley's magic while they were here."

Kenneth managed, barely, to bite down that her rich family could afford to let her study theoretic wizardry that no one would hire her for.

"O, you should!" said Anike. "Even *I'm* learning some, and you could learn so much more!"

Kenneth buttered his bread. "It will be hard to concentrate when we know that people are seeking our lives. What's being done about those wizards? They abducted or murdered the Fittons—or both—they cursed David Servant—they abducted Jamie and me, and tried to kill me—" He drew a deep breath. "—and if half of what Jamie and I saw in the Labyrinth was memory, or even plan, that's not a tithe of their evil."

He looked about. Most did not meet his gaze. None spoke for a minute.

"If you are still troubled by their trying to murder you," said Mistress Kyra, "I know they gave you something to soothe your spirits. There are stronger spells that can help—"

"I'm troubled by the prospect of their trying again," said Kenneth. "More soothing would only increase my peril."

Silence fell.

"You'll be safe here," said Master Florian.

"That," said Rob, cutting out each word sharply, "is what they told me and my parents about Graytowers: that we would be safe there." His eyes were narrowed.

"Mine, too, after that night." Diamond's face set in fierce lines. "I wonder what you've told them now that it's false, and they can't even hear it from me."

Kenneth ate some soup and felt useless. At least, none of the wizards pointed out that for the two of them, it had been safe. Only for him and Jamie had there been actual danger—for the time they had been there.

"You told my guardians, too," said Jamie. "And you'd have told Kenneth's parents, if they had worried that he was in danger."

Kenneth's stomach felt cold. He wondered what they would think, hearing the news—whatever news that the wizards had deemed fit to tell them. He let out his breath. Or his brothers and sisters. He had been a late child, born twelve years after the next oldest sister, and they had never been close, but he was still their brother.

He forced the thoughts away. He *had* told the three that first they would try to find out openly.

"What harm is there in telling us?" said Kenneth. "Jamie acted more soberly in our trip through the Labyrinth than I would have expected from some grown men. And if, in the end, we don't need to know, still we keep it secret, but if we do need to, it will be too late for you to tell us, for the lack of time."

The wizards' face set.

His voice took on a bitter edge. "Fortunate for us that Jamie and I happened to know enough of the Labyrinth and enough spellcraft to escape once. We can not rely on such things twice."

"You're too young," sad Master Thomas. "We must keep our oaths, not to deliver knowledge beyond their years to children."

"Pearl and Anike aren't allowed, either," said Master Florian.

"Well," said Kenneth sourly, "we do not wish you to break an oath. If only because we could trust nothing that you said, after." He took a bite of cheese, and chewed, contemplating whether the oath was that detailed, and when he could cast his own spell.

#

The sunset had turned crimson and deep purple in the west, with a lone star over it, and darkness overhead, when dinner ended.

"And so to bed," said Kenneth, pushing his dishes aside. "Unless someone's going to show us the library."

"After the day you had," said Master Thomas, "we would be rash to show you. You need to be alert, first."

Anike giggled. But then, they did not want just the parts of the library they let Anike into.

"Bed," said Diamond, and yawned. It looked rather convincing. Pearl rose, murmuring, and head for another stairwell.

Diamond led the way upstairs. Kenneth brought up the end, forcing himself to not look behind, until he closed the door behind him. Then—"To me, all of you."

The spell went quickly. All three, in the gloom, eyed him as best they could.

"Go look at your beds. But don't touch them."

Moments later, with wide eyes, they came back to him.

"Thought that one up over dinner," said Kenneth. "Those figures will stay there, and look convincing, until you touch them. For us—I think my room's best to gather in, and wait for them to talk."

They gathered themselves in the fading light. Kenneth hoped, as the minutes inched by, that Diamond would not try to while away the time by asking how the spell worked. He would have to confess that he had mastered it by rote.

Rob leaned forward. "Is that—the spell—" His hands moved as if trying to grip something. "Guillaume the Good wrote of a spell like that."

Kenneth could remember the page of the book. It had held the spell, not its history. Rob talked on.

"Warlocks used it to feign that they were asleep in bed when they gathered for their evil spells, to ruin crops and wreck ships. And they had another, to make it look like someone asleep in bed was with them, working evil spells. To let the guilty escape and the innocent suffer." Rob shook his head. "Guillaume the Good had to enchant things that marked all the people who were actually asleep bright green, and those who were awake and working magic, bright yellow." He sat back. "So they burned all the yellow ones."

"Does this spell hide us?" Diamond glanced at the bed where the figure of Kenneth lay.

"Yes," said Kenneth.

"Then it can't be the same one. They could see people at the gathering." Her frown could barely be picked out. "I wonder if it's a refinement. The original might have been evil to the bone, if warlocks used it."

Jamie, leaning back, said, "They probably didn't forbear with the burning long enough to let the warlocks teach them spells first."

Diamond shrugged. "So, a new spell devised from the knowledge—but it's not stonework. You must have learned it by rote."

Kenneth eyed her and nodded.

"I wonder," said Jamie, "how you would defend against it?"

"Authority marks," said Kenneth. "And watching carefully whom you let in, and what authority they have. You have to set up marks to prevent it except for people like prefects. Who might need it to smuggle people to safety or the like."

"That's stonework," said Jamie.

"O, yes," said Kenneth. Then the spell murmured. "Hush now."

The spell gave off sounds like rustling robes and people moving about. Jamie scowled.

"If we had chattered out of boredom, Jamie," said Kenneth, as low as he could, "I certainly and you probably would have died in the Labyrinth."

No one spoke after that.

They even fidgeted less than the gathering wizards. Kenneth grew more certain that others had arrived at the valley, increasing their number past those at dinner. He wondered if any had come from Graytowers.

"Are the children asleep?" said Master Thomas.

"With Kenneth chivvying them to bed an hour ago?" said Master Florian. "Yes. I checked."

The three stilled, and Kenneth realized for the first time that they had moved at all.

"One prefect for the three of them?" said a feminine voice, dryly. "Will that suffice? I know that they are Tower of Stone and tend to be stolid—"

"Maybe," said David Servant, with absolute gravity. "If you listen to them."

The silence was unbroken for a minute.

"You are hardly unbiased," said Master Thomas.

"And you are?" said David. "Even *I*, after all that had happened, would have thought Jamie safe at Graytowers. Instead, that one prefect was all that stood between him and death."

"It hardly matters," said a deep-voiced man. "We will know better than to let gargoyles into Quiet Valley."

Murmurs of assent sounded around. Someone muttered that they knew that before this.

"But we must do more—*if* we can." From the sound, Kenneth guessed the speaker shifted in his seat. "For that, we must know more. Therefore, as soon as I got the news, I read your account, and in truth, you have added little knowledge to our store. Let us ask the one question, then. Is there any chance that your sister and brother-in-law are, like you, birds? Or beasts?"

"Chance, yes," said David, heavily. "But I am half-man, half-raven. I can only push how long I stay in one form for hours before I must turn back—and the longer I stay in one, the longer I must stay in the other. I've not gotten further than a day."

Rob's tongue touched the corner of his mouth, and his eyes unfocused, as if he were trying to remember. Diamond scowled in thought.

"Unless they were hit by a different spell than I was, or held captive, or thrown to far distant lands, they could have revealed themselves by now. And unlike me, they had no reason to hide. And many reasons not to."

Jamie's eyes closed.

Master Bonaventure spoke, heavily. "They could have used more time and prepared a stronger spell, but we can not let any hope rest in that."

"So," said Mistress Imogene, "all we know is that they think that Jamie Fitton still had some use to them."

"We also know," said Master Florian, "that they were willing to kill an innocent boy for stumbling on them. They would have killed Kenneth Mornington out of hand."

"Not that's surprising, with the Web," muttered someone.

"That," said a woman's light voice—Mistress Perpetua? "militates against the Fittons still being alive."

"They wanted Jamie Fitton alive, Mistress Perpetua," said the deep-voiced man.

"Which would also militate against it, Master Quentin," said Mistress Perpetua, pertly. "If they have the parents alive, what would they need with the son? Especially when they ignored him before. Rob Oldcastle and Diamond Dombrey could not have stopped them from taking him."

Jamie leaned forward, as if it would let him hear better.

A deep sigh—"Also," said Master Bonaventure, "there may be factions among the Web in this matter. There are many, and in this case, one may have decided to use the son against those who hold the parents."

"If they are infighting like that," said Master Thomas, "we might gain advantage be playing them one against the other."

An indelicate snort. "If we ever found out enough," said Mistress Henrietta. "Don't count your chicks before they hatch. We would need to know the factions, and their aims, and their quarrels, and their powers, and only then could we even conceive of a plan to play such weaknesses—if any—that we found, against each other."

"At that," said Master Florian, "Master Bonaventure just guessed."

Silence fell.

"At that," said David, "the children are right. You must educate them. They went at Graytowers to be educated, and they will need to know how to defend themselves. And their math and history as well."

Silence fell.

David broke it again. "They are in perfect health and quite able to study. It's not like you brought them here to recover from the Gray Labyrinth."

None of those gathered below asked what that was. Rob scowled. Kenneth told himself to listen and not worry about trivialities.

"The textbooks," said Master Bonaventure, "are bound to Graytowers. I will see what can be added to the library."

A long sigh—Mistress Imogene spoke. "Is there anything else in our power? Because if not, I must remind you, Master David, that you can not stay here long. Not with that shape-shifting and deathly magic. It has a bad effect on Quiet Valley."

"Of course not," said David, coldly. "That is why everything must be settled now."

Despite her words, the talk rambled on, and they listened for minutes more, but uselessly. Nothing more of import was said before the meeting dissolved.

Kenneth broke the spell. They sat in silence minutes longer.

"Well," said Jamie, his voice sounding tightly leashed, "that was not much use."

Kenneth sighed and stood, lighting a soft glow. "At least we shall not have wonder if they are hidden much from us."

"And we know they know nothing," said Rob bitterly, without stirring from his seat. "I suppose that will help."

"I wonder," said Diamond, even more bitterly, "what exactly it was that they were oath-bound to hide from us." But she stood.

"Perhaps they feared a topic would come up," said Kenneth.

"Maybe they didn't want us to know what the Gray Labyrinth is," said Jamie, and startled some laughter from them.

Kenneth waited until they slipped silently down the hall and into their rooms before he turned to his own bed, and made the figure of himself melt like mist.

As soon as he lay down, he felt weary to the bone. So much unknown about them. And nothing he could this night except sleep. He closed his eyes and tried not to think on how there might be nothing he could do in the morning.

Chapter 6—Staying

The day might clear, but now, though they had slept late, it was still misty morning. Kenneth, never having slept that long after the use of the prefect spell, hoped it was just the lack from the night before as they walked down the stairs to the kitchen.

"Ready for breakfast?" said Master Florian. "There's oatmeal in the pot, and strawberries here."

Over the breakfast table, Pearl shyly offered them garlands of heartsease, in every shade of pink and red. Some still bore the dew.

"A charm as well as flowers," said Mistress Imogene, complacently. "Heartsease is good after distressing times. It will help you study with calm minds."

"It will help," said Rob.

"You look forward to class?" said Master Florian.

"Dost thou love life?" said Rob, waving his spoon. "Then do not squander time, for it's the stuff life is made of."

Then he dug into the porridge and ignored the look that Master Florian gave him.

"You'll show us the library?" said Diamond into the silence.

"Better than that," said Mistress Imogene. "You will have a class. A history class. And a magic class."

#

David Servant led them down one corridor, pierced with arched doors, and finally pointed right.

"In here for the class."

Master David, Kenneth told himself, as they took their seats among the many provided. However odd it felt to watch David walk to the podium, he was a master wizard and their teacher, however briefly.

62

"A two-fold class. One in magic, and one in history. Listen well, because I will not be in the valley long."

Kenneth hoped that his start of guilt passed as surprise.

"Why?" Jamie all but wailed.

"Because they can not break the curse on me," said David. "Last night, even, I left to sleep and came back."

"So," said Diamond, pensively, looking at her book, "you're going to go to a more powerful wizard—or a curse-breaker."

David looked grave. (Master David, Kenneth told himself, but thought he would not remember.) "No. I wish I could tell you so, but the strongest curse-breakers are in the Order, and they have looked. We need to learn more to have any hope of breaking it. No, it's that a shapeshifer who carries deathly magic will disturb Quiet Valley and your safety." He drew a deep breath. "Also, as a raven, I can act for the Order in ways that no one else can."

He looked between them. "Remember that I can hide for safety in the Boneyard, as you four can not. And one thing I can do is seek out books for you. But I'll show you the library after the class, to tide you over. It will at least let you read up on the valley."

"Such as," said Kenneth, "why there are violets and heartsease blooming at the bottom while there are still crocuses up top?"

"Ah, you noticed that." David smiled. "It can produce interesting effects on time spells. Even personal ones, but that is not the danger."

All four of them went still. Kenneth hoped he did not look guilty.

"The first spells that must not be used are offensive ones, whatever school they come from—deathly magic, regardless of what it does—and liminal spells, again without regard to what it does. All of them should not be cast in Quiet Valley, as neither you nor anyone else will like the results. But beyond that, some defensive spells are folly because the Quiet Valley's peace is not one of stout defense. It is preventing the clash. It does not repulse attack. It has never come under attack."

"Like Kenneth's spells to keep people as still as stone?" said Rob.

"You will have to tell a master here about that spell, and get a verdict on it. But it sounds like one that may serve." He went on, detailing spells as they took notes. Diamond looked rapt.

Kenneth scowled at the page. He would have to refine his spellbook's organizing spell. It would have worked reasonably had he still followed the standard course, but even this much of mad twists needed more—

He scribbled more. He could worry about that later.

Finally, David said, "And that will suffice to keep you out of most trouble with spellcraft. And now to the Web."

Kenneth flipped to history.

"What do you know of the Web?"

"It's an organization of evil wizards," said Rob.

"It's the Order's biggest problem," said Jamie.

Diamond sniffed. "My parents," she said primly, "do not think they are suitable to be talked about in front of children. Vulgar. I would think leaving a child in danger from ignorance would be worse than vulgarity."

Feeling large, gawky, and a fool, like a scholar in a class filled with younger students because of his own slowness, Kenneth opened his mouth to say, "Nothing," hesitated, and said, "They had something to do with our kidnapping. Also, with the images that Jamie and I saw."

"Kenneth's is the only one entirely correct," said David. "They are not an organization, like the Order. They do not have initiations, or oaths, or duties, like the Order's guard. The Web is a—is like a spider's web of scholars, and wizards with interest in their studies. Threads connecting points."

His fingers spread out, and he waved his hands as if sketching paths.

"They may send letters of introduction telling a fellow scholar that a stranger is part of the Web, they may share knowledge, they may have meetings with their fellows who live nearby, or when a stranger visits, but they have no formal roll of membership. Members can drift in, and drift out, some are central and others borderline, and some are always on the threshold but never truly join, or perhaps have joined but never move deeply into their councils."

Jamie scowled. "Hard to catch them all," he muttered.

"And, we do not want to catch them all," said David. "They all study subject matters that are less than pleasant. But then—Regulus Belmont was a member of the Web."

The other three scowled.

"Who mastered the prevention of transmitting hereditary blood curses," said Kenneth.

"Yes. Many learned—and not at all vulgar—wizards of the Web have written works and devised spells of great help to humanity, and many that are vital to the work of the Order."

David paused. Rob's pen did not move as his eyes narrowed.

"I have to say that even those members of the Web who produced works as great as Master Regulus's did not always reach his standard of probity. Master Maximus Perkins was a ghoulish fellow, though he wrote the definitive catalog of curses." David sighed. "As for the ones who cursed me, tried to abduct Jamie, tried to murder Kenneth, and did Heaven alone knows what to Jamie's parents—none of those deeds are particularly surprising to anyone who knows anything of the Web. It will always include mostly wizards with few scruples, and many with none."

Diamond scribbled, and Kenneth turned to take his own notes. It was, after all, a class and not a chat with Jamie's uncle. Rob shook himself and started to write. David paused until the pens stopped scratching.

Then— "The Order asked its contacts in the Web—on the outer reaches—for knowledge, and they knew nothing. Or professed to. Mistress Rose let it slip that the question was of murder. It may have frightened them off. Those we asked may even leave the Web entirely, and so never tell us of its ways again—but for this, definitely, it is too late to learn more now by that means."

Rob scowled. "If it is so—unceremonious, why has it got a name?"

David spread a hand. "I believe they were named by a foe. Or a wizard rejected from their number."

Or both, thought Kenneth.

"And it was useful to adopt."

David went on with more details about their history or what was guessed of it—their magic in all its ramifications—their old factions and how they shifted so they were never known until afterward—their crimes, with neither arson nor murder nor any of what Jamie and Kenneth had seen in the mirrors were omitted—but nothing that could be brought to bear on their plight. Kenneth furiously took notes, but suspected that even now, David elided parts. Parts worse than murder? he wondered gloomily.

David paused, looking at them. Jamie scribbled some more, Diamond scowled at her notes, Rob looked up thoughtfully, and Kenneth hoped his own were complete.

"And that," said David, "ought to be enough to convince you to remain securely within the valley's bounds, at least until the culprits are caught."

"Or until we are strong enough to ward them off," said Kenneth, putting down his pen. "It ought to be enough to convince us that we need to study even without teachers presiding over us."

David's eyes narrowed. After a minute, he said, "I can show you to the library, but then I have to leave. I would be no help in it, at that."

#

The library was somewhat larger than the dining room, making it at most a quarter the size of Graytowers'. A wall of widows—shelves along the other walls, freestanding bookcases in the middle—but not so many bookcases as could fit. It could not have held a tenth the books of Graytowers, and it was far from full.

Kenneth stepped to the nearest shelf and surveyed it. The books there might prove profitable, but it seemed to be advanced treatises, each one discussing the virtues of a single herb. One—a slim one—was on the effect of color on use of heartsease in calming spells.

"There's a cataloguing spell on it," said Diamond, with her wand in one hand, and a silvery thread in the other, "but it's not the standard one."

"Of course," said Pearl from the doorway. She smiled a little. "It can be hard to maneuver through—they ordered the library by the wizard who brought the books to the valley."

"What did they do *that* for?" said Jamie in disgust.

"For ease in his finding what he brought." Pearl walked in and looked about. "They seldom refer to other people's, since they came to conduct their own studies. Most of these books were left when a wizard died here. Mistress Imogene's have served for what I needed, though I've gotten some help."

For a moment, Kenneth just stared at her. The library's smallness suddenly seemed very large instead. "You mean there's no way to find a book you need except hunting through them *all*?"

"Not always, but—" She shrugged. "—there's an art to it. Mistress Imogene gave me some help—once you know what a wizard studied, it's easier to find a subject. She could help you if you studied with her."

He felt his face shift.

"Or one of the other wizards," she added, her tone more subdued.

"A few months in the tower can often save a couple of hours in the library," said Rob, sounding almost morbid, "but here it would be easier to go back through the Boneyard, consult the library at Graytowers, and return with the knowledge." His mouth tightened. "If they would let us go."

"If you had a tutor—" said Pearl.

"It wouldn't help *them*." Kenneth waved at the three. "We shall just have to spend the day on a catalog of our own."

"Don't try spells," said Pearl.

"Why, how kind of you to point that out," said Diamond, sweetly. "I was planning on casting Melvin's Arrangement."

After moment, Pearl looked at Diamond with a worried frown. "You can't cast that."

Diamond—smiled. "It would help you find the book you came for."

Pearl rolled her eyes, walked across the room, ran her finger down the third shelf of a bookcase, and took out a blue-covered book. "You can only take three books from here at a time."

No sooner had the door shut than Diamond said, "Sisters!"

Being the youngest by twelve years did have its advantages, thought Kenneth. "How shall we divide up the room? Catalogue by high-level subject, first, I would think."

"We could reverse Melvin's Arrangement into an empty book," said Diamond. "Then we could look things up."

Rob rolled his eyes.

Jamie snorted. "And get it right the first time? Just because you're better than us doesn't mean you cast a spell right the first time more than two out of three times."

"Divide up and do by hand," said Kenneth firmly. "I am not spending more time listening to you three yammer about cataloguing than it would take to catalogue it. By myself."

Diamond's nose wrinkled, but in a minute, they quietly inspected shelves. Every now and again, Jamie dryly pointed out a book of fairy tales, Diamond squealed over a volume of mathematics, or Rob announced a work of history.

In his own time, Kenneth said, "A history of the Gray Labyrinth. If anyone wants to read up on why someone who had been there would be sent here."

Diamond looked over.

"After," added Kenneth firmly. "Catalogue first, at least until we find any books on stonework."

Jamie grinned. "I knew she was wrong."

"She?" said Kenneth.

"You didn't chance on stonework."

Kenneth sighed. He supposed they would hear the story one way or another. "I did."

They all looked. Sunlight slanted over their intent expressions.

"My father's business did not have a place for yet another child, so he packed me off to master wizardry, with stern warnings that if I starved on what I learned, I starved. I stuck in my hand to find a magic that suited my talents, and I could live off, and the fish was stonework."

"That's one way," said Rob sagely. "Many of the greatest wizards of history choose their studies by aptitude, not inclination."

Diamond's eyes narrowed, but said nothing.

Rob said, pertly, "I think I got it because it's *old*. I wasn't thinking about it as a tower, either."

Jamie shrugged. "It surprised my parents, but what would be better for spells of protection?"

Diamond sat back. After a moment, she said, "I wasn't particularly thinking of anything but being in a tower that would let me learn something *new*. Something more than the books in my great-grandmother's house. Full of the Order's magic."

"And you face the standard course for four years, like every other tower," said Jamie, lightly.

"Someone learning stonework needs to know how important foundations are."

Rob laughed softly and turned back to the books. So did the others.

Kenneth noticed the way the sunbeams had inched their angle around and wished this room had a clock. He thought it was not yet noon. Kenneth returned to his books himself.

Minutes later, Jamie said, "This one has a shelf of stonework books."

Kenneth fought down the urge to scuttle over. "We can check the rest at the rate we are going. So that we know whether it holds books better for our aims."

At least an hour later, having found nothing better, they converged on that shelf like wolves on a deer, and catalogued every volume. A couple of history works thin on spellcraft. Works of geology less than useful when they could not wander freely. . . .

"We don't *know* the valley's rocks," said Rob, firmly. "We may need that even in these bounds."

One held stonework spells of war.

"I wonder how they managed to get in here," said Kenneth dryly.

Jamie pounced. "Not all of them have to be problems. Some might be defensive. And it could be wise to study the theory. We might find ourselves somewhere where miscasting a spell on the first try would leave us no worse off."

Kenneth hoped not. "We did well enough in the Labyrinth with the spells we knew already. Better to use those first."

Rob snapped his fingers. "The Gray Labyrinth. You saw a history book." He grinned. "As long as labyrinths are falling into our path."

Kenneth studied him a moment and then, with a sigh, retrieved it. Standing there with the book in his hand, he said, "You have to study regular history, too."

"History was even worse than stonework," said Diamond. "They had better give us better books, and soon."

"There's enough for studies," said Jamie. "It wasn't even all magic."

Diamond shrugged. "Mathematics a little better." She flourished her own chosen book.

Kenneth sighed and picked up a geology work. A work of reference, not a text, but it would at least let him look up the subjects that he knew they needed to study. Preservation, he thought. And vision, if he remembered his studies that year right. Or perhaps the year did not matter, since they would need that subject badly.

He should have asked David to bring a curriculum. That would have provided some guidance.

"They didn't set up the library to read in," said Jamie.

"There's a reading garden," said Rob. "And we'll have all afternoon. It's not noon yet."

Minutes later, in a hollow in the hill, with a cliff face to the hillside and blue flowers blooming all about, they sat in chairs and read. Kenneth looked up preservation to emulate them.

They changed off after some hours. Magic to mathematics. Mathematics to history. Kenneth read the history of the Gray Labyrinth. No one could take it for the Labyrinth of Thought. Endless, gray, monotonous, a place of anonymity and loss of self—first, those in it lost their will, then they forgot their names, and then they started to lose their color and their features and finally their flesh and bone, until they turned into shadowy ghosts.

They had to be recovered before that point to be brought here, thought Kenneth. He read on, on how kings and bandits and councils had used the place as punishment throughout the centuries.

He finished it and looked over the vivid colors of the valley. Then he noted the sun.

"Can't study all day." He stood. "I'm going for a walk, but you probably should stop even if you don't join me."

Rob shut his book and said, with curiosity in his voice, "We don't know half the paths."

"I wonder," said Jamie, "if we saw them all yesterday."

"Probably," said Diamond. "I don't think the valley has geometric anomalies that would twist the paths, and if so, there isn't enough space for more paths." She smiled and carefully closed her book. "Let's see."

#

After an amble that led them past daffodils deep in the valley, and found that all paths there were untwisted, they walked toward the hall as the sky showed peach and rose.

Inside, David was not at the tables. Master Florian heartily asked them how their studies went.

"We are seeing what we can do," said Kenneth. "I will try a preserving spell."

"A good choice," said Mistress Imogene. "There are plentiful flowers about, and they are the usual test—for good reason."

"And safe," said Mistress Kyra. "You can test them in this valley, unlike—"

"Anything that would be of slightest use to us," said Jamie. His eyes were narrowed, and he leaned forward, his red hair catching the light and looking like fire.

For a moment, all was silence. He had not been so angry before, thought Kenneth. He swallowed. Or else Jamie had quelled it because Kenneth could do nothing for him.

Diamond said, quickly, "How can we test spells? We need our practice, but at Graytowers, they would never let us try new spells alone."

That they knew of, thought Kenneth, but said nothing. Spells they learned in class were tried under the watchful eye of the teacher.

Mistress Imogene blinked. Master Florian said, dubiously, "I suppose we can work something out when you have a spell to try. We can make arrangements."

"We had practicum three times a week at Graytowers," said Rob. "Is that a change since you were there?"

Kenneth fought down his smile. It would be his duty to see that they kept up their studies, since he was the only one from Graytowers with any authority, but the task would not be hard.

"You're not at Graytowers," said Mistress Henriette, with delicate poison.

"Good heavens," said Mistress Imogene. "There is no need to quarrel. Kenneth can oversee them."

Kenneth blinked.

Mistress Imogene went serenely on. "As far as Kenneth's own studies go, he can work without oversight. It's not for nothing that boys his age can leave Graytowers for further studies elsewhere."

Usually under tutors, thought Kenneth. Like you for Pearl.

"And he can tell us what he has planned," said Master Florian.

"Preservation," he repeated, flatly. "After that, scrying."

Master Florian chortled. "As long as you stick to the past and the present."

"Of course," he said, even more flatly. As if the prohibition against fortune-telling were not taught them in the first year!

Chapter 7—Studying

Days passed and added up into weeks. Irises bloomed in colors like a jewelry box, and faded again. Daisies and clover started to blossom. Kenneth read whatever he could find that he thought was in fourth year of studies, and did his best to oversee the three's studies, steering a little here and there, though he did not try to stop them when they studied spells out of order, so they learned past their year. He felt fairly certain that they left gaps in their studies, but he could not have directed them more wisely; he did not remember his first year in detail, certainly not precisely enough to dictate the third term, and they did not have the books for much of what he did remember.

Pearl oversaw them, now and again, in return for help with her studies, and she grumbled that she had to omit all mention of Diamond in her letters home.

Asking whether they would soon have a tutor, regardless of whom they asked, met only dead silence.

Once he overheard two wizards talking about how they needed to teach them.

"It's part of the Order's duties, one *condition of our charter*—to teach new wizards."

A snort. "And Pearl's not turning out as desired."

"I thought she kept up with her studies. It was that she was only one student."

"She's flowers, all the way. She will never join the Order, and she would do no good if she did. You can't lure her to the useful studies. And you can't lure Kenneth either. There's a stolid little lad. No imagination."

Kenneth grimaced. That was what he got for eavesdropping.

"As for the younger ones, they still must master the standard course. No, we need to lure other students, more promising than Pearl."

As if they did not need to concern themselves about youngsters not fit for the Order—even those in their charge.

#

"How long," grumbled Jamie, with no question in his tone, "does it take to hire a tutor." He poked at his carrots.

"None at all," said Mistress Imogene. "If you are willing to branch out a bit—"

"For stonework," said Jamie.

"It was, after all," said Rob, "what the pool choose for each of us at Graytowers."

"You do not *have* to accept that," said Master Quentin. "To trod docilely the highway where many feet have trod, so there is nothing new for you."

"The one thing," said Kenneth, buttering his bread, "that you can count on with a highway, is that it will definitely lead somewhere, and a place where many travelers have found it worth their while to go."

"You should not go where others have trod a path," said Mistress Perpetua. "You should go where no one has gone before, and leave a path for others to follow."

He waved his hand, bread and all. "When it is their duty to not follow a path that others have trod? Am I not an 'other'? Am I not encouraging them to fail by following mine, as I would not if I did not leave a trail for them to follow?"

In the silence, Diamond giggled.

"Anyway, the value of a road lies in where it goes, not how new it is, nor in how few people have trod it." He bit into his bread and tried to ignore the silence.

"I'd like to learn some flowers," said Rob, diplomatically.

#

A rattling noise sounded ahead.

The door to their experiment room stood open. Jamie, like the other two, sat at a table, but where Diamond and Rob both had books, what spread before him were castle gems, all vaguely blockish: misty shades of green, purple, blue, and rose, set with runes.

With the rules new set, of course. Jamie pushed two together. Two blue ones stuck. The point of the game being, of course, to work out the rules.

Kenneth watched his work moodily. A good prefect would scold him back to his studies. Then, a good prefect would study himself to set a good example.

Fifty gems. Jamie had set himself a challenge. Two rose cubes joined together. Then two green.

Pearl, rosy-cheeked, swept into the room. "I have something to show you." Diamond, barely looking up from her book, gave her a dubious glance, but Pearl, oblivious, put down some earth wrapped in burlap, some seeds, and a crystal globe—hollow, he noted, with an opening.

She looked about. "For all of you. It's a simple spell. Anike laughed her head off when I did not know it when I came here. But it's useful."

She smiled, magnanimously. "Can you tell me what those seeds are?"

Kenneth started to move, then looked at the three. Rob stepped forward and cupped his hand over the seeds for the spell.

"Bitterthorn."

Jamie blinked. Diamond scowled. Kenneth folded his arms and hoped this proved to be useful.

Rob lifted his hand. "Which will not grow in Quiet Valley."

Pearl smiled and intoned a spell over the crystal. It seemed fairly intricate, actually. Then she slid seed and water and earth into the globe and cast the spell to make it sprout in five minutes.

Then she stood back. They waited. Five minutes later, leaves peeked over the earth, still a moderately shade of green, and not the midnight green of its full growth, and not a sign of its thorns, but still, obviously bitterthorn.

"Can that work for any kind of magic?" said Diamond. "How large can it get?"

"Yes, but not much larger than this," said Pearl. "And it can not be moved. A great weakness of stonework, how little you can move its workings. This is why it is a curiosity widely known only among those who work in place such as Quiet Valley. And in the Order."

She moved a hand over the crystal, the plant's next sprouts withered, and the growth turned black. She moved another, dispelling, and picked up the crystal.

"I can help you with experiments. Relieve Kenneth of having to do it all." She smiled on him. "After all, readiness is all. I must await, with all due patience, the fruition of what I have planted under Mistress Imogene's tutelage."

They all nodded. No students escaped their first session working with plants at Graytowers—in the first week at the towers—without learning that forcing plants changed their virtues.

Though not so much, noted Kenneth, that bitterthorn could grow without the sphere.

#

The next morning, Kenneth had just climbed down to breakfast when Rob's voice rang brightly outside.

He looked out the front door. In the gray and the dew, Pearl, under Mistress Imogene's eye, drilled Rob on flowers. A basic rubric of spring flowers, he thought—crocuses and tulips and scilly, he recognized the names of, though the list went much further. He supposed even in flowers, a basic knowledge was needed before field work, though he noticed, as Rob rattled on, that the list included any time in the spring from the earliest to the latest.

"Good morning, young Kenneth," said Mistress Imogene. "Have you come to join our studies?"

Kenneth shook his head. "Stonework for me."

Pearl's mouth pursed. "But you're so eager to learn—we could study together again—and you always said that you did not choose stonework out of love of it."

"Neither did you," said Kenneth. "You chose it because there is no Tower of Flowers."

"It is," conceded Mistress Imogene, "mostly advanced work."

"Most towers split off actual studies only in the advanced work," said Kenneth. "Every class is in common before then. There is no Tower of Flowers because those who would study there would not find work using their knowledge. Or most of them wouldn't."

Pearl put her hands on her hips. "This is—unlike you, Kenneth. Never before have you obstinately kept trying to do the impossible. You accepted the study of magic so placidly—and studied so well with the rest of us—that I did not know that you were sent here to keep you out of the family business until we had been at Graytowers over a year."

Kenneth said nothing. A wry thought said that actually, they hoped that they could train him, and so no longer have to hire the wizards to work for them. He had not realized it until he had studied for years. They had not considered that a course of spellwork that would make him useful to them would let him work elsewhere.

He turned his face away. And that course, he would stick to.

#

A small violet, still dew-laden, perched on his desk and glittered in the sunlight. Not so much as a single dewdrop shifted. He had preserved the violet, and could not continue to fuss over it without wasting time.

"Stop contemplating it," he whispered. "Time to go on. You're setting a bad example."

The dew glittered. On, to something not entirely new, because he had already read up on it. He let his breath out and sat back. Something that, perhaps, might help them. If he could only know what to scry—if only he could scry for what he needed to scry for—but the spell needed something more precise.

He would fall utterly behind if he dithered like this, and set a bad example for the three, and never work out any spells that could aid them against their enemies. He pushed the violet back, and his gaze fell over the small box that Mistress Imogene had provided him, with many assurances that it had been difficult to obtain something so odd for Quiet Valley.

He reached for the box and pulled out the clear, colorless stone, as smooth as a dewdrop itself. Perhaps with it before him, he would feel he had committed himself.

He sat and glared at the stone. The thought that it would be harder to gain what they needed if he did not use it did not move him.

He did not even know whether he mastered what he would have at Graytowers. The sunlight shone over the book, laid open to the directions for spell before him, and he closed his eyes for a moment. He wished he could scry Graytowers and the classes there, but Graytowers, of course, had protections—and wards that would recognize when he scried. Perhaps even who he was. That was one magic he did not want to learn closely this day.

Sunlight glinted from the stone.

He could find out whether the spell worked for something as vague as—something having to do with their abduction.

Kenneth shifted the stone from the direct light, and cast the spell to make it a window.

Gloom engulfed it. Not perfectly. He scrambled to close the window, dimming the room, and a glance at the stone send him scrambling for the door as well. Only with both closed did the gleam within became distinct enough for sight: a room lit only by a distant window, where a wizard lowered his wand from a spell, already cast. Before the wizard, another figure slumped under some kind of miasma, and with a wound in his side, dripping blood.

The wizard caught the falling man and gestured with his free hand. Moments later, a gate, itself gleaming in many colors from its magic, opened to a drab city street. Few moved about, and those few looked dejected and fearful. Plague flags flew everywhere, flapping unevenly in the winds.

Kenneth felt the blood seeping from his face.

The wizard hefted the other man to his shoulder and lugged him into the incongruously bright sunlight. For a moment, no more, Kenneth clearly saw them both. Then, for a minute, he had the room and the view from the gate, but nothing more; he tried to memorize the pattern on the floor. The wizard appeared in the gateway again, and the image winked out.

Kenneth drew a deep breath and chanted the fixing spell. The stone glowed and settled again. He would need many more stones if he did this often, but that vision he needed to fix.

"And to show," he muttered. He rose to his feet and opened the window. Sunlight poured in, and the warm air and the scent of flowers, from a tranquil and flourishing day.

He drew a deep breath. A poor time to go for help. Jamie, Rob, and Diamond were all hard at work at their studies. He ran a hand through his hair. At that, there was little they could do to help him. He thought for a moment, and winced. At all costs, keep Jamie out.

Jamie would wonder, within moments, whether that spell was what they intended for him.

He reached for the box.

At the bottom of the stair, he found no one in the hall. At the doorway, he tried to reckon the swiftest route to a wizard who could help him and looked about.

David Servant was coming up the path. Then he looked at Kenneth and hurried. Kenneth found himself back inside and pushed to sit with his head between his knees before he quite realized what David was doing.

He found that he was breathing in shallow pants.

"Now," barked David, looming over him, "what happened? And *don't* tell me nothing did. You looked less pale when we came out of the Boneyard."

#

With sunlight slanting across the dining hall from the windows, David's face set with his eyes fixed on the stone, and he sat back in his chair.

"Simon," he said.

Kenneth blinked. He sounded very definite.

"The necromancer. Definitely one of the Web." He sighed and spoke more softly. "His victim—looks familiar, nothing more, though I fear he may be one of the Order. With those plague flags, it was certainly months ago." He sat up, and said, firmly. "Bring the stone to dinner, and we will see if we can learn more."

Kenneth found that his voice was a whisper. "I hoped to find something that has to do with why we are here."

"Perhaps you have. It may even be clear before the meal is over. I hope it does not mean ill for my sister and her husband." His expression held little of that hope. "It may just be infighting among the Web. For all their loose structure, they fight over power often enough, and sometimes—actually fight."

"One would think they would just stop working together," said Kenneth.

David gave him a sidelong glance. After a minute, he said, "No tutor yet? Or textbooks?"

Kenneth shook his head.

"Ah. After a casting like that, it might be wise for you to study no more this day. Scrying takes more out of you than you might realize." David glanced over the stone. "Not so much as when you scry things simpler than this, which may have misled you—"

"This was my first."

His words plopped into the silence and spread like ripples.

"Ah," said David. "You seemed to have mastered it on your first try."

Minutes later, he rose to his feet. "Don't tell Jamie I was here."

Kenneth nodded, slowly. "I'll tell them about the crystal. I do not keep secrets from them."

David winced but did not argue. "I'll be back later today."

#

The first roses had bloomed, and some were past their prime, fading and losing petals. Snow white, deep crimson, glowing yellow, blood red, delicate pinks—the path through the rose garden was long and winding, and had enough rose petals for any purpose.

"Amazed it grows," said Rob.

"Every plant grows like nobody's business in this valley," said Jamie.

Rob waved a hand in the air and sent red petals cascading. "It's not the growth, it's the thorns. Bitterthorn can't for its. The flower's not carved into castles and embroidered on clothes for nothing, and it's the sort of defense that would go against Quiet Valley's enchantments."

"It doesn't defend until attacked," said Diamond. "It might not go against them until then." She looked thoughtful. "Or they use it for a different sort of spell. It has a lot of virtues."

"Histories might tell," said Rob.

"Even if they agree," said Kenneth, "don't bewitch it."

They laughed a little at that, and Rob said, "As if we could."

Kenneth said nothing. He had learned something about its uses in the spring that he had been their age but no uses from that year of study were safe to use in the valley.

They wound their way up the pine forest and back to the building where they found David at a table in the dining hall, sorting out piles of books.

Jamie shouted in glee and ran to hug him. David rumpled his hair.

"Decided it was high time you had some help to steer you, since I can't play Master David often." He put the last book in place. "They aren't textbooks like Graytowers'—but they are better than nothing as a course of study." He smiled. "Contain warnings about how to practice up on the spells, and what is best to start with."

Kenneth looked away, but David went on as if he saw nothing.

"They're the sort of book that the writers of the textbooks use, when writing and revising them."

Diamond headed toward the piles, with an intent look on her face.

"And yes, Diamond, Rob, I did include mathematics and history works in the list."

As the three poured over them, David turned to Kenneth and pitched his voice low. "Do you still have that stone?"

"It's upstairs." Kenneth shrugged. "Safe until dinner time, which is any minute now." He carefully did not look at the books.

#

When he reached the door at the bottom of the stairway, the wizards had filed into the room, and all of them looked up. The three were still rapt in their books.

Just as well, he told himself, and brought the box over to the table where the master wizards sat. The scene unfolded before them, turned black, and began again.

It had caught more of the spellwork than he had thought, said a wayward thought, but Mistress Kyra's breath hissed out, distracting him.

"You should have showed us at once!" she said.

"What good would that do?" said Master Giles, sourly, looking rather green. "You know it shows only the past."

Her hand swept the air. "It can show as little as a moment ago. Now—it is certainly *hours*." She snatched up the crystal. "Anike, we're leaving. We'll send for our things after."

Kenneth's mouth did not managed to shut before mother and daughter had vanished out the doorway. Then he choked out, "That's my crystal."

"Better this way, lad," said Master Giles, heavily. "You don't want to be involved."

"He is involved," said Rob. He still held a book, but his gaze was fixed on the master wizards.

As the other two also looked. Then, Mistress Kyra's reaction had been hard to miss.

"They tried to kill him," said Rob. "And we are all in hiding."

"At least you can study properly now," said Master Giles, with a heartiness that did not fit his still greenish complexion. "No more of this nonsense—you should steer clear of it."

"A window is always dangerous," said Mistress Henrietta, fastidiously. "Never open one to a place where you do not know what could look back."

Kenneth folded his arms, drew a deep breath, and kept his voice steady. "I thought I was supposed to direct my own studies."

The master wizards fell silent. Jamie giggled. Diamond frowned in thought. Rob looked almost abstracted, as if he were already chronicling the scene.

Mistress Henrietta's hands fluttered. "Not like that."

"And," said Master Thomas, "we will not give you a crystal to use."

Kenneth felt the color draining from his face as he glared at the man. "How much of an attack could he launch? That would affect other matters of my studies."

David laughed, not sounding very amused. "Fortunately, you have mastered that spell—cast it right the first time. You need to go on." He sat back. "Mistress Imogene can advise you about dangers."

"You can't tell them yourself?" said Mistress Imogene.

"He wasn't Tower of Stone," said Master Giles.

"And," said David, "I will be gone after dinner. I can not stay the night. I push my luck with the raven with merely this."

Mistress Henrietta raised an eyebrow, and summoned the dishes.

#

At meal's end, David stood. Jamie hopped up.

"We can show you to the border."

"As long as you do not go off," said Master Giles, his tone quelling.

"Kenneth will make sure of it," said Rob. "Sternest prefect the Tower of Stone ever had. And he'll get in his walk, like us."

Kenneth raised an eyebrow, but a second walk would have its points. Especially when they had already had to spy on their elders, and might want to talk.

The sky outside was still brilliantly blue. Not long until summer term, thought Kenneth with a pang.

They walked toward the border, until the trees hid them from the building. David looked back as if idly, checked the lines of sight, and turned on them fiercely.

"Piers was caught again. Briefly. They bungled it—but they did find out what he worked on. And that spell—" He shook his head. "Be careful. Be very careful. Even that spell you cast—they were right in that, it could have endangered you, Kenneth, to have scried that."

The three stopped and stared at the two of them, listening intently, but they had as much right to know as he did.

"I am in danger," said Kenneth. "Great danger. Most likely, increasing danger, since they have more time to plot against us." He drew a deep breath. "We don't even know what the Order knows. And the Order isn't looking hard for more, since they were surprised by a discovery made by a boy who hasn't even finished his fourth year."

"That was stonework," said David.

"Then the Order is derelict in its duties. They should have inducted more stoneworkers. To learn what they can not, with where they have studied." Kenneth put his hands on his hips. "Or I could teach them the spell. It's only a fourth year spell. If worse comes to worst, they could master it by rote."

"Prove it," said David. "Your random searches through the library may have turned up an advanced spell by mistake."

"It was *mastered* by a fourth-year student. It's a fourth year spell."

David raised an eyebrow. Then he glanced aside. "Tell them. They can not see the crystal now, but they should know what it showed."

Carefully, Kenneth recounted it. Diamond scowled at the scanty description of the spell, but said nothing.

Jamie frowned. "I wish—I might have known the young man."

"He wasn't someone who ever visited your parents," said David. "And—they will not let you see. Fortunately, you have the books. They can not stop you from learning enough to protect yourselves. Though I suspect it would be truly advanced work to protect yourself in a manner that made your crystal spell safe."

"Nothing will make it *safe*," said Jamie. "There's no such thing as true safety in this world."

"What a cynical view," said David.

Rob stirred. "They teach it at chapel."

David's gaze moved between them, but a moment later, they reached the border, and he gestured for them to step back. Moments later, he flew off, cawing.

Jamie sighed. "I hope he manages a safe place to perch."

"He managed for months," said Diamond. "Without our help."

None of them turned back until, despite the bright daylight, the raven disappeared with distance. Then, they walked slowly. The sky started to darken.

"Studies tonight," said Kenneth.

Jamie scowled. "We studied today. As long as we would at school. Probably learned more."

"We don't know that," said Diamond. "We could have odd holes in vital subjects. *Enormous* holes. At the very least, we need to—review the curriculum."

"In the morning. Or we will have to double-check our work, and so do it twice," said Rob.

He had a point there, but—"It will help to at least look them over tonight." He glanced at Jamie. "You were eager enough to inspect them."

"You have to see what he brought *you*," Diamond told him. "I have a book on geometric figures, Rob a history of the Order *and* a history of the Web, and Jamie one on the use of flowers in protection magic."

"All mine will be different from yours," said Kenneth, dryly.

"He even brought Pearl a book on floragraphy," said Jamie.

Kenneth blinked. She had not seemed grateful.

#

"A good thing," said Jamie, "that they include spells to cart about books in the first weeks at Graytowers!" He inched up the stairs, backward, with the pile of books floating after him like an obedient dog. His eyes were bright, as if he could not bear to look away from them.

Kenneth could not help looking down at his own books, time and again. It had been tedious trying to piece together a course of study from nothing more than the library.

At the top of the stairs, they separated without a word for their own rooms. In his, Kenneth sorted. One book, a history work, stuck to his fingers, not painfully, and not so much that he could not pull away as soon as he thought to try—but he put it aside, his heart pattering. He forced his breath in and out. It was an old technique to alert a person to a concealing spell.

He glanced over his own piles, drew a deep breath, and stood. Jamie exclaimed with glee, and he went to see the other's books, and listen to them chatter, in bright-eyed excitement, as they considered how to fill in the gaps.

"And yours?" said Rob.

"I've mastered the scrying, at least," said Kenneth. "I'll have to draw up a list."

#

The three slept in their dark rooms. Kenneth sat in the pool of light from a radiant stone and pondered the book. David might only have wanted to hide it from the master wizards here, and not the three.

He tested the spell. It came off like the husk from ripe grain, and revealed a book on how to recognize spells.

He sat with it in his lap.

He should go to bed. Staying up too late would be obvious in the morning, and he did not want them to find this book, not if David wanted him to keep it secret.

He rifled through the pages. He needed his sleep. In the morning, he would be trying to patch the holes in his course of study *and* oversee the three in their efforts to do the same. Mistress Imogene could not be *that* much help.

He opened the first page. It spoke of sigils. He picked out the one he had seen in the crystal, and turned to the appropriate page.

#

He yawned the next morning. It had, indeed, been folly. The sigils had formed some kind of protective spell, and one that, he thought, had nothing to do with the murder. And that he worked out only after staying up far too late.

Outside the window, roses bloomed redly. It would be summer break, before summer session, before he knew it. He grimaced.

They sat together through the meal as usual, but there was more planning needed this day than most.

"We have to study through summer break to make sure we catch up," he said.

"We had a break in the early spring," said Diamond. "When we first got here." But her voice held no enthusiasm.

"We wouldn't want to break," said Jamie. "We need to defend ourselves, or we will have a longer break than we can possibly wish for."

"Be wary," said Mistress Perpetua. "You are still in Quiet Valley."

Jamie rolled his eyes.

"You may want to take your walk early," said Mistress Imogene. "Before your studies, perhaps. It's one thing to fall into a routine, but another to trudge in the rain—and it's almost certain to rain."

None of the three seemed to notice what she said. And, Kenneth conceded, he had a hard time listening himself. The book waited, up the stairs.

"It's likely to clear up," said Master Florian. "They can walk after dinner if it comes to that."

Kenneth nodded and stood. "Study time," he said, as firmly as he could, and herded them off. He suppressed a yawn in the doorway.

At least, once in their study room, the three went to their books at once. A bird twittered outside the window, in the sunshine, without drawing any attention from the pages.

"We should divvy up them up," said Diamond. "We only got so far last night. All three of us could work out how far we got more swiftly that way."

"Only if you could swear to having each studied the same things," said Kenneth. "Which you can't, since I remember what spellcraft you practiced."

Diamond looked discontented.

"And you will each have to take the tests on your own. They will need that at Graytowers, to prove you learned it."

"Dreamer," breathed Rob, low enough that Kenneth could feign not hearing. Insisting that they had to be ready to return did not mean insisting that it was certain that they would. Or even likely.

"Can't we do our own studies?" said Diamond. "There's enough in the library to study for weeks by itself. And we might need spells we can cast here."

"Only if it's on top of the coursework," said Kenneth. He turned to his own books.

"Some of the library, we'll need for the course," said Rob. "Because we're in Quiet Valley."

#

Diamond triumphantly produced the sphere. The light in the room was turning orange with evening, but she had gotten Pearl's spell down, and altered, and approved by Mistress Imogene, in a day. The difference from Pearl's spell was subtle, but methodical. Moments after, Diamond cast a spell, and the stone within was strengthened to cast back attacks.

Diamond grinned.

"Will we need one for every time we have to test?" said Jamie.

"I could make a permanent one," said Diamond, "but it would take time from my studies." She batted her eyelashes, and they laughed—for an unreasonably long time, thought Kenneth, catching his breath.

Jamie shrugged. "We could use the practice. Do you need help cleaning that up before the walk?" He stretched his arms over his head. "It would do us some good. Shake up all the thoughts we've been stuffing into our heads."

"I'm afraid," said a voice from the doorway, "that the three of you will have to manage that."

Kenneth blinked, surprised and not quite certain that he had recognized the voice—but Master Bonaventure did indeed stand there, inspecting them as if the room were an everyday classroom at Graytowers. David Servant leaned against the wall behind him.

"Kenneth, I wish to speak to you."

The three gawked. Kenneth, feeling cold, nodded.

"We'll need that book with the spell you used on that crystal," said David.

"It's in my room."

"We'll just plot, then," said Jamie, cheerfully. "To overthrow the Web. Or maybe Graytowers." David grinned at him.

With less cheer, Kenneth walked down the corridor. It took him moments to dig up the slim tome.

"Sophonisba," said Master Bonaventure with a glance at the cover. "It surprises me—astounds me—that anyone let you read it."

"It was in the library." His gaze jerked back and forth between the two of them. "They let us loose in there."

Master Bonaventure steepled his fingers together. "I suspect that I had spoken more of their need to take care, they would have banned you entirely, not kept better watch. But—the Order, as well as the Web, had its outer reaches." He shook his head. "This is no refuge for young students."

For a moment, Kenneth's heart leapt, but Master Bonaventure said nothing more. Certainly nothing about removing them to a more fitting place.

"I gave him her work on spellcraft," said David, idly.

Mutely, Kenneth produced it, mentioning no more than David had that David had disguised it.

"Ah, the one for which she was on the borders of the Web." Master Bonaventure smiled. "That will serve you well." After a moment, he added, "Is there anything you need to cast the spell?"

"Besides the crystal, of course," said David, producing one.

"I have it all here," said Kenneth. Methodically, he arranged it, with the two of them watching as carefully as if they were testing his original casting. He let out his breath. Probably David had gone directly to Master Bonaventure, and they had come as soon as David persuaded him. David had not had a chance to give him warning.

He still felt their gazes on him every moment.

Finally, he put the radiant stone on the desk and went to the windows. Clouds had come, and thickened, but the day was still bright enough to glow. He pulled the shutters closed.

The room plunged into shadows—the radiant stone's light, no greater than a candle's, engulfed by them. The crystal glittered. Master Bonaventure and David looked barely human in the light and shadow patterned on their faces.

He walked back to the desk. "I only strove to see something relevant to—" He waved a hand at the walls about them. "I do not know what it will show."

Master Bonaventure nodded with magisterial gravity. Kenneth had not seen him look so grave even on the night they had been abducted.

He cast the spell. A tiny image appeared in the crystal. Swift as a striking hawk, David hid the radiant stone, quenching its light. The crystal showed clearly enough, by its own light, a mechanica still being built.

Kenneth's gaze traced cogs and posts and springs—not an orrey or the like—and said, "That's stonework."

"That's liminal work," said David, mildly but definitely.

Kenneth scowled and stared. It was stonework, however odd.

"It's both," said Master Bonaventure, as mildly as a May breeze that barely stirred falling petals. "Which is a matter of grave import. Kenneth, seal the vision. We must discuss this in council."

Kenneth sealed the crystal, knowing he was not included in the "we," and held it out. "Watch out for opals being stolen or sold. Especially the large, fine ones."

"I suspect," said David, "that they took care to have opals enough very early. Even started with the opal, and then decided on the mechanica."

Rain thundered against the roof and wall. Kenneth went to open the shutter. The view was smeared past visibility from the rainfall.

"We'll have to hope that Master Florian was right," said Kenneth. "For now—well, you had games and things for rainy days."

Jamie stared longingly at the sodden landscape, but Rob nodded and said, "Join us?"

"I—am afraid I stayed up too late last night. I have to nap. I hope the prefect spell will keep it in order—I've never tried to use it after staying up late, instead of before."

"Should have checked!" said Jamie, grinning.

For a moment, he thought he should tell them, but—staying up would only be tedious. He could tell them of anything of import. And he did not want to talk of his knowledge here.

#

After dinner, and after they had walked on puddle-filled paths, to return with soaked shoes and withdraw to their rooms, wizards started to arrive. Kenneth, like the others, turned to the spellcraft to dry out the shoes, and tried to not peer. The other three did not seem to notice the convergence, and he did not encourage them to.

He hoped that David had either not realized that they had spied the first time, or kept his silence.

He sat in his room and waited, until, from the sounds down the corridor, the three were abed. It would serve him right if one were spying on him, but that one would learn nothing more than he would tell the others in the morning.

He started the spell and listened. It had been an hour; their number had increased past those he had seen arrive.

They gathered with grumbles, and observations that even Master Bonaventure could play the fool, to finally, Master Bonaventure laying the crystals before them. A welter of voices rose.

"He's only a scholar."

"He's not under anyone's tutelage."

"He just learned the spell."

"And he might have miscast it—it may have nothing to do with his plight."

"Even if he got it right, how close to us could it be?"

"The deeds of a century ago might be pertinent to their plight."

"It's very unlike the Web." —a new voice, querulous.

"A mechanica that uses both liminal magic and stonework is likely to be important," said Master Bonaventure, "whatever their plight."

A moment's silence, before a voice spoke, smoothly. "A century-old thing could have affected their plight, but it would have to be so vast that the effects would be large, and unlikely to be limited."

"Very unlike the Web. They like to work in secrecy and call it power."

"The attack on the Fittons was not done in secrecy," said David crisply.

That silenced them for longer. Then the voices rose again. Kenneth stared at the wall. He needed his sleep. The prefect spell would last only so long.

He sat up. It was over an hour before he admitted to himself that he had wasted his time.

#

Morning light made the room glow. Diamond scowled as if the silver bowl before her was thwarting her with personal malice.

"We need a teacher," she said.

Kenneth walked over to his desk, pondering how to tell them.

"Can you tell me what I'm doing wrong?" she said, brightly. He sighed and looked at her carefully laid out sigils. He remembered that spell.

"It's not the book one," he said.

She started. "It's just some tweaks—"

"Do the book. If that doesn't work, we'll have to dig harder. If it does, add your changes one by one."

She grimaced but turned back to the book.

Kenneth drew a deep breath. "David and Master Bonaventure came here to see me cast the spell on the crystal again."

Jamie scowled. Rob looked mildly interested. Diamond barely glanced up.

"It showed a mechanica that used stonework *and* liminal magic."

Diamond stared at him. "That's not—"

"Web," said Jamie curtly.

"I do not think the Order will act on that knowledge. But now you know." He looked at Diamond. "There are always opals."

She grimaced and said nothing.

#

The roses and lilies blossomed along the way of their walk, as they went with David to the border.

"Do they have you fetching things, like those school books?" said Jamie.

David laughed. "Now and again, but many do not find the prospect of a raven messenger boy that alluring. Some don't trust me enough to deliver an invitation to tea. I sagely spend much of my time squirreling myself away in odd corners. Studying." He smiled. "It helped me find those books—and I shall expect great things from all four of you. I know how much can be done in such a course of study."

Kenneth's mouth twisted.

The border roses were in full bloom: scarlet and pink and snow white, with the flowers so thick that they hid the leaves, let alone the thorns that fed the protective spells. The air smelled more sweet than a perfumer's shop.

Jamie and David spoke in low voices. Kenneth, at the gap, looked out and then, abruptly, felt dizzy. His hand went to his head without thought. His vision looked—spotted—as it had when they had left the Boneyard.

"I—"

He blinked, and blinked again without clearing his vision, and then he fell, face-forward, landing in the grassy gap, and his head outside the roses. . . nausea seized him.

Diamond screamed.

He could not make out who spoke, or what was said, or which pairs of hands roughly drew him back into the charmed valley. He lay on the grass, breathing hard and barely able to twitch. His pulse hammered in his ears. Voices were low and urgent about him, and close enough that he thought he should hear them clearly. He tried to open his eyes and could not. Hands came down and checked him for injury, with muttered spells behind them.

He managed to open his eyes for a moment. He saw only his own hand, and it looked gray.

"Go," said David, so harshly that his voice could barely be recognized. "Get help!" Footsteps hammered, and Kenneth swallowed against nausea.

David shifted him on the grass, and then scoped him up in his arms, as if he were a small child. He strode off. Kenneth slumped helplessly against his shoulder.

Chapter 8—Changes

He had never seen so many spells cast so rapidly, and never a time when spells were so concentrated on a single patient.

And that despite falling unconscious many times, and rousing to find the spells going full spate, and sometimes in the middle of whispered discussions of his condition.

One grumbled, once, "I hope he's grateful. He's getting more spells than thirty patients would get."

Later, another—or the same one—said, "Anika was right."

But, later still, Kenneth woke in a new room, one he had never seen before. The view from the window showed he was still in Quiet Valley, and the roses still bloomed beneath a crimson and violet sunset. A single star gleamed, diamond-bright, in the darkening sky.

He drew a deep breath and raised his hand. It rose, and it was no longer gray. That much time had passed, at least.

The door opened. David Servant looked him up and down, gravely, before he stood aside and let Jamie, Diamond, and Rob pile in with exclamations, "You're all right!" "You're awake."

Master Bonaventure brought up the end, bringing a bright radiant stone into the room. He looked almost as gray as Kenneth had seen himself.

"Pearl expressed concern about your well-being," he said gravely, "but had to retire before this."

"She said," said Diamond, scornfully, "that she had to get up tomorrow morning before dawn."

"It was Mistress Imogene who said that," said Master Bonaventure, gently.

"So," said Kenneth, and found his voice only a little weak, "there is that advantage in lacking a tutor."

Rob and Jamie laughed. Diamond still looked scornful.

"You knew I was going to wake today?" said Kenneth.

"Kenneth," said David, "it's the same day."

Kenneth blinked. And glanced at the window. Stars lit the sky over the sunset, but the sunset was not utterly gone.

Jamie said, "We—they told us you would wake at night, so we napped during the day, so we could stay up."

"Mistress Imogene kept Pearl at work," said Rob. "She couldn't've."

Even if they had taught her the spell, thought Kenneth.

"You were right about the severity of the curse," said Master Bonaventure, gently. "In the normal course of things, with the normal curse-breaking, you would wake in perhaps a week. But the spells came from the Web, and until you were cured, we could not know that it would not kill you." He sat down. "Also, we had need of your knowledge."

"We need," said David grimly, "to know how the curse hit you."

"And," said Jamie, looking fierce and indignant, "you need to move. They say that we are not safe here." His voice grew more scornful. "And that the valley is not safe with us here."

"True enough," said David. "Half of them say that you must have passed the roses. I told them you stood inside when you fell."

"I—that happened when I felt dizzy. All of a sudden."

Master Bonaventure's breath hissed. "Dizzy. Dizzy and nothing more?"

Kenneth nodded.

Master Bonaventure scowled in thought, as if he no longer saw what was before him. "Do the enchantments ward against mere dizziness? It is not like it can harm in itself."

"You can fall and crack your head," said Jamie. "It's not safe."

"Or fall—and fall out of Quiet Valley," said Kenneth.

"And that shows what a danger you are," said Mistress Imogene from the doorway. "An inch outside, an ell outside, it makes no difference. With your scrying spell on that crystal, you opened a win-

dow, and let them strike you down. You must be moved to break that
link, and the others with you, because *they* know you are here."

She grimaced. "Pearl as well. Horribly unfair to her. We will have
to reinforce all the spells here, and she can not stay for that part.
Breaking up her studies horribly."

"You can't have too many places to protect us," said Jamie. "You
should have helped us more to study the peril and the protections, so
we can *fight*."

David's voice was as harsh as a raven's caw. "Jamie, you should
have studied Kenneth's condition after the curse struck him down, if
you scorn protection that much. Because you could easily end up like
him. Only without the magic to heal you."

#

Dawn was gray with mist. Pearl's face had never looked so sullen.

"There are flowers on the shore," said Mistress Imogene, as coldly
as stone.

Over his oatmeal, Kenneth thought they might have to ship her
off and send her things after, as the four of them had left Graytowers. They had packed before breakfast, taking the most care over the
books—Diamond had sighed over the library, but not hesitated in
her work.

"Perhaps there will be a library at this—place at the shore," he
said.

"I wonder if it's a *keep*," whispered Jamie, bright-eyed.

"Could be," said Rob, with slow thoughtfulness. "The shoreline
has a lot of keeps, but I don't think any of them fell under the Order's
keeping." And looked innocent.

Diamond gave Pearl a poisonous glance and lowered her voice.
"The sooner *she* packs, the faster we will find out."

Pearl shoved back from the table and flounced off.

"A good sign, I suppose," said Kenneth. Diamond grimaced.

"There you are," said Master Bonaventure from the doorway. "Come this way."

He led them out into a cloudy day, where the mist was burning away, leaving it bright, and into one of the gardens, one surrounded by a hedge of boxwood, its tiny leaves smelling more like spice than greenery. Rob looked thoughtful, and Kenneth told himself to ask afterward about its protective spells.

Once inside, Master Bonaventure turned to them. "It's about the crystal that Kenneth first enchanted. Or what it showed, rather."

"The way he killed that man?" said Jamie, diffidently.

"Murdered him," said Master Bonaventure. "All to use his blood to damage the labyrinth they stood on."

Kenneth winced. A fugitive thought said that he had identified it rightly.

"A hunt is up for Simon now, but he has not been caught. You must stay safe. Otherwise, your blood will be used to break the workings of spells that are important to the safety of many people."

Jamie seemed lost in thought as Master Bonaventure led them out again. Mistress Imogene stood there.

"Pearl has not finished packing," she said. "And asked me why I ordered her about when I was no longer her tutor."

"Then," said Master Bonaventure, "her things will be sent after her." He swept off.

Diamond sighed. "He should have lectured Pearl with us. Or instead of us. *We* know that they murder innocent strangers in the middle of labyrinths."

"Maybe different ones," said Rob. "Different studies, different scholars. May even be different factions, feuding within the Web—and different tactics as a result."

"Such as murdering someone without intent to damage the labyrinth?" said Jamie.

"Different studies could just as well mean that they aren't rivals," said Diamond. "They could pool their knowledge to make a greater spell, and a greater danger."

"Maybe," said Rob. "But it's not a pool, it's a building, and not all the parts would work together. A pool can hold anything poured in, and magical knowledge doesn't work like that."

Jamie laughed. "But if you pour in oil and water—"

The sun shone through the clouds. Lilies bloomed in glorious pinks and yellows like a dawn about them, and the three squabbled cheerfully about possibility and metaphor.

Kenneth smiled. Everything they said was, he supposed, possible.

A sullen Pearl joined them, and the three fell silent like a fire being banked. Master Bonaventure lowered his voice and told them they were going to the Lighthouse. He and David led them down the hill to the doorway to the Boneyard. There he conjured a luminous spell and gave it to David, who led them down the stairs toward the Boneyard.

In the shadows cast by Master Bonaventure's spell, Jamie said, "I am going to learn how to keep bloodwork from destroying protective magics."

David did not so much as twitch; the light did not tremble.

"Probably not with the standard course," said Kenneth. "You'll have to complete it first." David reached the floor, and Kenneth walked after. Master Bonaventure closed the door behind them. "Rob, what were you noticing about the hedges earlier?"

"Oh, it's a secret keeper," said Rob. "Not a common spell now, or ever. It didn't ward off listeners or hush words. It *misdirected* them."

The shelves appeared ahead.

"They're like hedgerows, keeping the traveler on the road and away from the fields."

The Boneyard's air seemed to settle about them like a mist as they trudged on, and Rob's cheerful prattle cut off.

Soon they were in the path and walking onward by the light of their spells. Some things were recognizable from the last trip, which felt oddly unnerving.

Kenneth's gaze went over a shelf filled with the glints of polished gemstones, and then he stopped. The largest of them, it had been there—he wished he could be sure it had been an opal—

"Kenneth," said Pearl, sounding more crabby than he had ever heard from her before, "you're not supposed to stop in the middle of the Boneyard."

He did not take a step. "Something's missing."

Diamond, Jamie, and Rob all looked sharply at him, their faces showing only worry.

"Where?" said David.

Kenneth pointed. David stared with intensity.

"There's gaps all over the place," said Pearl, "and it's not as if it left a gap in the dust that isn't there. How could you *tell*?"

"We've been here before," said Diamond.

David shook himself as if throwing a fly. "That won't be for long. Come." He set a brisk pace. Kenneth fell behind to keep a watch on the others. Pearl lagged, until she stood by him, and turned her resentful face on him. Her mouth opened.

"Did you look at me when David Servant carried me in?" said Kenneth, his voice low and intense. Pearl winced and hurried on. Kenneth gave her a moment before picking up his pace. Diamond had been more reasonable on just hearing of the peril, he thought.

Then, he reminded himself, she had seen things the night that Jamie's parents had disappeared.

The next shelves were filled with driftwood—broken crates and fallen tree boughs weathered by the sea—with sea shells, with glass worn to brightly colored pebbles by the waves. They were advancing, and his heart rose more than he would have thought a new route would bring.

Past those were shelves laden with yarn and thread—some undyed, some bright with fresh dye, some faded almost to its raw shade—and past that, dried herbs. For a moment, he thought of asking Pearl whether they were seashore plants, but, no, the sea things had given him false hope. Past more shelves of boxes, bags, and bales. Past children's toys, broken or worn or perfectly new. Heaps of clothes, whether men's or women's or children's, he could not tell, but some were jewel-bright silks, and more, dingy shades sewn from a cheap weave.

On and on. The shelves blurred together. China figures. Orreys in brass and tarnished copper and pure gold. Books—without gaps, David Servant had not found their books here.

When the floor extended from the shelves, he blinked, thinking it had been hours, and hurried after to be the last one up the stairs.

Sunlight greeted them outside. Broad daylight—he had not misjudged the length of the journey. A warm sea breeze with the scent of wild roses brushed against them and made the tall grass bend. Pale sand spread out toward glittering waves. Kenneth thought he saw a rocky shore, but dunes and plants did much to hide it.

Pearl reeled, and her face was whiter than salt. He caught her arm and eased her down. Then he plopped down on the sand himself. Diamond sat by her sister and told her how they had all fainted, coming out in Quiet Valley.

"But," said Jamie, his arms wrapped about his bent knees where he sat, "where's the Lighthouse?"

David Servant cleared his throat. "This is your first visit here. You do not have the freedom of the Lighthouse. You will have to be guided in by the light."

Kenneth, and the others, looked. Bright as the sun was, and however the waters glittered, it could not have completely drowned the Lighthouse's beam. Kenneth frowned. Could it have?

"In the evening."

Jamie looked aghast, and Kenneth wondered himself. He would not have believed that David Servant would drag them out of bed to wait about like luggage for hours.

Pearl's face worked.

Diamond burst out, "Then what was the point of hustling us here at that hour?"

With a sudden expression of sagacity, Jamie said, "It wasn't to get us to the Lighthouse. It was to get us out of Quiet Valley. And the risk there."

"Surely," said Pearl, "the risk from *Kenneth*?" Her hand rose, and fell. The wind pulled on her hair. "Even if it was easier to move us together."

"No," said Jamie. "At least, they could not know it was just Kenneth. Their histories of Quiet Valley mention no such intrusion." He scowled. "They could not know about the risk to the valley, either."

"We are prepared for the delay," said David. "Come, if you can stand."

Kenneth rose. Pearl was the last, which seemed more from reluctance than the Boneyard's effect. He did not, quite, sigh.

The air smelled more fishy with a shift in breeze. They followed David.

Sand lay, drifted, over the path, but the way was clear enough, between the dune grass and clover in yellow and purple, the vetch in pink, and the wild roses with hot pink petals—single roses, with only five petals, but enormous. Further into the dunes, juniper with their small needles blue-green, and pines with their longer needles green, or amber red, grew into shapes so twisted that the trees often had dead and needle-less branches mixed with those still alive. Here and there, enormous pieces of driftwood sprawled, pale as bone.

The wind came from this way, and that, sometimes smelling more, and sometimes less, of the sea. Sand hissed, falling, at times, before it.

"Are the roses protective?" said Rob, chirpily.

"They grow wild all along the shore," said David. "I do not know whether the Lighthouse pressed them into use. I supposed if they have a history of it, it will tell. . . but I do know that the roses do not demark the boundaries. I'm not sure what does. Safer to stay far, far within. At least until they can tell you where safety lies."

They came about a high dune overgrown with roses, grass, and junipers. Behind it stood a cabin built of weathered wood, if not actually from driftwood. Small songbirds nested in the wooden shingles. Shutters were pulled back from its few windows, but the inside was too shadowy to be seen clearly. David opened the door.

Half a dozen windows let in light on wooden benches, of which the best that could be said was that they did not look rickety, or full of splinters.

"Can't we walk about the shore?" said Kenneth. "This place must have strong protections, or they would never have sent us here."

"Immense ones," said Rob.

"They built this Lighthouse to counter the sorcery of wreckers," said Jamie. "Who would have broken through anything except the most powerful of enchantments."

"We don't know the bounds," said David, wearily. He walked in and sat. "And if you went too near the Lighthouse, you would be protected against. The enchantments do not know you are not wreckers."

The wind blew through the windows, for the moment crisp. They filtered in and sat. Kenneth felt glad that he could lean against the wall. A bird chirped, on the roof.

"There *have* to be places where we could have been taken in at once," said Diamond.

Pearl smiled on her.

"There's the Ivory Tower," said Jamie. "The Castle Rosarium. Even the House of Dreams. Some of them have to be under the Order's watch."

"You were expecting to be taken to the Marketplace?" said David sourly. "They can't. There are still too many wizards in the Order who don't really believe in my innocence. Even if I could deliver you and escape unnoticed, you would pick a fight on the matter."

Jamie glared at him, but did not argue.

"It wasn't my idea to bring you here," said David. "Still less at this time of day. It keeps me from rushing off with the news that something was stolen out of the Boneyard."

The air was still for a time. A gull's scream carried from far off.

"Can we at least get at our books?" said Diamond.

David shook his head. "Not with the way they are brought." He hesitated a moment. "The Lighthouse does have a library."

"Since we can't get there," said Rob, sitting up straight, "Diamond will regale us with the mathematics of our journey. We were on the way for *hours*. Nothing like getting *to* the valley. So how does the geometry work?"

"It's not distance," said Jamie. "I know that much of the Boneyard—and it's not so great a difference, as the crow flies."

David's mouth twitched.

Diamond's forehead creased as she scowled. "I'd guess likeness—you saw the things, they get sorted on the shelves, it must be by the spell—so if they are closer to each other by likeness—" Her scowl deepened.

How alike were the valley and the school? Still more, how in a manner that they didn't have in common with the lighthouse. It—

"It may not be the places," said Kenneth. "Perhaps the way to the valley from Graytowers is better known. So, not lost. Or not so lost."

Diamond's face lit up. "It could be. I could test—" Her face froze. "Not here. I think. Maybe at the Lighthouse."

Pearl slumped again. "It's going to be a long afternoon."

"Do you know anything about the Lighthouse?" said Diamond to David. "Quiet Valley was hard enough to work in until we devised how to protect spells from it. And it from our spells."

"And it wasn't wonderful even then," said Jamie.

David looked cornered.

"It's directional magic," said Rob. "We might have to watch how things flow."

"The third kind of protection," said Jamie. "There's shielding, ablative, and directional." He stared out the window.

"There's the stone, too, on the shore," said Kenneth. "We should not forgo the chance to study it if we can."

"Is there going to be any nourishing magic in this afternoon?" said Pearl.

"In a bit," said David.

Kenneth sighed and sat back. That no doubt meant what it did when any adult said it.

Chapter 9—Storm

The blue sky was only faintly touched with pink and yellow. David sat, leaning back against the wall. Next to him sat a basket, utterly empty of a rather inadequate meal. Rob, Diamond, and Jamie had managed to curl up on the benches and nap without even the aid of spells.

Pearl, in the corner, sulked.

Kenneth went to the window before he started to sulk himself. He watched the colors of the sky and the seascape below. And then—

It was not as if it shimmered, or solidified out of mist. It was just that the Lighthouse stood there. Its light swept over the still glittering waves.

"It's here!" called Kenneth. "It's here, we can see it!"

David blinked. Diamond yawned and rubbed her eyes. Rob scrambled over to the window. Moments later, Jamie swung his legs off the bench and headed to the door. Kenneth followed him, and behind, Diamond went over to Pearl.

Moments later, he heard Diamond's voice: "You can stay if you want."

Kenneth sighed. Sleep and food might let her regain her spirits. Pearl had always been out of temper the first few days of a term. And if not—flowers surrounded the Lighthouse. Inspecting the library might give her ways to continue her studies. And learn new things.

The winds had shifted, and blew steadily toward the waves. The grass bent low as if pointing the way before them. Jamie already plugged onward, and the rest of them followed.

Diamond eyed the beam. "The protection must be circular."

"Concentric, maybe," said Jamie. His hand swept out. "As the light dies."

"I think," said Kenneth, "that we will not have to consult their library for a history to find that out. They will tell us at once so that we will not wander too far."

"If they don't just lock us up," said Pearl. "That will keep us safe, for months and months, as long as they remember to keep us fed and don't mind if we go mad."

"They didn't lock you up in Quiet Valley," said David.

"That was before his—feat at the border," said Pearl.

"Master Bonaventure would mind if we went mad," said Kenneth. "Even if they don't, they mind if he gets angry with them."

Then, as the sky grew dark, they climbed on a rocky prominence, with the tower looming ahead. About its foot stood many flowers, more than they had seen on the wild land: roses in many delicate hues, sea lavender, and black-eyed susans.

Something for Pearl at any rate.

A door opened, a gap of light in the shadowed stone. A man stood there, side-lit, enough to make out that he dressed as a sea-captain would. He pulled back as they approached, and the light fell on his weather-beaten face, and his white hair and beard.

"This is Captain Robert Seaborn," said David. The man nodded. "These are Kenneth Mornington, Pearl Dombrey, Jamie Fitton, Rob Oldcastle, and Diamond Dombrey."

Kenneth nodded at his name, as the others did.

David took a step backward. "And with them in your care, I have to be off."

The captain opened his mouth, but a raven already winged its way inland, with only the briefest of breezes from its beating wings.

"Do the protections keep him out?" said Jamie. "Because it's deathly magic?"

"Only symbolical," said Captain Seaborn, his voice deep. He held the door open wider. "He can return. For now, come in."

#

Fish stew for dinner, at a table with half a dozen wizards. Or four fishermen and sailors who had mastered spells, probably by rote, and two severe women, rather less weather-beaten, but, Kenneth suspected, with equally rote spells. All gathered in a white-washed room, with a floor of brownish tile, furnishings of sandy-beige wood, except for a tall clock. It had a dark walnut case, and enameled figures on its face, of sun and moon and stars, of waves and wind and seabirds. It reminded him of the mechanica at Graytowers, though he suspected this one was more pragmatic. On the wall, pegs held mantles, most of a bright yellow, and an arched gap in the wall showed a small kitchen.

The company was all bent on conversation, low-voiced but intense, that they did not break even to introduce themselves.

At the meal's end, one woman said, her voice deep, "We'll show you your rooms, but we're not going to be much help to you, before the day after tomorrow."

"Why not?" said Pearl, surly.

The woman pointed her spoon at the room's small, round window. The sunset was made of pastel clouds, wisps, or clumps laid out like fish scales, all pink below and purple above.

"Red sky in morning, sailors take warning," said the other woman, her voice light and high. "Red sky at night, sailors' delight. It was red this morning."

"Also," said Captain Seaborn, "mackerel skies and mares' tails make tall ships carry short sails."

Kenneth nodded and sat back. "Did our luggage arrive?"

"All ship-shape and stowed in your rooms," said one sailor, smiling and standing. "I can show 'em up, if you like. You two will have plenty, what with the widows' spells."

The second woman nodded, and already looked lost in thought.

He winked. "Bos'n Billy, at your service."

Chairs scrapped back, and they followed their guide into a short corridor. He pointed out a niche where a sea chest sat. "The letter box. If you get any."

Moments after, he led them up a coiling stairway. The walls were as white as the dining room, but stone.

Bos'n Billy said, "With all the men at sea, it fell to the women-folks to keep up the spells so the harbor stayed ship-shape. And those who did it the most were those who was still hoping for a man coming back long after they'd been widows."

Pearl, her face cold, nodded. "Will it will be possible to tell us how far we can walk, tomorrow?"

"How far? Yes—for miles. How to navigate about in that distance, so you know? That's harder. It'll take longer."

Pearl sighed. Then Bos'n Billy pointed out their rooms: small, white-washed, with tiny port-like windows. The beds were bunks built into the walls, and the floor barely had room for their chests, a wardrobe, and space enough to walk to the bed. They would need some other place to study.

Kenneth, in the doorway of his room, turned to see that none of the others had gone into theirs, though Bos'n Billy had already vanished around the curve of the stairs.

"Looks like we have time to unpack," he said, as cheerfully as he could muster. "And be ready to study in the morning."

Pearl stared at him. "Did they overdo the spells to restore your health? Bursting with energy to study after only two days?"

"We need to study," said Jamie. "This way we can fight them. The wizards who killed my parents."

Kenneth's mouth twitched.

"That is what the Order is for," said Pearl. "And the king's men. The idea that a pipsqueak like you can manage something they can not—"

"Like save me from Piers Lawrence in the heart of the Labyrinth of Thought?" said Kenneth, hooking his hand on his belt. "When the Order had not even found where we were? We worked out how to return before they learned that."

"Did you see the shells?" said Diamond, too quickly. "In the stone of the wall? They weren't magic, either. It must be part of it."

Kenneth blinked, and then said, almost as quickly, "You should have spent longer on your basic geology if you found that astounding. It's limestone. They make whitewash of it, too."

"Wise," said Jamie. "Sea stone to deal with sea magic."

"Don't count on it," said Rob. "Half the time when I look up why some castle used some stone, or some other thing, for its significance and its virtues, it turns out that was just the stuff at hand."

"Doesn't matter," said Diamond. "It means what it means even if they didn't know it. Like—" Her hand curved. "The round tower. It has sound architectural reason, encloses the most room with the least boundary. And that's why we can build such wizardry on it: It is significant, it can be built on, precisely because it is so practical." She threw her hand into the air. "For stonework, that is. For other kinds, they might need to plaster on some ornament, but then it would be less—" Her mouth twitched. "—foundational."

"Nine times out of ten," said Rob, "they never bother to use the stuff they built in."

"Such insight," said Pearl, sourly.

"We should have had Bos'n Billy show us the way to the library," said Kenneth. "Then we could look up this place's history. Especially since he did not show us a workroom."

Jamie waved up the corridor. "More rooms there. Some might be workrooms."

"No," said Rob. "Those are for more wizards. This place once held scores of wizards, and hundreds at times. They had to divert the fleets of the Purple Pirates."

"Purple—" Pearl laughed.

"They dyed their sail purple to show they served a pirate *queen*," said Rob sourly. "And they murdered and looted and tortured and enslaved like any other pirate. They destroyed cities with fire and sword for treasure and captives. The wizards here blew them into the middle of the sea and becalmed them there. Then they fouled their water with curses. Five or six fleets they did that to, where not one pirate in a hundred lived to hang when the navy arrived." He sighed. "And still they had to raid the kingdom and slaughter the pirate queen and her nobles to stop their doing it again."

"We'll have you check the value of the library's histories before we read them," said Kenneth. "For now—we unpack!"

Diamond ducked into her room and stuck her head out again. "They must have practice room. The wizards would not have stopped their spells for storms, or risked doing them in the weather."

Kenneth rolled his eyes.

#

The sunset, down to the darkest shade of purple, had dissolved into blackness. Encroaching clouds hid both stars and the moon—only half full, but still shining at this hour. But the sky was not dark. Relentlessly, the beam of snow-white light ran past his window every minute.

Just as well that a curtain spell was so easy and swift, even when he was yawning with exhaustion, to plunge the room into darkness, and vanish in eight hours.

Though as he settled against the pillow, reflections on the reach of the light, and how far its protection had to stretch made him smile as he nodded off.

#

He woke to a gray-lit room. Even from the bed, the window showed a sullen gray sky, and beneath those clouds, wisps of a lighter gray, blown sharply along by stiff winds.

The view it gave when he stood on the floor was not large, but enough to show the gray waves pounding the shore. He wondered whether the tide was coming in, and then whether he could ask at breakfast. A splatter of rain struck the window.

Diamond already stood, bright-eyed, in the corridor when he emerged. "I thought I heard you."

He smiled at the sounds behind the other doors. "It looks like we will invade breakfast in force."

Minutes later, he led their troop down the stairs, with even Pearl bringing up the end. The clock showed they had risen none too early. Also, its enamelwork images were more of clouds and lightning than of celestial lights.

Mistress Prudence and Mistress Patience nodded to them. Both shoveled in oatmeal as fast as they could eat. Bowls sat on the table, and a pot of oatmeal, with a smaller one of honey. The five of them went to sit, and before they had, the two women rose. They snatched sleek yellow mantles, donned them, and went out. Rain splattered on the floor through the briefly open door, and the wind blew it sharply shut.

At least, thought Kenneth, the air was still warm, though cooler than the day before.

Pearl sighed and reached for a bowl. "It looks like a day when youngsters get firmly told to stay out of the way and be bored out of their wits."

"I hope," said Diamond, wistfully, "that we can get time enough to ask after the library."

"We have our books," said Rob, not quite managing to sound cheerful. "We can keep busy. It won't be so bad as the first days at Quiet Valley."

Pearl gave him a quizzical glance.

Kenneth glanced at the windows, saw no one, and wondered if someone outside would be visible. They dawdled through breakfast. Rain lashed against the windows, and more often as time went on, but no one else came to the kitchen. They did not so much as hear a noise that might have been a voice.

Kenneth took his bowl to the sink. The grass outside was bent nearly flat against the ground, from the wind, and the blades showed silver. He thought the waves beyond had grown larger since he had woken up.

A stone wall, extending from the lighthouse, stood outside the window. It held a green gate, and brief glimpses of greenery, tossed by the wind, over the wall made him scowl. An odd place for a kitchen garden.

The door opened, and the rain splattered far enough that drops struck him. A woman slammed it shut again, and stood just inside, to survey them all without even shifting her shadow-dark mantle. Only her face was visible: heart-shaped, salt-white, with sea-blue eyes of subtly different shades and a quite piercing stare.

After a moment, her mouth twitched. She pulled off the mantle, showing herself to have long black hair and a gown of shifting colors: green, blue, black, and even violet in places. Kenneth thought he saw sigils on it as she hung up the mantle.

"So," she said. "I am Marea, wizard of the Lighthouse. The only one here to study sea magic, and not to work sailors' and widows' spells against it. As you can tell." Her sweeping hand took in the empty chairs. "Did they work to exhaustion and collapse in their beds? Or are they all hard at work in their spellcraft?"

"Mistress Prudence and Mistress Patience went out just as we came down to breakfast," said Rob. "The rest, we haven't seen since last night."

"Last—" Mistress Marea scowled. "Did they tell you where to go during the storm?" Her scowl deepened. "It's not like you could join me, studying."

"No," said Kenneth. "We were hoping for the library."

Her hand slashed the air like a sword striking. "Not when it arrives in full spate—but I will show you. You will have much to learn to manage here."

"What's the garden outside for?" said Rob. "The walled one?"

Mistress Marea hesitated. "It's a measure. The flowers do not flourish on the shore. Some are hardy, and some are tender, but all let them gauge how the protective spells hold.

"Not that you will be allowed outside, or to see anything but the most secure parts while the storm rages. They themselves will not look at the garden before the storm has blown over." She strode across the tiles of the floor. "Come."

Up the stairs, past the rooms where they had slept, and up and up, through four circuits round the tower, she led them until, with all of them breathing hard, she opened a door.

Smaller than the valley's library, the room was jammed full of books and papers, with stacks of yellowing maps. Even to Kenneth's unpracticed eye, many books were obviously the logs of sea-farers, salt-stained and weather-beaten. Brass lanterns hung from the ceiling on chains. Charts hung on what portions of the wall showed. The single window was smeared with raindrops, showing nothing but gray.

He glanced about. Three chairs, and one stacked with papers, and another with nine books on it. This would be a room to find books, not to read them.

Mistress Marea pointed. "Those shelves are most likely to be of interest to you."

The books did look more scholarly than the rest. The three hurried over, and Kenneth followed. Pearl, slowly, brought up the end.

Rob pounced, and Kenneth looked at the tome in his hands.

"Of the Lighthouse? It's far fatter than the one of the Valley."

Rob shrugged. "Which talked of how this princess hid from robbers there, and that noble, from the slander that he meant to overthrow the king. Or the queen falsely accused of adultery by a man whose advances she refused. Just a list—with a tale now and then of how a magical deer aided one." His fingers tightened. "This has more tales."

"Like the time," said Mistress Marea, "when they wafted the treasure fleet from the dragon's island to the royal city." She looked about. "Choose your books. You can not stay here during the storm."

The wind blew against the tower, with a blow of raindrops striking.

Kenneth thought of their textbooks and opened his mouth. The wind howled, loudly, and thunder sounded after it. He shut it again. They might as well distract themselves. Perhaps Rob could regale them with tales of the spells that held the Lighthouse up.

With a book on navigation under her arm, Diamond offered her sister a book on wildflowers. Jamie had one whose title he could not see, and Kenneth stepped up quickly. What sort of book on stonework could you find in a place laden with sea magic?

Sunstones and Sand in Navigation—he snatched it up, flipped quickly through it, and said, "I'm ready."

They would need to seize pen and ink on the way, he thought, but Mistress Marea nodded, and turned to another door, stuck between two bookcases, unable to openly fully because of a table with maps. She edged through it to a stair behind it: painted black, more like a ladder than a stair, down a narrow stairway. A light shone, just barely visible.

Diamond folded her arms across her chest, her book forming a shield. "If it's so dangerous, how could going down the tower help?"

Mistress Marea cast her a sidelong glance.

"The Lighthouse is so old," said Rob, "that it was Hagspoint Lighthouse back in the day when lighthouses stood on every rocky shore to warn off the ships, before the navigational spells of today, when its light was actually to be seen by nearby ships, and not used to help those navigational spells. I think that means it's not likely to fall down."

"And if it did," said Jamie, "I do not see how its foundation would be the safest place."

"It's not the danger of a fall," said Mistress Marea. "It's the danger of the spells they are casting. Those navigational spells do not preserve themselves, and by being down below, you will be below their range."

Then she climbed down, as if it were a ladder. Kenneth let out his breath and followed. The wall within rumbled, and he glanced at it. Whatever mechanica kept the light lit and revolving had to be hidden there.

The stairs went down, down, and down. The sound of the mechanica faded; the sound of the wind or of thunder reached them, now and again, but muffled. The lights punctuated the descent, each one looking exactly like the one before, and giving enough light to climb down, and not a glint more.

When the stairs finally ended, his feet struck stone—and not flagstone, either. He muttered a spell as he stepped aside; they had reached bedrock.

Well, what else would they build on, to last? He faced the room. A thick pillar of mortared stones stood before them. Flickering light, as from a fire, came from around it, with odd, unflamelike colors, of blue and purple, running through pale orange. An enormous chest stood against it.

"That sea chest there has food. Not, I fear, of the finest. They stocked it to last a long time with no magic, as they do on a sea voyage."

Kenneth hoped it proved palatable. Or that one of them had a freshening spell. But Mistress Marea already led the way around the pillar.

A little nook lay there, with couches and rugs. Next to a heap of driftwood, a fireplace held merrily blazing fire. The smoke was wafted up the chimney so thoroughly that a spell had to be aiding the draft.

On a side wall, a tapestry hung, an incongruous image of a unicorn on a black field arrayed with flowers in every color. Mistress Marea scowled, then hauled the cloth aside. Behind it stood a clear stone, showing the charcoal clouds, the rising waters, the flickers of lightning, the sheets of rain.

"You can watch that if you must—it would be better than venturing out to see how the storm progresses—but I recommend against it. It will only distract you, and this is the safest place in the tower. It will be safe to leave in the morning, once the storm is gone, because they will have finished slinging spells about."

Kenneth nodded. "We can study here for the hours." Though getting their own books might have been wiser, he doubted she would let them leave. At that, the spells they were working on might affect the tower as much, or more, than the storm.

Mistress Marea nodded back and swept off. As her footsteps receded, Diamond walked up to the stone and frowned in thought. After a moment, she turned to Kenneth.

"It's like the one you cast," she said.

He opened his mouth to deny it, but then, it might be showing a moment ago, and so viewing the past. "I couldn't cast one that lasted this long. I don't think that spell could even be extended that long."

Jamie snorted. "Amazing we don't see more of them. To spy like that—what a defense it would be."

"It's fairly easy to ward against," said Kenneth.

Jamie looked at him in shocked disbelief. "But you—"

"The only reason I saw *that* scene was that he had to leave an opening, so that his own spell could get *out*. And maybe overconfidence as well."

Jamie scowled in thought. "It might be—" He shook his head.

"Anyway," said Rob, "we can study."

Kenneth nodded, but did not move.

"Looking for something?" said Pearl, her tone surly.

Kenneth nodded and did not look away. Within a few minutes, a figure came out on the strand. Mistress Marea, her hair and skirts tossed about by the wind, and soaked by the rain. The colors on her gown started to shift, and she walked into the waves. Her footing shifted as the larger ones hit her, but she plugged on. The water rose higher and higher, and she walked under the waves.

"One way to observe the sea in a storm," said Kenneth lightly.

"So," murmured Diamond, "why was she wearing a mantle earlier, if she does not mind the rain?"

"Perhaps she did not want to use a protective spell early," said Kenneth. "She might use it up."

Back in the room, Jamie already opened up a book on the history of the Web, and Rob was opening his tome.

Pearl shuddered. "You know how it rages out there. How can covering it up do anything but make us worry the more? They would not have stashed us away so safely if safety were not needed."

"The spells—" said Diamond, and Pearl whirled on her.

"They wouldn't have us here if they had to keep us in the foundation. The storm was what brought the need for spellcraft."

At this point, Kenneth thought, he would be unsurprised if they did keep them in this room forever, but what he said was, "It keeps the crystal from distracting us from our studies. Anything has to be better than sitting here gaping at it."

"You can even hear it."

Kenneth hesitated, and listened. The fire crackled. Behind it, perhaps, the wind sounded, too softly to be called a howl. "All the more reason to divert our attention."

"Besides," said Rob, without looking up from his book, "the Lighthouse is secure. During the Regents' War, it suffered a wave that totally engulfed it. The water didn't even get in. This storm's not magical. It won't."

"And if it did," said Diamond, "the storm would be powerful enough that not even Quiet Valley would be protection. Everything in the land would be harmed."

"You can't even see the spells," said Jamie. "Not being caught in their undertow would be no more visible than being caught in it." He looked about. "If we had a clock here—"

"It would interfere with the one upstairs," said Diamond. "They use it to tell ships what time it is here, so they must ensure that nothing can interfere. Then, the ships see what time it is where they are, and know where they are, east versus west. The hardest part of navigation."

Odd, though Kenneth, Diamond had never shown interest in navigation before.

"Calculating how far north or south you are is easy by contrast."

Ah, thought Kenneth, all was clear.

"Leave the curtain open," said Jamie. "If it gets to us, hopping up and down to look would be worse."

After a moment, Kenneth gave up the curtain.

"Study," he said, firmly. He walked to the nearest couch, and put his back to the crystal, to settle on the cushions, put the book in his lap, open it, and ignore the sounds of motion about him—softer than the fire, some of them. He even ignored Diamond's sitting on the same couch as he stared at a sketch that had to be of the Lighthouse and the rock it stood upon. The words took concentration to come into focus.

How significant the stone was as the mark of that liminal region, the shoreline. Sands and mud, besides being stone in origin, were unsteady. Stone, standing against storm, bearing the mark of high tide, was the true threshold.

He sighed, leaned back, and dredged up the thoughts of the wizards' reaction if he defied them, and returned to the library, let alone his room. He reminded himself he had looked at the library's books and rubbed the back of his neck. This might indeed be the best. And he could not practice spellcraft here, not yet. He looked back to the book.

After a moment, he cast a glance around. They all had a nose in a book, with Rob sprawled on the rug before the fire, and Pearl with a sour expression but an open book.

He forced his gaze back to his own book, and told himself, sternly, to not be curious about how often they turned pages, if at all. Being in no position to criticize himself.

He read the first paragraph, and then the second, and slowly began to turn pages, reading and reading. Every now and again, someone looked at the crystal—he was not so rapt as to not notice that—but the raging storm hid even the passing of day. It darkened as time inched onward, and then lingered dark, now and again paling slightly before darkening again, with no hint of the sun. He wished they had left a clock to mark the hours. They had only the judgment of hunger to go by.

Diamond slapped her book shut. He looked up, blinking—her bookmark rested half way through her book—and others did as well.

"Time to eat," she said.

"Is it time for lunch?" said Pearl.

"Lunchtime," said Rob, "is the time at which lunch is eaten, not an hour of a day." He scrambled up.

The sea chest opened smoothly enough, once they put enough strength into it, and rested open.

Diamond fished out the bottles. "Water," she announced.

"Will do," said Jamie, pulling out dried fruit, and fish, and bread as well. "We will need it to eat this."

No butter, of course, though Pearl fished out some seaberry preserves in deep garnet red. And Diamond found, and triggered, the freshening spell on the fruit and bread, until they looked like peaches, and fresh-baked bread, again.

"None on the fish," said Rob, sourly. "None for me, then."

Kenneth looked at the fish, and nearly joined him, but choked down a dried piece, with plenty of water, before eating bread and preserves, and fruit, with more vigor.

The meal did not make them merry, or chatty, and they all settled back to their books after, without looking at the crystal.

A gust of wind roared so loudly they could hear it clearly. Kenneth started. All about, the rest looked up as well. Rob, sprawled on the floor again, seemed to have not been looking for some time; he stared into the depths of the fire.

"How can anyone expect us to study in this?" said Pearl.

"It's not like we could do something more profitable," said Rob, without looking from the blaze. "Neither flowers nor stones bear much watching in the storm. Still less experimenting."

"How can you be so *calm*!" Pearl threw her hands in the air.

"Quiet Valley," said Diamond. "We did not spend a single day, storm-racked or not, with only such books as we could find in the library. We spent *weeks*. You'll learn it, too."

"If it weren't for my uncle," said Jamie, "it would have been for months."

"I'm sure he will bring you some as well," said Kenneth.

Pearl gave him a glance of astonishing bitterness.

"And if the storm's too much," said Rob brightly, "we can watch the fire. There's pictures."

Kenneth, opening his mouth, looked over. In the fire's jumbled colors, a sea-blue mermaid looked back at him. She lowered her comb and, with a flick of her tail, dived back into the flames.

"A gryphon," breathed Diamond, and pointed out the soaring wings and the hint of mountains beneath the creature.

Pearl slapped her book shut. "All very well for children. I'm going to sleep. I did enough dawn and dusk work with Mistress Imogene to master that alteration." She sat her full height. "It's all very well for you, you're just studying the standard because you have to."

Jamie cocked an eyebrow. Diamond shrugged. Rob did not turn from the fire.

Looking at none of them, Pearl recited the spell and fell asleep at once, her back to them.

Kenneth sighed, and memories stirred, of Pearl disgruntled after a late frost had put off a herbology lesson, malcontent at an early snow that made gathering pebbles a chore, waspish when they could not find a library book—

He ran a hand through his hair. He had let memory grow too fond and forgetful, not just not seen her in distressing times. Now, Elgiva—

Don't be a fool, he told himself. However sweet and honorable she was in his memory, he might misremember her, too.

"How Great-Grandmother would disapprove," said Diamond.

"Not your parents?" said Kenneth, startled.

Silence fell. Fire crackled. Distantly, thunder rolled.

"My parents," said Diamond, "belong to the Order. So do all my grandparents, and all of them act as its agents, to track down problems, often." She folded her hands in her lap. "So they had us both live—well, the Dombrey house was still our great-grandmother, retired from the Order. They lived there, too, my parents and my father's parents, but not enough to look after us. When she died three years ago, they had us stay at the Oldcastles'—" She waved a hand at Rob. "—or the Fittons.'"

"Mostly the Oldcastles," said Jamie. "My parents did not venture out as often, but often enough." His mouth twisted. "I stayed with the Dombreys, too. The three of us at my parents' house was a special treat, not an ordinary thing." He sat back. "They were—disappointed about the tower, they thought it would hinder me in joining the Order. It was David who took me off to strange rocks and stones and things about stonework."

"My parents are clerks," said Rob. "Cataloguing all the things that are learned in these—ventures." His smile was short-lived and unconvincing. "They'll take down what happened to us when they learn of it."

With a sigh, a log settled in the bed of ash and ruby-red coals. For a moment, a castle lingered in the flames.

"I wonder if they told our parents that they moved us," said Rob.

"What would the point be?" said Kenneth. "They weren't told where we were. Telling them we were moved—well, the Web knew where we were. It would tell our families nothing, but something to anyone in the Web who hears it. Not that—" He cut off the sentence before the bitterness overwhelmed him.

"They'll know I'm all right," said Rob. "They have these roses, the family has had them for generations, and they plant a new one for every child. Seven all in row, for me and my brothers and my sisters." He hesitated. "There are other such magics for other families—"

"They wouldn't bother."

All three stared at him. So much for swallowing bitterness.

"Not for my brothers and sisters, either," he said, carefully.

"They didn't have to decide for me and Pearl," said Diamond, idly. "This enormous tapestry with a family tree." She spread her hands wide. "It would fall over in a stiff breeze, were it a real tree, it's so branchy."

"I wish we had one," said Jamie, very quietly. "Then we would know."

Silence lasted a long time, as the fire danced and showed a ship, a galloping horse, a dovecote.

"I heard you were the first in your family to come to Graytowers, Kenneth," said Diamond, after a minute. "Odd if you had brothers and sisters."

Kenneth looked at his hands. "I was the youngest of five, by about twelve years. So they had places in the business for all of them, but threw up their hands and said I had to go into a profession. Any profession."

"And so your studies are urgent," said Jamie.

"Oh yes," said Kenneth. "I will need to be a respectable master wizard living quietly with my wife and children in a pleasant home with a garden where every flower has been chosen for its beauty alone."

They all laughed.

"Urgent," said Rob, "but not that urgent. We'd go for a walk now if we were in the valley, unless it rained too hard. Even then, we wouldn't study forever."

"So," said Jamie, "we watch the fire."

A fiery green bird burst out of the flames, soaring up the chimney before it winked out.

"My house," said Rob, "will have a fireplace like this."

Rosy-red trees grew. Sea green deer leapt. Castles of pink and gold stood impregnable for a moment or two. After a few minutes, Kenneth thought he agreed with Rob, but it seemed easier to ponder it than rouse himself to say so, in this pleasant warmth.

Chapter 10—Explorations

Diamond slumped over the couch, her face hidden by her arm. Rob sprawled by the fire. Jamie curled up by the couch, nearly at his feet, and Kenneth, trying to move silently, shifted his feet past him to get up.

Pearl, also, still lay asleep. He turned aside.

The unveiled crystal showed a cloudy but glowing morning. Orange light colored the rock, glanced from the waves, and suffused the clouds as they hastened along the sky. The still heavy waves—he thought. Then, he did not know how large the swells were on this shore on an ordinary day.

The grasses were bending, deeply, in waves of their own, as gusts of wind ran over them.

Sound came from behind him. Pearl still sprawled and did not stir, but Diamond had rolled onto her back with her arm thrown over her face, Jamie eyed him and shifted to sit up, and Rob stood.

"What does it show?" said Jamie softly. Kenneth spread his hand at the crystal, and they came over to look. No one, of course, moved on the strand. At most gulls soared, too distantly for him to be certain that they were gulls and no other bird.

"There's only one stairway out," said Kenneth.

"We should check," said Rob. "It's a good test of our spellcraft."

Kenneth closed his eyes for a moment. Then he remembered his spell of the day before, at the bottom of the stair.

"Go ahead, if you can be quick. But you won't find anything."

Jamie eyed him, and cast it. Moments later, the other two did as well. "Solid bedrock," pronounced Jamie, and the other two nodded.

Kenneth swept his hand toward the stair.

"Here's to hoping that we don't have to send for help from the master wizards," said Jamie, cheerfully, leading off.

Diamond rolled her eyes. "At least we haven't unpacked. Because if we have to do that, they will pack us off to yet another place, like unwanted baggage."

"Perhaps we'll end up at the Ivory Tower," said Rob.

Kenneth snorted. The last thing a place dedicated to cloistered scholarship wanted was four obstreperous scholars, even if the wizards there neglected to teach them as much as the wizards of Quiet Valley had.

Climbing took longer than descent had, and no one stirred within their hearing as they walked out into the library, went down the stairs, stopped in their rooms to lay aside the books, and continued to the kitchen.

The wind could be heard, more often than not. Kenneth looked out the window at the swells, which hammered on the shore and flooded it with white foam. Seaweed and driftwood lay scattered about on the stone, farther than the flotsam and jetsam had lain the night before.

Without a glance outside, Rob looked about the kitchen. "We should have stayed and eaten out of the sea chest. It was food at least."

Kenneth ran a hand through his hair. Perhaps they should go back—he pushed open the door outside. The air was damp and cool. Every color, even the green of the grass, seemed to burn in the orange light. Over the wall, in the garden, he could see a sailor's cap bobbing. His shoulders slumped in relief.

"Gadding about without leave?" roared the man. "We'll have none of that! No space for wastrels at the Lighthouse! You come here at once and check the flowers to make yourself useful. It's more important than breakfast."

Kenneth walked over, with the three hurrying after. He pushed open the gate and, blinking, hesitated. They had met Able Seaman Jones when they arrived, but the table had hidden his wooden leg. Kenneth forced himself to walk in as if he saw nothing odd and reminded himself that Jones might not be the only one. An injured sailor might have to give up the sea, and find the Lighthouse the only place he could be useful.

At least the garden could easily distract. In the amber glow, everything seemed to burn—not just the snapdragons in pink and orange, but those in white and dark crimson—tiger lilies in orange and other lilies in pink-flecked white—a trellis laden with blue morning glories, and another with pink sweet peas—delicate pink blossoms on heronsbill and water hyssop—rose bushes lush with golden roses.

"You're not here to gawk! You're here to be protected by the Lighthouse's ward. Look, look—see whether there is any damage to the wards that you need about you—you need more than anyone else."

"Do weeds count?" said Rob. The wind ruffled his hair.

Jones opened his mouth and shut it again. "Yes," he said more calmly. "They count. But not today. Today we look for storm damage."

Rob nodded sagaciously. They spread over the garden. Some plants showed signs of nibbling insects, and others were going to seed, but Able Seaman Jones finally, reluctantly, conceded that the garden showed no sign of damage to the spells, and that they might go eat some breakfast.

When they reached the door, Mistress Patience looked over, from taking things from the cabinet. "Huh. I suppose you lot want some breakfast."

"If you show us how to make it," said Rob, "we could not bother you with the effort. And if you all had to work to the utmost, we could feed ourselves—and you too, unless you all had to set sail."

"Unlikely," said Marea, walking in and looking hollow-eyed. She scowled. "Where's Pearl?"

"Still asleep," said Kenneth.

#

Porridge even came with the knowledge of where it was stored, and how to stir the spells to cook it, as the wizards filed in to eat. The food did not quite compensate for being told they could not learn the spells to navigate about the Lighthouse. Diamond barely managed to winkle out of them that the protection worked in circles before the wizards headed off to sleep, leaving them the only waking things in the tower.

"It does mean we can walk around the Lighthouse," said Diamond.

"How many times, to qualify for a walk?" said Jamie.

"First, she'll need the distance," said Kenneth.

#

The shore about the Lighthouse was solid rock, however weathered. Wind blew inland, relentlessly, punctuated by sharp gusts; Diamond's hair flew in wild tangles. Waves lapped—below the high-tide mark, but none went to venture below it. Flotsam and jetsam piled up there, with seaweed draped indifferently over the driftwood that was uprooted trees and that which was crates and barrels, however broken.

Diamond snagged her hair in her hand. "We'll practice no spellcraft out here, not today."

"Maybe never," said Rob. "We do not know if it's ever really calm here."

"Then," said Jamie, "we had best rack up spells to be ready for it, so we can strike if the weather does turn halcyon enough." He grinned.

"First," said Kenneth, "let us see how many times we have to walk around the Lighthouse to call it a proper walk."

"Do I get to say," said Diamond, "that we walk out to the point?"

"You must calculate both, as today's mathematics problem, both with that distance and without."

Diamond's laughter ran over the water.

#

After she decreed five times, they went back in with cheeks ruddy from the window. Pearl looked up from porridge.

"You didn't wake me," she said.

"You seemed *so* tired," said Diamond.

We should have gotten Marea to tell us where we could study, thought Kenneth. The sheltered room was too far.

"We're going to our rooms," he said. "To study."

"Able Seaman Jones," said Rob. "He had us looking at the flowers in the garden—he might be able to teach you more about them when—"

"He wakes up?" said Pearl sourly and looked at her bowl. "I will inspect the library for books on the garden. If there are any."

They headed up. Kenneth supposed they would just have to study where they slept. The library was impossible for even a single scholar. And he felt glad that Pearl had left the tower and so had no prefect; she was directing her own studies under whatever tutor she could find.

The library book sat on his trunk, still. Kenneth grimaced. Perhaps he could blame the storm or the spells for his not remembering a word of it.

#

The next afternoon they gathered outside the garden. Pearl, in their number, looked sullen.

Bos'n Billy showed them sextants and watches, and the spells to use them. And laughed at the notion of the tide trapping them on a new made island.

"You'll be able to see your way to land from any such island." He shook his head. "No, your danger would be more going so far as the salt marshes—folly, with their footing, on top of the folly of going that far. The protections weaken the farther you go."

"How far can we go?" said Jamie. "Reasonably."

"Well, if you never left the shadow of the tower, that's where it's strongest—"

"I'd bet you," said Kenneth, "that it's *strongest* if we stayed down by the fire."

Her mouth pursing, Pearl gave him a baneful glance, but Bos'n Billy laughed. "Don't go more than a league from the Lighthouse itself. You'll never see more of the salt marshes than a glimpse."

Kenneth nodded. Minutes later, he led them all off down the path they had come by. Even Pearl came.

Diamond, bright-eyed, said, "We can use the watches for their traditional use as well, and check our distance every five minutes or so. It's a rote spell. We want it down pat." She started to cast the temporal spell before any of them had a chance to speak.

"And not go more than three-quarters of a league from the tower," said Jamie, shoving his hands into his pockets. "For margin of error."

"And stay on land," said Rob. "It's not like the roses at Quiet Valley, because it's still land—but still be wary."

"That would be prudence," said Pearl. "Even for those of us with no reason to believe that *they* are coming after *her*."

"They're after Kenneth," said Jamie. "For no more than that he was seen with me."

"So, I should be grateful that they ensured that I, also, was seen with you?"

At least Jamie did not snipe about that. Kenneth looked over their path.

Winds, not so fierce as the day after the storm, rippled the grasses. Roses blossomed, all single flowers but as large as his hand, but other flowers were sparse here. Even if Rob pointed out the yellow clover and the pink vetch, and here and there some off-white and herbal-smelling yarrow. Now and again Pearl would comment.

Diamond's temporal spell rang. The spells themselves perhaps did not need such practice to ensure perfection. Still, it did reveal how so featureless a scene could hide distances.

The path forked past the hut. To the right, after much meandering, and a fair amount of storm-tossed leaves and plants, it ended in sand dunes and shore. Then, to the left, the sand gave way to rockier ground, and finally ended on a rocky cliff, where they got a glimpse of a small port town. The bay before them was filled with choppy waves, but the winds over them were less, and the sky overhead showed blue in places.

Boats were setting forth.

Fishing port, thought Kenneth, and said, briskly, "Study time after this."

"This path will lead there," said Jamie, pointing. It was not as if it could lead them astray with the Lighthouse's spells about, thought Kenneth. And it did not cross the path they had come on.

On it, the winds blew on them from the sea, and gnarled junipers blocked their sight of the waves.

"We will need them to give us a place to study," said Kenneth. "Though I suppose some things can be studied outside, there won't be many."

Diamond rolled her eyes. "Did they design every room in the Lighthouse to be as small as on shipboard?"

"It reinforces the spells," said Jamie. "With its structure."

Pearl sighed. "I'll have to borrow your book, Kenneth," she said, with only faint bitterness in her voice.

#

"They gave us a study room," said Diamond the next morning, as Pearl finished off her porridge.

Pearl put down her spoon with a crack. "I will not be coming with you." Her eyes narrowed as if her sister were the only one at the table, even as the wizards looked at her. "It's all very well for *you*. Standard course, and it's not like there's not plenty of stone around here. Not like those meager flowers."

She swept off, up the stairs. Kenneth looked back at the table.

"I suppose," he said, "that it would be imprudent of us to cast spells on the stone that serves as the Lighthouse's foundation."

Captain Seaborn snorted. "Right you are there."

"Then," said Rob, "it's back to playing with pebbles again."

"I mastered most of my coursework on pebbles," said Kenneth. "At Graytowers."

#

One day, Kenneth set the watch to wake himself. Then he rose up early. The sky was still charcoal gray, and he was surprised to find Bos'n Billy already in the kitchen.

"Couldn't sleep?" said Bos'n Billy with sympathy.

"I'm testing a spell," said Kenneth.

Bos'n Billy snorted. "Studying, studying, studying." He shook his head. "There's no way you can use a tenth part of what you study."

Kenneth managed to a smile but eased outside, to watch the sunrise in peach and gold over the water, and be pleased that he had mastered a weatherwise spell, however much by rote, well enough to know it would be clear.

Across its color came a bird flitting over the waves—a dark shadow from the light behind, and then, briefly, a great dark raven in its own color, and then it landed as David Servant, briefly buffeting Kenneth with his wing beats.

He took a moment to find his footing on the stone; then, he wore a heavy pack.

Kenneth nodded to him. "What news of the Boneyard? And that stone?"

David gave him a baleful glance. "The news is that I am forbidden to speak to any of you about it at all on pain of being banished from every place that the Order holds. If they can't catch me and hand me over to the king's men." He glanced up at the Lighthouse. "If we weren't this far off, you'd have gotten me in trouble by asking."

Kenneth blinked and wondered how much, if any, they had told David. And whether he ought to warn the three to keep silent.

"And—" David ran a hand through his hair. "I have come to impose on you."

Startled, Kenneth said, "Me? Or the four of us?" He would not be asking for Pearl's aid, or perhaps he was desperate enough—

"That spell you cast, showing the murder. I tried to duplicate it. It should have been simple enough, because I knew when and where I looked."

"Yes," said Kenneth slowly, dredging up the lesson. "It should have been."

"So. You are overseeing your own studies, and theirs as well. You can oversee mine, and see what I am doing wrong."

Wind ruffled the waves and his hair as he looked back at Kenneth.

"I didn't know you studied stonework," said Kenneth.

"Tower of Shadows. But, as Pearl reminded you, you can study other things outside Graytowers."

"How true." The waves lapped the shore. Kenneth sighed. In the valley, even more than at Graytowers, every wizard was there to study. Here, they cast their spells, some, or most, or all, by rote, and their work was done. It felt odd to study so much with such examples about them, though none of them had slacked off. Pearl, he reminded himself, spent a fair amount of time sulking instead of studying, but then, he wasn't responsible for Pearl.

"We have rooms for our studies, now, and to practice, and with the books, I think we're keeping up."

David nodded, and smiled.

"I'm learning weatherwise spells. Navigation as well. Might as well. If we're trapped here for long, it may be wise to work."

They started up the path, and after a moment, David said, "I brought more books. As long as they have no real work for me, I might as well play the librarian."

"Good. The library here is of—some use."

Around the bend, Rob sat on the grass with Jamie, both of them intent on a rose. Neither one glanced up.

David's eyebrows went up. "Particularly for Pearl. Since she had none to carry from the valley."

"She's sulking," said Kenneth. "The garden—she can't use any of its flowers except when the plants need thinning, and only those they want to thin. And the other flowers are few."

David looked ahead, at a patch rich in pale red clover and pink vetch.

Kenneth threw a hand in the air. "In variety. Though—Jamie is showing more interest in the roses, for protection—I think he's trying to master every spell that he could not in the valley—"

David smiled fondly as they walked on.

"But Pearl might find them more useful than what they have here. And Rob will read them. He seems ready to master both flowers and rocks at once."

Bos'n Billy sat by the doorway. He nodded, in an abstracted manner, but his attention was bent on the ivory he carved into a scrimshaw. Then, Kenneth thought, Bos'n Billy probably had no other work once the spells were cast.

He hoped that he could escape the Lighthouse before he had to take up the work himself.

Diamond burst out of the door and ran toward them. "David! Did you bring more mathematics books?"

"Diamond!" Pearl, looking shocked, appeared in the doorway.

Diamond looked over her shoulder. "Shouldn't I appreciate what he's done? It's a heavy pack!"

David laughed. "Borrow Kenneth's."

Diamond blinked.

"If you're done with what I brought, you've caught up to him."

That far? Kenneth looked between them. "At the rate she's going, you should have brought more. She'll get past me."

And he should do more mathematics. He had not gotten so far in the book that he could just pass it off to her, and mastering the math could only help with the navigational spellwork.

#

"Night sight," said David, in the dimly lit room. "It will let you see in the dim light as well as by day, so you can see what I am doing wrong." His smile seemed forced. "Not like true sight in the dark. That's a complicated spell."

Which struck Kenneth as an unusual precaution. He stood in silence as David cast it—it seemed to have no effect—and then while David shielded the window and closed the door. The lighting seemed—odd, but he could watch as David cast the spell with meticulous care, and clearly see how the stone remained dark and lifeless.

"And the worst of it is," said David, "that this is the Lighthouse. Quiet Valley has nothing to hinder sight as such, but the Lighthouse should actively aid such spellcraft, casting it out to the world like a ray of lamplight to the gloom."

Kenneth studied the dead stone. "What else have you tried to see with this spell?"

David blinked. Within moments, the crystal flawlessly showed Jamie, Rob, and Diamond being ushered into a building with lions of justice standing before it.

"After—that night," said David in a low voice. "Because I was not there, either."

How pale all three of them had looked. Kenneth shook his head, and tried to not think of whether he had looked as pale, escaping the labyrinth.

#

"We can feel out the spell that stops you, David," said Jamie over their chowder, and looked oblivious to the glances they garnered from the Lighthouse wizards. "Especially if Kenneth can still cast it."

Diamond put down her spoon. "When did you learn to do that?"

"You have to know how your protective spells can be tested," said Jamie. "You have to test them yourself. So—" He spread his hands. "You learn them."

"Too dangerous," said David, and wizards around the table looked relieved. "You saw what happened to Kenneth for merely looking."

"That," said Rob, "could have been for merely being with Jamie."

"Or being brought to Quiet Valley," said Diamond. "It could have put him in danger rather than protected him."

"As well as," said Jamie. "It protected him from the Web sorcerer who had infiltrated Graytowers."

"All those gargoyles," said Kenneth, with a groan. They had started to fade in memory, but they returned with a gallop. To think they had seemed like nothing more than nuisances at the time.

"Schools, by their very nature," said David, "must be open to people coming and going. It affects—things."

"Then the Lighthouse must be safer even than Quiet Valley," said Diamond. "Fewer scholars."

Pearl pushed back her empty bowl, murmured farewells, and drew back into the tower.

Diamond sighed. "It'll be her birthday soon. I need something to give her."

"A scrimshaw?" said Bos'n Billy.

"I think she's appreciate a potted plant more," said Diamond, gloomily.

"You're not likely to find that in the village, even," said Mistress Patience. "If you could go that far."

Mistress Prudence nodded, emphatically.

"I will see what I can do," said David, "but I have to be wary about where I go. It might not be possible. I hope the books suffice."

Diamond blinked. "A scrimshaw with flowers on it might please her—if it's possible."

Bos'n Billy smiled.

Kenneth glanced at David and wondered what had increased the danger.

Or if the strike at him had frightened them for David as well.

#

Kenneth looked over the books in the library again. It was almost too hot to study, too hot to walk. . . he idly pulled out a book with a dark cover.

The title was stamped on it in gold: *The Liminal Seashore.*

He looked at for a long time without moving. Was anyone even trying to discover the villains? They had mostly likely killed Jamie's parents. They had certainly killed the young man in the crystal. They had tried to kill him, twice, and Heaven alone knew what they would have done with Jamie had they succeeded in carrying him off in the Labyrinth. And the only response he had seen was to imprison four young scholars, who had done nothing wrong, and neglect their education.

His hand tightened on the book. He knew that they used liminal magic of some kind. It might be more help to catalog their spells, but he did not know if they were as much rote spells as his mastery of prefect, weatherwise, and navigational spells. It might let him gauge their power—he winced and resolved to do it—but it would not let him fathom their purpose, or orchestrate their capture.

He turned away. The windows even here were portals barely larger than his face. He looked out. The shore faced the ocean, not the bay, and swells poured relentlessly over the waters and onto the shore. It would be high tide soon. Half way to a neap tide. Not one of them had tried a spell about the tides, yet they all learned the coming and going. He turned from the window. For one thing, they served as well as a clock.

"Time and tide wait for no man," he whispered, and managed to smile for a moment.

All three would be bent on their studies at this hour. Jamie above all—he intended to master ten protective spells for every one he had had to forego in the valley. Questioning him on their walk would work better, and he could read now.

His breath came out in a small snort. All the more in that if Jamie continued at this rate, he would have to study protective spells himself instead, to master enough to oversee Jamie.

Chapter 11—Plans

The study lamp started to glow. Kenneth laid aside his book, and cast the weatherwise spell. Then he stood.

"If we don't walk now, we'll have to cut it short. Or not go at all."

Which was as good a way to get to speak as any, he thought, as the three roused, and Pearl murmured about not trusting the weather.

"Wise of you," said Diamond, crisply.

Outside, the wind already blew briskly, though the clouds were wispy as down, or thin and arrayed in ranks like fish scale.

"Mackerel skies and mares' tails," said Kenneth, "make tall ships carry short sails."

Jamie and Rob laughed. Diamond smiled as the wind yanked her hair forward, and she wrapped her hand about it.

"Interesting book on the shore?" she said brightly.

He wondered how far she had gotten, and whether he would have to study to oversee her as well. Between the three of them, he might have to drop everything he wanted to study and still not keep up, but that was no reason to keep her in the dark, especially about this. All the more with the way the Order told them nothing—

"You know what Rob said about the shore? How we should stay on land?"

They all nodded, and turned toward him.

"He was by no means stern enough. Far from it."

Rob looked startled, and Diamond thoughtful. Jamie scowled, glancing toward the shore.

"Do not go below the high tidemark at all. Nevermind that it's still land, the tide covers it, and we know they use liminal magic. Don't give them any opening—and remember how little I had to go among the roses to be in the border."

They all stared at him. He looked down at the sands. Then Jamie shrugged and started to walk again.

He felt a fool, he could hold his tongue about what else he had read, but if he stopped now, he would lose his nerve.

"At that, there was something else I was looking at, Jamie. What did your parents have at your house that was taken, that night?"

Jamie stopped.

"If the Order continues to examine the matter at their current *leisurely* rate, we may be able to leave the Lighthouse for our own funerals, if we die at an advanced age." He drew a deep breath. "David Servant would not lie to me—" Jamie winced. "—and he, alone, is making little headway. I will see what I can learn. It may help him."

A gull screamed, high up and far away.

"The only trace of what they are is what they do, and it will be the only way to catch them. So what do we know? They tried to catch me, but they wanted Jamie alive."

"They don't all need to want the same thing," said Rob. "Some might help another in return for help on something else entirely. So those ones might do things that are—unlike them."

Kenneth winced. "First we gather all we can. Then we look for order in it."

"They stole a lot of things," said Jamie. "If they were—my parents—were holding anything for the Order, no one would have told me. Or would tell me now."

"You could—" Diamond hesitated a moment, and her words slowed as she spoke. "You could ask for an inventory. You are, after all—the heir." She drew in a deep breath. "Write to Master Bonaventure."

"They could all be important," mused Rob. "They could be hiding what was important to *them* with such thefts."

Kenneth let out his breath slowly. Frustrating or not, they needed every scrap of knowledge. "From what I heard, I would think any thieves in the Web would take whatever looked interesting at the moment in hopes it might profit them afterward. In knowledge, or perhaps in money. They could buy things with what they could not use themselves."

"They didn't give us much to go by," said Diamond. She hesitated, did not suggest that they should leave it to the Order. He was glad of Pearl's absence; Pearl would have insisted. And then written to Master Bonaventure, or more likely to some great master in the Order who would put a stop to them by hook or by crook.

"They wanted Jamie," said Kenneth. "It might have been for something—like—that murder I saw."

Rob snorted. "There's no enchantment that uses Fitton blood. They would have forbidden them entrance into the Order until they tracked down any such spells, and destroyed them all. The Order can not allow such a weakness."

"Is that the only reason for his blood? I do not want to discard it as chance without—" Kenneth spread his hands. They reached a crossroad in the paths, but they could take any of the ways, and had no reason to favor one. He looked up. The clouds were thickening but not a threat.

There they stood as seeds with white down flew by them like snowfall.

"It's not like they would do it to intimidate people," said Jamie. He looked only a little pale behind his freckles. "My parents' death was enough to do that. But I do not know of any other reason why they might want me."

"To use against your parents," said Diamond.

The wind rushed over the grass, making it bend deeply, and the sand, making it hiss as it fell from dunes.

Jamie let out his breath slowly. "Then it would be no clue. I—can not think of a magical reason."

Rob said, "There's boxes that only someone in a family can open. They are common enough—"

"We had one," said Jamie.

As the wind made the only sound, Kenneth picked a path. It would angle back toward the Lighthouse, and they walked slowly along it.

Kenneth turned to Jamie. "Did you know what it held?"

"It held another box like itself, except that someone from another family could open that one," said Jamie. "I was only a child when they showed me it. It was from their early days in the Order—the family was ashamed of its sorcerer, and never claimed the box back."

The wind tousled his hair.

"What family?"

He hesitated. "The Stone—no, the *Flint* family." He smiled. "And David took me to see a flint outcropping after, so I would know what flint was. It was—David was still in school then."

"So," said Diamond. "Let's hope he's helpful again. Who else could we ask whether there are members of the Web from the family of Flint?"

More likely, thought Kenneth, David would find it useful. With all the restrictions he suffered under, he could still learn more than they could.

But Jamie said, promptly, "Master Bonaventure."

"It might hold that opal they need," said Rob. The path, curving about, faced the Lighthouse now. Clouds loomed behind it.

"It might," said Kenneth, "have nothing more than some oddment belonging to that sorcerer. A useless one, perhaps."

"If the Flints are that ashamed of him, it's likely he was linked to the Web," said Rob.

Jamie snorted. "Practiced fell magic, yes, but they don't *all* join the Web." The wind rustled the grass. He added, "It is likely."

Kenneth nodded, and then he sighed. "Striking me down in Quiet Valley was likely just spite, but when they killed that man in that labyrinth—"

"They were trying to warp it," said Diamond. "Change—" Her hands moved about. "Labyrinths are such intricate shapes that it's hard to change things. Blood magic of the crudest type can alter the lines." She scowled. "That one—with that opening you saw—had to have been a journey labyrinth. With that change, he let himself go new places with it. Except that with the perfect order disrupted, it's dangerous. The shape is the foundation, and when it is disrupted, it disrupts everything about it."

"There's sorcerers," said Rob, "who've used it to hide. No one could tell, after, where they had gone in such labyrinths." He lowered his voice portentously. "Nor could they tell, before, where it would send them. But they feared a worse fate, if they stayed."

"This wasn't that much," said Diamond. "He could tell where he was going. It's just that it could break at any point."

"So at least one of them is bold," said Kenneth. "Alas, wanting to go many places is too useful for a knowledge seeker to be an identifying trait."

For a moment, the wind slackened. Then it picked up again.

"I'll send the letter to David," said Jamie, sounding subdued. "Perhaps you won't need to find out." He looked at the cloud, and shook his head. "There's another reason. They might want me for revenge after my parents took that box."

Both Rob and Diamond flinched. Kenneth felt the color seeping from his face.

"Or," said Rob, his voice shaky, "anything else your parents did."

#

In his dark room, Kenneth woke as suddenly as if a nightmare had threatened him. And he could not remember a dream.

But he could remember something else.

He yanked on his clothes and was in the corridor before he quite thought.

Jamie's sleepy voice rose. "You're up early."

"The Labyrinth—of Thought. Those scenes in the glass, were any of them your memories?"

"No?"

"Then if we get them clear, we will know their memories."

Jamie yawned. "I don't remember them that well."

"We don't need our memories."

#

Kenneth glared at the page. They needed those memories. And the book could only go on and on about the dangers of crossing the present and the past. He had no intention except to look into the past.

"We can write down what we remember," said Jamie. "That will give some notions. To guide your spell. . . ."

"Mastering the spells will help more."

Jamie's voice was acerbic. "You've been studying so hard, you haven't even noticed that it's late for the walk."

"You," said Rob from the doorway, "would have chivvied *us* out of our chairs on the grounds that it would not help our studies to work ourselves into mindlessness."

Kenneth looked up. Far too early for any sign of a summer sunset to show—but from the slant of the sunshine, dinner was near.

"We'll walk after dinner," said Diamond. "For now, write down what you remember."

The fire, thought Kenneth, instantly.

#

"If it were something out of history," said Diamond, slowly, as they compared just before the dinner hour

"Can't," said Rob. "It shows memories, to be that vivid. And the Web has not learned to prolong life."

Kenneth scowled. "Memories," he whispered. If they went back, perhaps they could—

"No," said Jamie. His gaze was intent on Kenneth. Kenneth blinked.

"We are not going back to the Labyrinth, even though we want memories of then. We already know they can go in and out of it at will."

"And the mirrors there will not show things at your will," said Rob.

"Of course not," said Diamond. "They would not have let you see their memories if they could control it." She frowned. "Probably. They might have intended to frighten Jamie, or at least keep him off balance."

"They had no choice," said Rob. "That was not the first time this happened, and it will not be the last. You can not control it. That is why the labyrinth was so ill-secured that you two could be torn out of Graytowers into it." He waved a hand. "It's not like Graytowers, which needed to allow entrance and exit. The Labyrinth of Thought did not—but it also did not require them to prevent it, so they just didn't bother. The lack of control for the mirrors went with that."

Botching their work, thought Kenneth. From the first spell a student slung in his studies at Graytowers, such a lack of control and purpose would lead to failure.

From the doorway, Pearl said, sharply, "Are you going to bother to come to dinner?" and muttered something indistinct about studying already.

Kenneth blinked. "Dinner, then," he said. "Walk after."

#

A short walk, thought Kenneth. Dinner had lasted until the sky started to show color. Even in summer, the dark would come. He set out briskly in the still air, as the receding tide lapped at the shore.

Diamond hurried to catch up. "We—we don't know they were all memories from the same person. Piers was not alone. And they might not be relevant."

"It would make more sense like that," said Kenneth. "So many things—but they would have kept out anyone who wasn't both in the Web and in their plot."

"They didn't keep you out," said Rob.

A gull screamed, over the bay. Rob *had* to bring that up.

"We have to go by best guesses, here," said Kenneth. "Remember that this is just in case David Servant can't find it."

"Anyway," said Rob thoughtfully, "anyone who wasn't in the Web was likely after them. So it would still be evidence."

"Only of being in the Labyrinth, not of their plot," said Kenneth, "but that doesn't matter so much as identifying who they are—"

All three faces lit up at that thought, and they walked on under a sky of delicate pinks and creams. Kenneth idly wondered if rain alone would be a problem.

They had nearly circled back to the Lighthouse when Jamie stopped and scowled. A bird flew over the dunes. Dark, though the lack of light made that uncertain, flying raggedly—and was that blood red?

Kenneth ran forward through the grass. The sand underfoot shifted with no stability, and nearly threw him a few times, but he did not look away. The raven flew toward him, and, then, for a moment, David, bloodied, stood before him.

"In the Dark Forest," he croaked. "It must—they couldn't—" He shook his head. "Someone in the Order betrayed me."

Kenneth, already reaching out to steady him, was able to break his fall and ease the weight to the ground. He slipped off David's pack, glimpsed the green within, and handled it off to Rob with a low voiced order to get help and then hide the plant.

Rob ran off, calling already. Diamond dropped to her knees beside David and pressed her bare hand to his bleeding shoulder. Kenneth tore the bloodied shirt and said, "Here, use this instead."

It took a moment to replace it, and the blood was slackening. Kenneth sat back on his heels. Jamie shifted from foot to foot, his face caught in a frenzied desire to help, and a knowledge of his uselessness. The sky darkened as they waited.

Able Seamen Jones and Fairington burst out of the tower. Fairington pushed Diamond aside to press true bandages on the shoulder, and Jones went to inspect his other injuries. Kenneth and Diamond pulled back toward Jamie. Diamond's hands were bloodstained, and Kenneth opened his mouth to suggest leaving, to go in and wash, when Fairington hefted David up, with a grunt of effort.

Jones went ahead to hold open the door for Fairington. They followed him.

Rob had vanished. Pearl swanned down the stairs with a letter in hand. She raised an eyebrow and moved slowly aside—though swiftly enough that she was out of their way when Fairington started up the stairs.

She put the letter in the box and eyed Diamond. Who, Kenneth noted now, was not only bloodied but pale.

"I hope," said Pearl, "that cures you of your plan to go poking around things that could get you killed."

"It has changed my plans," said Diamond, with a little half smile.

Pearl raised an eyebrow, and said, "You'll want to wash your hands," but went back up stairs.

Diamond looked down and let her breath out with a gust. She walked over toward the sink. "We'll have to hide putting in the letter. Otherwise, she'll be—"

"You haven't changed the plan?" said Jamie.

She batted her eyelashes. "Of course. We have to write to Master Bonaventure. *This* is as urgent as when Kenneth was struck down. I'll—write it now."

#

Jamie checked the box, and said, "Ah—" when footsteps sounded on the stairs. He slipped a letter away before Pearl appeared on the steps, with no need for the rest of them to deflect attention.

At least the wizards were about their business, not eating there, to see and be suspicious.

Diamond, sounding brittle, asked Jamie about the octagonal keep at Broadwood as they sat down to breakfast. They did not even mention the letter as they talked of this and that, but they ate quickly and left the room as if they had an experiment that would take all day to work.

As soon as Rob pulled the door to the study shut, they surrounded Jamie. He pulled out the letter, and handed it to Diamond.

It was all the more frustrating in that Master Bonaventure told them that he knew nothing of the fire, and that the Web held no one named Flint as best that the Order knew. And also that such a box could also be opened by anyone in a female line of descent from the family as long as the person knew of it.

"Which is a lot," said Rob morosely. "I had a Flint great-grand-mother—" He fell silent—not because they all stared at him, which he did not seem to notice as he stared out into the air.

"They didn't try to abduct you," said Kenneth.

"Yes," said Jamie, "they must have their own Flint." He looked down, and he had a small charm in his hand. "And we can speak to my uncle."

Diamond's face brightened. "We can?"

They pelted up the stairs to the sickroom. Kenneth, wondering if they perhaps did not mean all four at once, brought up the rear. Mistress Patience, leaving the room, raised an eyebrow but stood aside to let them in.

A white-washed room like the others, trimmed in blue, and with two windows like ports. David, propped up on the pillows, was not so pale as to give them a fright. The three piled around the bed, demanding to know what had happened. Rob told him the plant was all right, Jamie asked whether the danger could reach them here, and Diamond worried that he was not yet up, when Kenneth had been—

"Kenneth had the ministrations of wizards who could sling more healing magic," said David. "And, at that, he did not recover that much more quickly than I am. I will be up and about soon enough."

"After you flew here?" said Jamie. "Injured?"

"It was not that far," said David. "I came through the Dark Forest."

"Do you know how little protection that is?" said Jamie. "Its safety lies mostly in its secrecy."

"And how it's spread," said Diamond, dryly. "What is it? One hundred and forty-four woods that have been mapped with the Forest in them—and you can walk from one end to the other without going out—and then you can go out wherever the Forest is, like some woods near here. I'd think you'd get lost searching for someone in it."

David leaned back. "They would have, so they could not have. Someone must have told them. Perhaps firebirds and unicorns and golden stags can escape notice, but a man must stick to a path as rigid as a labyrinth to get through it safely, all the more if he cares which of those woods he leaves by. That makes it possible for someone to betray you."

"I put that in my letter to Master Bonaventure," said Diamond. David blinked. "We were going to ask you, but we did not know how soon we could. So I wrote to ask him if Flints belong to the Web."

His voice rather flint-like, David said, "*What* have you four been up to?"

"Gathering up knowledge we have of our enemies," said Kenneth. "We talked of why they might want Jamie, and he told how, among the stolen things, there was a box that only a Fitton could open. Except that Jamie said it held a box that only a Flint could open."

David scowled in fury, and possibly in thought as well. Rob looked at the floor.

"Master Bonaventure said that the female line works too," said Diamond. "So it's less important that there are no known members of the Web by that name."

"And we might have to protect Rob twice over," said Jamie.

David put a hand to his face. After a moment, he said, hollowly, "Tell me," and dragged out more details when he was not satisfied with their accounts—rather more than Kenneth had quite remembered.

"They haven't tried to abduct Jamie and Rob both," said David, finally, "which would probably be easier than one of you. Easier still if they did not mind Diamond as well." He snorted. "Safer than with Kenneth, too. No, they have a Flint of their own—assuming that the box was not taken to disguise their intent, or by accident."

"Could a bastard do it?" said Rob.

Silence for a few moments—"Yes, if they know," said Diamond. They looked at her, and she shrugged. "They used them on sea voyages, and I read—I should have realized female line would work as well."

"No matter," said Kenneth crisply. "If we can not track down why they took the box, the best threads to guide us back lie in what Jamie and I saw in the Labyrinth. A scholar of mechanica could identify what we saw, if the image were clear enough."

"You aren't to use memory spells," said David, sharply.

"Of course not," said Jamie, blinking in mild wonder. "We wouldn't do that."

Kenneth kept his face set. No reason to tell them that he had briefly read up on those spells, only to be put off by the cautions that hedged every discussion. "We want what was actually shown, not what we remember, at that. But we are working on the spells for that."

"Did you bring the book?" said David.

Jamie was out the door and running down the steps within a moment. A minute later, as they, with bright eyes, poured over the pages, Kenneth wondered whether the three would be better employed studying something they could master. This would be beyond them; they could gape at his handiwork, and David's, but not cast the spells. Then he dismissed that thought as folly. Neither he nor David could pry them away.

Diamond asked a question about fitting the spell to the labyrinth path, instead of a straight line. Perhaps they could learn them by rote, Kenneth told himself.

Mistress Prudence came in lugging a tray of soup and pudding—enough for the invalid only. She lifted an eyebrow. They pulled away.

"There's a letter for you in the letterbox," she said to Diamond, as she lowered the tray.

"No, we—"

Mistress Prudence snorted. "There's another, then." She glared. David meekly took up his spoon. Diamond walked out the door. Mistress Prudence followed, telling them to bring the tray down after.

Before he had finished, Diamond returned, and read the letter in silence. Her face set, and her mouth worked.

"It's from my parents," she said, fiercely. "Pearl wrote. Told them I was stirring up trouble."

Rob and Jamie were loud in indignation. Kenneth studied her pale face and wondered whether they had encouraged her to be indifferent to the danger, or not be such a nuisance.

"Do they know what happened?" said Kenneth. She shook her head. "What do they want you to do?"

"To remember that my acts may determine whether I can ever get to serve in the Order."

"They will," said Jamie. "There is no way that we will live long enough to join the Order unless we stop these wizards of the Web. Hiding like this only gives them more time to ready a strike, and even if they do not succeed, we can not both hide away and serve." He glanced at his uncle. "You were trying, but with all the secrecy, you couldn't do much. Now you can do even less than that."

"They'll insist that you stay as secret as us," said Rob. "Though—they might not care so much. About me and Diamond." The window cast a round patch of sunlight over him. "We—saw—some things, but no one seems to care."

"They tried to kill Kenneth again," said Jamie, "and he saw less."

"And," said Kenneth, "we don't know they won't care. We do not know enough about to them say any such thing. If you do not hide forever, you will be risking your life. And the Order certainly won't let you."

Diamond pointed at the book. "That will risk us."

David sighed. "We will wait three days. Then I will, because there is a traitor in the Order, move you. I will swear all here to secrecy, and still not tell them where we are going. Or you, either, until we are there." He shifted against the blankets. "Do not talk about this outside this room. I have strengthened the spells on it."

"Pearl will tell our parents," said Diamond. "She told them—" She blinked, fell silent, and paled, and when she spoke again, her voice was soft. "She wrote after you were injured."

"Your parents would betray me only out of the noblest of motives," said David. "Or if they convinced themselves that they did so out of the noblest of motives. So it's best not to tell her until we go. And they will have no chance after. There will be no letters, and so no intentions will matter."

Rob flinched and looked down at his hands, but did not argue. Kenneth wondered for a moment what he had been writing home about.

"But—to the Web?" said Jamie.

"Who knows? Perhaps the traitor is someone they trust, even someone in royal service. And also— " He pointed at the book. "Don't even study that, here."

"I shall study mechanica," said Kenneth. At least he might get some glimmering about the one he had seen. "And we shall leave you to rest before Mistress Patience loses hers and drives us out."

With a faint smile, David said, "That sounds prudent."

#

Kenneth put down the book in the study.

"What did you need to study," said Diamond, "to master those spells? The preliminaries?"

Both Rob and Jamie looked eagerly over.

He opened his mouth, thought of what danger they would be in if the Web struck even slightly harder, and said, "Transparent stones and their virtues. About sight. Everything up to true sight."

They all nodded sagely.

As if he had studied that at their age—"If we return to Graytowers, you will be so unevenly sagacious that they won't know what class to put you in."

"The more we learn about this," said Jamie, his eyes bright, "the more chance we will have to get back before it's all sorts of matters where we are uneven."

#

He had lost track of days. The next night, to his surprise, they had salmon and a cake for Pearl's birthday. Diamond presented her with a potted plant, and with a scrimshaw carved with a flower, and Pearl talked of how both would be useful when she had more flowers she could use.

"Something might be arranged," said David.

Pearl was still displeased when David announced, the next day, over the oatmeal at breakfast, that they were leaving.

Perhaps it was that they were all going, thought Kenneth. It gave it away. He pushed his spoon through his oatmeal and wondered if Pearl were in actual danger. They might even be able to send her back to Quiet Valley without peril. He scraped his bowl and thought—if the Order were willing to risk it. His breath came out in a little huff of a laugh, and he finished off the oatmeal.

"I suppose you want us to pack," said Pearl, pushing her bowl away.

"No," said David. "Their things were sent to Quiet Valley after them, and so too here." He stood. "We are leaving now."

The wizards of the Lighthouse nodded farewells; he must have got their promises earlier. Kenneth stood, and Pearl gaped like a fish. It was not until all the others stood that she followed.

"I hope there's some flowers there." She glared as if she would hold them personally to account if there were not.

Chapter 12—Journey

Gulls screamed over the harbor, but they walked farther from the Lighthouse than they ever had before. The broad hollows filled with marsh grass appeared ahead. A milk-white egret moved daintily through the dreary green. Behind it stretched a dark line that had to be the forest.

"This is not well protected," said Pearl.

"It has the advantage of secrecy," said David, and Jamie visibly swallowed a retort.

"I wonder that it was allowed," said Pearl loftily.

Kenneth turned his gaze away, toward the trees. Who did she think had allowed it? Many authorities thought secrecy protection enough.

The forest grew as they approached, resolved into a thicket of wind-twisted junipers and pines. The trees closed about them, cutting off breezes, the sight of the ocean, and much of the morning's light. Before they had gone far, pines dominated, and soon after that, they straightened, and grew tall, unbent by the wind. Amber needles, broken only by fallen pine cones, littered the ground so thoroughly that the path was the only place where the dingy grayish earth could be seen, and the air was laden with the pine scent.

The trees grew taller. Here and there, stands of ferns, emerald bright, stood. Grayish boulders sprouted moss, even more vividly green.

A black squirrel darted over the forest floor, leapt up on a boulder, and stood on its hind legs in the path of a sunbeam. The light shone through its back a rich brown and its belly a glowing amber, as bright as the pine needles, as it stared at them in silence.

David muttered a spell. Then he shook his head. "Not a spy. We should still walk faster."

Around the bend, the trees grew thicker, darker, shadowing the way, and the needles on the forest floor were smaller, like the scattered cones: firs, not pines.

"This," said Diamond, "is the Dark Forest."

"And you knew the squirrel wasn't?" said Kenneth.

"There are black squirrels all about in the woods around the Dombrey house," said Rob.

"And—that's not in the Dark Forest?" said Kenneth.

Rob blinked, scowled, and said, "Not the part we were allowed in. Especially not as children. But we saw them when we were quite small."

"They would come out on the grass," said Jamie.

No more squirrels eyed them. They walked on. The shade was cooler even than the shore had been. Trees continued, towering, silent. Sometimes white birches with pale leaves only tinted the sunlight green, and let it shine on ferns and jewel-bright butterflies. Sometimes thick firs blocked out the light, and the earth was littered again with tiny needles and fir cones. Now and again they crossed streams on bridges consisting of a felled tree, split in two so that two flat sides faced them, or else by stepping stones, rounded by the tumble of water.

As the gurgle of one stream sank behind them, and they climbed through a stand of oaks, Rob said, "Is it usually this quiet?"

"No more squirrels," said Jamie. "No birds—no rabbits that I've seen, but then, clearings are rare. Deer and bears, we might not see even if they were as common as in an ordinary wood—"

"What's that?" said Kenneth, blinking. Was it really a flash of gold through the trees? Like an enchanted flower that could dissolve all enchantments?

One that would conceal them from notice would be more useful, he told himself. And the gold moved—too large to be a flower, as it lumbered between the trees. Moments after, a golden bear came snuffling along the forest floor. Then it stopped, and lifted its head to eye them.

"Stay on the path," said David, without taking a step forward.

"It's supposed to be good fortune," said Rob. "To encounter an enchanted beast in the forest. It throws off pursuit."

"It's supposed to be an enchanted prince whom I could rescue and marry," said Diamond, "if you believe the right tale from my great-grandmother."

The bear swung its head but did not move toward them.

Kenneth laughed. "It could be an enchanted princess, as well. But if it's a prince, remember to not burn the bearskin."

"If she remembers that," said David, "it always turns out to be the right thing to do, to rescue the prince. If it's the wrong thing, she will just have to chase after him for seven years to get him back."

"Sometimes it kills the prince," said Diamond, demurely, "but *I* would not take anyone else's word on the spell. *I* would analyze it and figure out how best to break it."

The bear snuffled at them and turned away.

"No wonder all fairy tales are once upon a time," said Kenneth.

Pearl muttered about childish prattle.

They walked on. A ruby-red bird flitted over the path. Silvery squirrels flitted about, chasing each other or climbing trees. Oaks gave way to maples, and the maples to beeches, and the beeches to maple again. Birds cheeped, now and again. Once, Kenneth thought he saw a deer as white as moonlight, but he could not be sure, and it did not approach.

A lake appeared ahead, glittering in the sunlight, and the path circled it. A few islands stood in the waters, and each had a tree or two growing on it. Two white swans, in the middle, let the ripples bear them up and down.

Then, across the waters, stood a mass of green dotted with white and red. Kenneth blinked. A castle overgrown with roses, but he had not expect any castle to ever be quite so overgrown. He cast sideways glances at it as they walked on. The form of the castle was clear enough, as if enchantments kept it from growing into a wild bramble such as might protect a sleeping princess from a too early waking.

The lake's curve turned the path toward the castle, and they could see the lawns about it, and its leaf and flower covered walls, which were far enough from the castle that they had to guard a garden. Or a courtyard, but for this castle, a garden.

"Castle Rosarium," said Diamond, and though he had heard of it only in half-fanciful tales, Kenneth recognized it as well.

"They keep people here," said Rob, "if they are in enchanted sleeps. Or have been turned to statues."

Kenneth snorted. A place where people were hidden away to be forgotten—perhaps he was just unnerved by the past months.

"Also," said Pearl, "those roses are all white by nature. They only turn red from blood shed on them or their roots."

"Ew," said Jamie, and Kenneth, eyeing the roses and how many were red, had to agree. The castle looked less charmed and more cursed with that. Though—

"How long does the red last?" he said. "After the blood is shed."

"Oh, forever," said Pearl. "Certainly, there are roses here that are red from blood shed centuries ago."

He let out his breath, and eyed the roses again. One day, all that they suffered would be as distant as the suffering that changed those roses.

The breeze bore the scent out to them, and filled the air with sweetness.

The wall that marked the division was low enough that he could have climbed it, were it not so wreathed in roses both red and white, their green leaves very dark, their legendary thorns hidden. He could only guess that stone lay beneath; if the others had heard more, perhaps from the Order, he had never heard it even mentioned in class or any textbook.

The vines rose in an arch over an entrance without a gate. Behind it stood a rose garden before the castle itself. The bushes here, in a neat and patterned beds, bore other colors, pinks and oranges and yellows like the dawn. Walking gravely among them were Master Bonaventure and a gardener, but at the sight of them, Master Bonaventure nodded to the other man and walked toward them.

"So quickly?" said David.

"Time and tide wait for no man," said Master Bonaventure. "This is the best time for me to leave for quite some time, and your plans are best done quickly." His lips twitched as if holding back laughter, but his words continued grave. "All the more in that many in the Order think I came here to rebuke you, for taking it upon yourself to move the children, and then for your plans with them."

"You—you can't mean to—" Pearl gawked. "They're youngsters! Even *Kenneth* is not full-grown!"

"All the more reason to deal with their peril firmly," said Master Bonaventure.

The gardener walked up.

"Pearl, this is Master Tidwald," said Master Bonaventure. "He can tell you about the gardens here. The others will get a lighter tour, later, as they will not understand so much as you will. They do not know enough about flowers."

Pearl looked caught between sullenness and curiosity. When Master Bonaventure stood in silence, waiting, Pearl started forward. Master Tidwald nodded and led her off. Rob looked after, and Master Bonaventure and David herded the four of them inside, through a small, arched doorway.

Branches of snow-white roses brushed their heads as they went in, and white petals fell. Inside, a stairway led up between walls of russet-brown stone, and besides it, a corridor led into the depths of the building. All about the light was green. Kenneth glanced about. Octagonal windows, set in the walls, were all so overgrown that he could not see a scrap of the sky.

David led off up the stairs and then down a short corridor, into an octagonal room, without paneling to cover the walls' stone. The octagonal table in its center was made of oak and dark with age, which could not conceal that, for all its sturdiness, it had been battered, leaving gouges and scorch marks in its surface.

But not replaced, of course, because it doubled the virtues of the room. Kenneth wondered whether Diamond could enumerate them.

Five of its walls had large windows in them, with old-fashioned panes, small and diamond-shaped. One had a chest under it.

Master Bonaventure went to that chest, opened it, and with an approving mutter that they had managed, pulled out crystals, completely colorless, and large enough to fill his hands. He put them on the table.

"We should cast the spells as quickly as we can. To give us as much as we can in as short a window possible, before we have to seal the visions in."

Kenneth's tongue touched his lips. How much could they recall, out of all the scores of windows?

"First of all," said David, "the difference between my spellcraft and Kenneth's."

"A differential spell?" said Diamond, brightly.

"Don't cast it yourself," said Master Bonaventure ominously. "Still less on your own."

Diamond smiled innocently. Master Bonaventure took up two large crystals, all but identical, and handed them to Kenneth and David.

"Do they have to be the same, geometrically, to work?" said Diamond.

"It only helps," said Master Bonaventure. "More important is the detail, since neither of them remember any difference."

Kenneth drew a deep breath, laid out the spell book, and went through the spell. The stone flooded with the dark room of his memory, but sharper than his memory. It was, after all, a scrying spell, he reminded himself. Of his memory of the time he cast the spell, but that just formed a focus.

David set about the spell. Moments later, his crystal stood next to Kenneth's. It was black. Master Bonaventure scowled in thought and had them block out the light from the windows, leaving Kenneth's crystal the only source of light.

Master Bonaventure breathed out the words. "A protective spell. An overt protective spell, I think. The two of you did cast the same spell in the same manner."

"Because they realized that Kenneth had cast such a spell?" said Jamie.

"Perhaps," said Master Bonaventure. "There are other reasons. It might protect against David but not Kenneth for all sorts of reasons." He frowned. "The roses might keep us from seeing too clearly, what with the protection they grant us."

David straightened up from the table. "I will take them to the Ivory Tower. See if it is clearer there."

"That's too dangerous," said Master Bonaventure, more quickly than Kenneth had ever heard him say a thing before. Jamie looked sharply over, and his mouth opened.

David's face was set, and implacable. "Like the children, I am in danger. If they can risk their lives to escape, they will hardly object to my doing the same. All the more in that, this time, I will take care to not go where I have been before. In and out, and give them no time to prepare. Nor any traitor time to betray me."

Master Bonaventure winced and muttered that perhaps someone had eavesdropped.

"No one is eavesdropping here," said David. "One of its charms." He smiled. "Besides, we saw a bear, and birds, along the way. You know that means enchantment hid our path."

Master Bonaventure gave him an exasperated glance, but minutes later, David departed through the archway, carrying the crystals. Jamie sighed, turning away.

"The enchantments," said Rob. "How can they protect us?"

Master Bonaventure sighed. "You know fairy tales—"

Rob's nose wrinkled. "Where a bear can be a transformed prince and talk like a man? And you can burn his skin to free him—or maybe kill him? We learned in our first lessons that magic doesn't work that way. The lessons we learned from our mothers, not the first lessons at school."

Even I learned that before I went to school, thought Kenneth, and my parents knew no magic.

"But that bear he spoke of didn't turn into a prince," said Master Bonaventure. "The enchantment of the forest both hides your path and causes birds and beasts to be plentiful. It is well that David guided you—you could have stumbled on something much worse than a house made of gingerbread."

Rob scowled.

Diamond said, quickly, "Probably their library has a history book on it. We can get there the quicker if we conjure up what Jamie and Kenneth saw."

"And that is the prudent path," said Master Bonaventure. "Come. David's discoveries are unlikely to save you, or him, by themselves."

"Let's do them in order," said Kenneth. Then he looked at the crystals and sighed. This would take a long time. He had lost count of the windows in the Labyrinth of Thought to be scried.

#

The sunlight was turning golden with evening when a knock sounded on the door. A little old woman, dressed in gray and brown, with a shawl and an apron over skirts and shirts, stuck her head in.

She smiled cherubically as they turned, scowling, toward her. "We have spells to ensure we do not disrupt dangerous spellwork. Now, it is time for you to *eat*."

#

The kitchen had heavy wooden crossbeams, a fireplace as large as the doors to the Tower of Stone, and a long trestle table beneath a row of windows covered with rose vines. By green light, they, and Pearl, ate soup, and bread and cheese, for dinner.

"And," said Mistress Meg, scrapping her own bowl with her spoon, "you'll be wanting to see your rooms."

Jamie swallowed the last of his bread. "Uh—we've got to get back to work."

"Best to see them now," said Rob, putting down his spoon. "We'll be too sleepy to search them out when we're done."

"Kenneth," said Diamond primly, "won't let us stay up *that* late."

Kenneth rolled his eyes.

Master Bonaventure chuckled. "I will oversee that, but Rob is quite right."

Pearl stood. "Best see to them at once. There's still some time for the garden—*you* may manage without caring about time and sunlight, but it still matters for me."

"You're in a different tower," said Mistress Meg. "It will give you an easier way to the roses."

Pearl's start turned into a rather smug smile.

#

Castle Rosarium indeed, thought Kenneth, as he stood in his suite. Before a great window—diamond-shaped panels, clear and colorless as air, with a stained glass border of roses—chairs gathered before a fireplace, and the walls about were paneled with carved oak. To its right, a bedroom held a four-poster bed with hangings embroidered with trees and deer. To the left, a study with massive book cases, and a desk larger than most masters had at Graytowers. He thought that the room held more books than the entire library at Quiet Valley. He slipped in and looked over shelf after shelf of tales of adventure, and tomes of history. The amusement might be worth it, but—he slipped back out.

The three exclaimed over their suites, their voices echoing in the hall, with Master Bonaventure smiling beneficently on them.

"It's been centuries!" said Rob from the doorway. "How do they keep it up?"

Master Bonaventure's smile vanished. "It—has its advantages."

"I bet," said Jamie, "that we'll be able to go for long walks even on the days when it rains."

The smile returned. "I shall show you one way."

It took them back to the room with the crystals. Diamond took to sorting them, and Rob to scowling over them, as Kenneth and Jamie finished the Labyrinth's windows.

Master Bonaventure joined Rob. Kenneth glanced over and saw that the crystal before them held the mechanica.

"If," said Master Bonaventure, "these do not all show the same mechanica, they show ones of the same type—a type I have never seen."

"I have," said Kenneth in exhaustion. "Though not in life. An illustration of what a liminal mechanica might look like."

Both of Master Bonaventure's eyebrows went up.

"They had some unusual books in Quiet Valley."

"To be sure they did," said Master Bonaventure, "if they included something so mixed up."

Jamie's mouth twisted. He picked a crystal up.

They were fixed, Kenneth reminded himself. They would have time to pour over them at leisure. He yawned, feeling weary to the bone, and looked out the window at the billowing sunset clouds—more colorful than the darkening garden. The woman moving about the garden might be Pearl, but he could not see well enough to know.

Rob leaned forward next to him. "Is that—"

Kenneth followed his gaze. In the shadows of the forest, something dark moved, flying toward the castle gate. Just outside it, David Servant settled to the earth and walked in.

"He's back!" called Rob joyously.

Master Bonaventure alone did not turn from the crystals as they thundered off to greet him, finding him at the bottom of the stairs, and Kenneth thinking that perhaps, as the prefect, he should have had more dignity. But he was too glad to see that David returned safely.

"Upstairs, you little lunatics," he said, "upstairs. Unless Master Bonaventure has left already?"

Jamie shook his head, and they clambered back up the stairs.

David looked at Kenneth and shook his head. "And you ride herd on them, alone?"

"They aren't usually this—energetic," said Kenneth. Unkind to dwell on their fears. "It's the prospect of learning something that might help."

David nodded and strode up the stairs.

Master Bonaventure looked from the crystals. "I will have to leave soon—as soon as this lot is herded off to bed—but I confess that curiosity possesses me."

"It was a protective spell, all right," said David. "Neither man nor woman, neither girl nor boy, could watch him at work."

Silence fell. Frowns of thought—and frustration—formed.

"So," said Diamond, "Kenneth is neither boy nor man."

Master Bonaventure let his breath out. "No, he is a youth, as you are a maiden. Such spells always take meanings in their narrowest sense. An infant, as well, could see, if capable of casting the spell."

"Not even by rote," muttered David.

Master Bonaventure's voice was grave and measured. "And that, perchance, is why you three escaped the night Jamie's parents vanished. And why you two escaped that labyrinth." He waved his hand at the crystals.

"How likely is that?" said Jamie. "Foolish to trust to a single spell for protection."

"Foolish, but common," said Rob. "Why muck up something that works? And if you cast a new spell each time, you leave new gaps."

"And," said Diamond, "you've read enough tales of mixing spells and how it goes bad."

"Consider it in the morning," said Master Bonaventure. "I must seal this room so that only we six can enter, and that spell needs solitude."

Diamond said, "It's Kenneth who's supposed to chivvy us to bed." She yawned. "And Pearl's no use. She's too old."

Kenneth smiled and lingered. As soon as the three were out of earshot, he said, his voice low, "We have three weeks."

Both men looked sharply at him.

"Then *I* will be too old. After that day, you will face the choice of bringing another scholar my age into peril, or using one of those three."

Master Bonaventure winced but kept his voice measured. "It is unworthy of my oath and my position to send you to face this peril alone. And—what could you do?"

"Learn what we can do," said Kenneth.

#

They rose late, with the morning well progressed and the skies a dove-pale gray outside the windows. David sat alone at the breakfast table when they arrived, eating porridge.

"Master Bonaventure wanted me to stay here as long as I can."

"It's safe?" said Jamie, going to fetch the bowls.

David shrugged. "The castle has crypts, there are those who die here, but no place is safe in the end."

"Particularly for us," said Kenneth dryly, taking the bowl Jamie handed him.

"Oh, yes," said David. "I dare say Rob could find you the crypts."

"No," said Rob, sitting. "I have work to do. I can't even study the gardens. I couldn't study the history except that Kenneth will make me study history and mathematics as well as magic."

Kenneth's eyebrows went up. He dished himself some porridge in silence.

"You can show us during the walk," said Diamond.

"You should have realized that I would make you do that, too," said Kenneth as dryly as he could, and a murmur of laughter went about the table. Rob blinked.

"But yes, study first," said Diamond, and looked at David. "I hope you know enough of mechanica to help with the sketches."

#

All of them were competent enough at sketching that the mechanica swiftly took form. Kenneth concluded that if they did not all show the same device, the devices had all been built toward the same plan—for ends that no amount of sketching would reveal.

"Did they run them?" said Jamie, stretching his arms over his head. "It would be odd to see them only in moments of preparation, not in use."

"Maybe they weren't there when the devices ran," said Diamond, scowling over one crystal. "They were sent to fetch Jamie, after all—they might not be powerful in the Web."

"We should visit the library," said Kenneth. "I hope it has books on mechanica."

"Recent books, at that," said Jamie.

David looked between them, and his expression was odd.

"We should go for our walk first," said Rob. He waved his hand at the window. "It's going to rain if it gets much darker."

Kenneth looked at the clouds—slate-gray. He had not noticed how it had darkened.

Rob stretched his arms before him, and frowned. "If we can go for walks. We don't want to leave the gardens, but they are all close by the castle."

"We could go about a few times," said Jamie. "Like we would do in the castle, if it rained. Or when we circled the Lighthouse."

"They are larger than you've seen thus far." David stood. "I can show you the way to the walkways, and the library on the way."

Rob lowered his arms, his gaze back on the crystals. "I hope it has a history of the castle and the roses."

"Mixing up your interests?" said Diamond.

"Well—" He reached for one crystal. A snow-white rose turned blood-red. Then it returned to white as the crystal returned to showing the mirror from the beginning.

After a minute, Diamond said, "*Not* here. The stone behind it is *black*."

"Where else would it be?" said Jamie. "It's not a very good spell for the effort put into it. It doesn't afford the castle much protection—it's not even frightening without a legend—far better to vest more power in using the thorns against intruders."

"A book might tell us," said Rob.

"If I find anything," said Kenneth, slowly, "I will tell you, since that might indeed be our best guide to where to look. Just as you will tell us about books of mechanica."

"You'll find the library better organized than *that*," said David.

It would be hard put, thought Kenneth, to be worse than either Quiet Valley or the Lighthouse.

Diamond stood. "I'll help Kenneth."

"And I'll help Rob," said Jamie. He looked at David.

"And I will work on something else entirely," said David. "Not at the library."

Kenneth let his breath out. "Don't expect me to chivvy you to the books when I've got these three. You're on your own for studies."

#

David's path led down another set of stairs, along a corridor clearly, from the cold and damp, underground, and then up again, down a short corridor, and into a library.

Vaulted windows, up to an arched roof, stood no more than half as much again as an ordinary room's height. Walking in, and about, found that the library held a dozen round rooms, just touching. Diamond wondered aloud what fit in the space where they did not touch, but did not go look for a book on it. The windows were mostly the diamond panes that let them clearly see the gardens, but they also bore glassy roses: long green stems with ruddy or sun-yellow blooms, all flat and single. A central room, with odd corners from the circular libraries, held a sundial with all the hours, and a sunstone glowing over it, to show time both day and night.

After a short walk, which none of them had tried to lengthen, they began to use that time, searching through the shelves.

It was, Kenneth soon found, both better organized than he had expected, and less valuable.

Lamps lit on their own, to fill the rooms with golden light, and the windows darkened.

In another room, Jamie and Rob raised their voices now and again, about getting a ladder, or disputing a description. Once he walked over and decreed, "If it is so ambiguous that you can argue like this over it, we can hardly rely on what it says to plan."

Both boys flushed, but Jamie said, mulishly, "It can't be on Greenwood Isle. There's no black stone castle there."

Kenneth sighed. "Perhaps you—or one of you—should tackle it from the other end, and look for castles of black stone, and then see if they have roses." He looked between them, heard footsteps from behind. "Especially if you can say nothing except 'black stone,' I have been most negligent in overseeing your theoretical work."

"It wasn't obsidian," said Diamond. "And that would be too fiery for those roses. The magic—" She waved her hands in the air. "They would be fiery red and orange, not blood red, and certainly not white."

"It had no veins like marble," said Rob, frowning.

Jamie shrugged. "Probably granite. Good building stuff."

"Though—" Kenneth winced. He should have seen that before he spoke. "—we don't *know* that it's a building. It could be a chunk of stone put somewhere for its virtues."

Rob's face lit up. Moments later, he had dragged Jamie off to another room.

"Perhaps we should change, too," said Diamond. "Look at books about liminal things and liminal magic, instead of mechanica."

"There aren't many more books of mechanica," said Kenneth. "We can finish them off." The windows were as black as obsidian, with the lead tracing the patterns. He glanced into the room with the sundial. "After dinner."

As if the words had unleashed a spell, rain thundered on the roof and gurgled down the drains as loudly as a torrent in spring.

Diamond said, loudly, "I think I can work out the way to the kitchen from here."

"I'm not mastering a spell to find it," said Jamie. "At least—not tonight!"

#

The corridor had fewer lamps than the library. It held the same arched, diamond-paned windows as the library, but roses had been allowed to overgrow it. Their rain-pelted, wind-tossed leaves were barely visible through the glass, except when lightning flashed, and the roses were stark shadows.

Diamond led them down a stairwell, and past oaken doors. Ahead, to their right, the wall gave way to arches and pillars.

Moments later, Diamond stopped. The arches were in a room filled with crystal coffins. In each one, a body lay as if asleep—a nut-brown maid with poppies in her hair, a grizzled knight in full armor, a delicate boy with hair so blond as to be white—

"The crypts," said Jamie, breaking into his thoughts.

Rob shook his head. "They're sleeping. The crypts have ordinary tombs. But this is where they bring everyone under sleeping curses."

"In the castle overgrown with roses," murmured Diamond, glancing at the window. "How—fitting."

"This must be centuries' worth," said Rob.

Jamie eyed a girl with coppery hair and a black gown. "I wonder if anyone's trying to free them."

Silence fell.

Diamond shivered. "It—might be best to let the curse run its course. A sleeping curse can not unbounded." But Kenneth had never before heard her speak so hesitantly about any matter of magic.

"Dinner," he said firmly, but as he ushered them into the kitchen—the rain having settled to a steady drum, and daylight even having returned, however dimly—he felt as subdued as they looked. They were so pale he was glad that he could not see himself in a mirror.

Pearl was nowhere in sight, but David, sitting among the other wizards, looked up and raised an eyebrow.

"Ah," said Mistress Pierrette, "you'll have been by the lower way back. Most of us don't like it."

A voice boomed from the garden doorway: Master Zander, a dwarfish wizard. "Wise of us. You don't want to—disturb things." He eyed them. "You didn't—touch anything?"

"Of course not," said Diamond, but could put no vigor into it. The wizards eyed them, but said nothing more.

"I hope it was a profitable afternoon," said David, with a joviality unlike him.

"We found some ideas," said Kenneth. "Eliminated more dead ends." After a moment, he added, "Hope yours was, as well."

"It had its moments. I can show you after."

Chapter 13—Discoveries

The room by the library had a crystal in the center of its table, glittering. Kenneth watched David's spellwork more than the stone. Something was odd about it.

Then the stone held a towering building, built of white stone. The sea lapped all about, up to a dock, where, oddly enough, a tree grew, straight and tall, not twisted so much as slightly by the sea winds. Stairs rose into a building that looked more like a castle than a tower, with courtyards, guardhouses, towers, oranges trees that were in fruit, but always the stairs led up and up.

"Tower Island!" said Rob.

David smiled. "With the Island Tower on it."

"What did you do with the spell?" said Kenneth. "That's not the one from the book."

"I scried for liminal places," said David. "Boundaries, borders, thresholds."

Kenneth looked at the licking waves. They seemed to be rising—"How does that avoid getting swamped by the tide twice a day? Is this the high tide?"

"No to the second—and *magic* to the first," said Rob.

"How is a secret that its builder took with him to the grave," said David.

"But it was a vital part of the spell," said Jamie, "with boundaries—it serves as a fortress because of that, because it can be used to fix the boundaries."

Kenneth scowled, staring at it. The tower's stone was as pale as sea foam, or the light and fluffy clouds, and no roses grew there. It resembled nothing that the Labyrinth of Thought had shown them. He supposed that the boundary made him think of the Web—that, and how David had cast the spell.

"At least we can know that it's not part of our enemies' plot," he said. "Since David can scry it."

The three giggled. David looked exasperated.

"Maybe we'll find something useful this evening," said Jamie.

"Possible," said Kenneth, pulling open the door and holding it for the others.

"Nothing thus far?" said David.

Kenneth shook his head as the three headed down the corridor. "I suspect Diamond and I will exclude the chance of finding anything in the books about the mechanica. Which could be called knowledge, of a sorts."

Daylight had returned to illuminate the way. They walked down the corridor after the three, and went around a turn. Master Zander came up the stairs into the hallway ahead of them, and gravely nodded.

"We have quite a bit of knowledge just from the crystals," said David. "We can reconstruct it. However slower that way is. Then we will know, and the Order as well."

Master Zander smiled benignly on them. "And," he said, "it will give you a chance to build up knowledge. The edifice of wizardry. You should be glad that you can add a tower or a room to it."

"I would be just as glad," said Kenneth, "or more so, to move into a tower already built."

"For shame. What does that say about those who worked at it before?"

"That it was good work and worth moving into? If the use of the room is pointless, so too is the room and the work that went into building it." Kenneth straightened. "One would think they would want others to move into it."

Master Zander studied him, shook his head, and went into the library. David went after, and Kenneth followed, but both men split off at once to search out shelves. Kenneth looked for Diamond.

She stood by a window and scowled over one of the last books. When he went to reach for another, she turned to hold it up before his nose.

"Look at this one."

He raised an eyebrow, took it in hand, and started to read. At first, he thought that she had found a basic text, for new scholars, it talked in such general terms, but something in the writing bothered him.

Then, slowly, it dawned on him that what was general was the mechanism. Not designed to perform some task, but to operate according to the virtues of what was put into it. It did not even have to be stonework if he read it right.

"This is the one we want," he said.

Which brought not only Diamond's sharp nod, but the presence of Rob and Jamie, and David.

Minutes later, Jamie stepped back. "I'm looking for the stone, still. If we can find the mechanica, perhaps you can foil it with your studies, but another line of attack might be wise."

Kenneth nodded. "Tomorrow, perhaps." He ran a hand through his hair, and his gaze went over the window. "Or perhaps not."

In the gloomy garden, Mistress Imogene and Master Bonaventure were deep in talk, and coming toward the castle. The others fell silent and looked anxious. Even David did not speak.

Pearl, her arms grubby, emerged from between rows of bushes, her pale face looking hopeful—and once Mistress Imogene spoke with her, twisted with resentment.

David's voice was heavy. "Perhaps not indeed."

Master Bonaventure and Mistress Imogene went in a doorway, which was closer to where the master wizards worked than the library.

He wondered how long it would take for them to come for the five of them.

#

The last daylight had left. Were it not for the tracings of lead still marking stained glass roses, the room would have looked entirely walled in mirrors. Those facing each other made endless repetitions of the scenes within, the heavy, oaken table and chairs, the light that Master Bonaventure set on the table, and the faces around it.

Kenneth could not quite follow the spell Mistress Imogene used, but intent was clear, to seal their words within. He thought it would work against a wizard who used authority marks to listen.

Diamond whispered, "I hope the echo's not too bad," and then, when the whispered echo was louder than in an unenchanted room, blushed a little.

Subdued, they filed into the chairs. For a moment, Kenneth wondered whether Master Bonaventure knew of their eavesdropping at the valley. He sat. At least now, he had hope they would not need to use such a spell again.

"The report we have came from Mistress Gloria," said Master Bonaventure. "At the Ivory Tower."

And was urgent enough to not wait for morning, thought Kenneth.

Mistress Imogene nodded. "It has kept her busy, and half a score of other masters. Because it was not the Ivory Tower's wizardry. That was why I was there, and can bear the news: they brought me in to inspect the garden, to tell what the flowers could tell—not much, they were not set with the intent of catching such spells, more the tower's purity."

She turned to the others. "The news was of a magical attack. It tried to crack the Ivory Tower like a nut. If it had been more measured, it might have done harm, but it strained too far, and broke without doing damage. Still—" She looked at David. "It came shortly after you scried."

For moments after, the echo in the room held no sounds.

Kenneth let his breath out. "It must have alerted them."

Jamie leaned forward. "There are spells that can do that. And counterspells against it."

"We would be wiser to trace it back," said Diamond, "and find our foes there. The Order lies in peril as long as these Web masters can weave."

"Dangerous," said Master Bonaventure, heavily. "Dangerous past your knowledge." He sighed. "I should not have come. Of what use is a sage old man to caution you of peril, when all your paths are perilous? And to stand at the crossroads is most perilous of all."

"You can point out flaws in our plans to dissuade us," said Kenneth. "Even knowing that young fools seldom heed sage old souls."

Master Bonaventure lowered his brows and looked at him. Kenneth looked back.

"We have that mechanica," said David. "I did not see much before they arrived—what does it do? Can we stop it? Do we have to steal it?"

"It depends on the stone they put in it," said Kenneth. "They might even use something else—but it works liminal magic, I would guess, based on what other magic we have seen. If I have read the description rightly, they can send magic to and fro."

"It might even have a map you can use for direction," said Rob. "You could send it anywhere."

"Next thing to chaotic sorcery," said Mistress Imogene.

"Far enough away," said Master Bonaventure. "For all the evil things said of it, and for all that many of them are true, it is liminal and not chaotic. They would not be such fools. Every chaotic sorcerer who succeeds in any manner always fails in the end, because some quick-witted soul realizes that with the breakdown of all rules, there is no rule that the sorcerer must reap the fruit of his labors."

"At least if we sabotage it," said Jamie, "it will stop. Shove something into the gears—wood, metal—sand—" He shrugged. "Shoes."

"Between working and not working is also a boundary," said Diamond.

Kenneth blinked. She had read more on liminal magic than he had realized. He glanced at her pale, still face. Or deduced more.

"True," said Master Bonaventure. "If you must do it—and you should not—you must stop it entirely or not at all. Do not try when you might fail."

"Or transform it," said Kenneth slowly. "Liminal magic does not want to stay in place." Which was what he hated about it. He plugged on. "It wants to complete its transformation or fall back."

Silence fell.

David Servant sighed. "Has anyone found out what happened to the Opal of the Northern Lights?"

"Lost," said Mistress Imogene.

"Utterly lost," said Master Bonaventure. "Master Thomas showed that it was in the Boneyard."

Kenneth let his breath out. "I have an idea about that. It requires a stone."

#

They went for the walk in the morning, before the dew had dried, before breakfast. The three insisted, to Kenneth's surprise, but on the path, in the cold air, he thought he too would rather wait for the news inside.

A raven flitted down, and became a man. "May I join you?" said David.

"Of course," said Jamie.

David walked on with them, mild and silent among the roses.

Kenneth's gaze went over the sundial, still unreadable in the shadows, and the flowers about it. The dawnbright was closing its pink flowers, but the morning glories were opening in radiant blue. He fought down a sigh. For the first time in his life, he dreaded the approach of his birthday.

"We could scry for the roses," said Rob. "That would show us the outside. Then the Order would know where the Web masters are."

"And where we are, if they do something," said Jamie. "If they had scried that we were in the Labyrinth of Thought—" He scowled. "They would still suspect *you*," he said to his uncle.

"We can not trust that you will escape as easily, a second time," said David. "Piers was a bungler—and I would have gladly foregone being exonerated for your safety—or yours, either, Kenneth."

"Both or neither, uncle," said Jamie. "Neither of us could have survived alone."

In the silence after, a bird trilled.

"I'll have to study stonework more," said Rob. "I've learned enough plant magic—more than enough—" A nearby rosebush bloomed with dainty pink blossoms from buds, through full blown and growing ragged, to a bare heart of yellow, with the petals all fallen. He cast a spell at it. The branches writhed at them, as if to tear them apart, and more petals fell. The leaves shifted enough to show its thorns.

Jamie frowned. "It's dangerous."

Rob dismissed the spell. The branches settled in serenity. More petals fell, leaving more blossoms ragged, or even petal-less. "That's why I practiced it. I can use it as counter-magic against the danger."

"I probably have to change my studies myself," said Kenneth. "I am not getting far in—" He waved his hand in the air. "The spell that Pearl showed us. I tried some variations on it."

David's lips pursed for a moment. "I see my studies are hardly studious enough to let me hold up my head among your number. I will look at your work, Kenneth, if you will look at mine."

"What does it do? Or is meant to do?" said Kenneth.

"Stop you in motion," said David as they passed under an arched lattice set with golden roses. "Even if you are snatched away by spells. A natural application of stonework to the eyes of those who know little of it, but I need a way to test it."

Kenneth nodded. Their path arched back, by a low stone wall, toward the castle again.

"Easier than scrying."

"Much," said David. "However urgent the matter, I should have started with a more basic matter. There's only so much to be done with the limits of the crystals you can get. Spellcraft can only work on such virtues as they have got."

"There's no inherent limit to their virtue in that respect," said Diamond. "And so none to what they can scry."

"There is to your purse—whoever you are. Natural crystals are limited in size, no matter how wealthy you are, and the smallest flaws add up. Artificial ones, made perfectly, are still more costly, and past all your power to make."

"Like the Eye of the World," said Rob. "It can show all manner of things—once Master Mortimer made it."

"Could," said David. "Since it's been lost."

A breeze sent a flurry of white rose petals through the air before they settled on the earth among the red petals.

"I wonder—" Kenneth shook his head. "Your work first, David. More profitable than tales of lost crystals."

#

It gave you respect for jugglers, thought Kenneth. In the spell-lit chamber, with an empty floor except for David's spell sphere, he drew a deep breath, gathered up the spell again, and sent the ball flying across the sphere. He let go, and the ball instantly fell to the ground in mid-flight.

David ran a hand through his hair. "As good as I will get, I suppose."

"For now," said Kenneth.

David snorted. He looked both bitter and hollow. "For now."

Kenneth let his breath out. "Then I shall be off. I want to see to my scrying."

"You have a way to increase your power?" After a moment, David blinked. "Or are you just scrying to master it?"

"I thought I would scry for the Eye of the World."

David fell silent. In the corridor, the clock ticked out the moments, and David said, slowly, "That might work, at that."

"It will be quick, at any rate," said Kenneth. "You could watch if you were curious. If it fails, I can go back to my textbooks. And to trusting that the Order will keep me safe and find the enemies trying to kill me, so I can walk free again."

David rolled his eyes.

Out in the corridor, the open doors of three study chambers showed each of the three intent on their books. His own was half open, and within a minute, he had the crystal out in the middle and cast the spell.

The crystal went dark. David shut the door and quenched the light, and still it was dark, showing only a few glimmers of light.

"Well hidden," said Kenneth. "To make it impossible to find. Or at least difficult." He stepped closer to peer at it.

"Oh, it's not that," said David. He walked closer by the glimmers. "Look more closely. It's on a shelf. You have seen that shelf before, or ones close enough."

Kenneth felt icy. "It's in the Boneyard."

David snapped his fingers, and the light returned. He nodded. "Lost indeed. No getting it out of there. It might as well have been intended as a hiding place."

"If we search—you can find a way out, so you can find things."

"Not so easily. The magic gets to you. You four all fainted from the effects of a journey, nothing more."

"If you're protected?"

"You can't be," said David. "The magic is too strong."

"You hid there."

David hesitated, and spoke slowly. "As a raven. Still, it affected me. I kept enough of my wits about me to remember to leave in due course—but not enough to do something else at the same time." He snorted. "And even magpies are overrated as thieves. I might manage to make myself steal something bright and sparkly, but a piece of fool's gold would draw me as much as the Eye of the World. More. The Eye looks too large to carry."

Kenneth scowled. There had to be some way. He opened the door and headed toward the library.

Walking down the corridor, David hooked his hands on the belt. "Don't let how I act outside fool you. The deathly magic strengthens the raven. At that, I don't know the spell, and it's likely it's illegal, and for good reason."

Kenneth's scowl deepened. "That's not the only way to be protected. There's the spheres."

David laughed, shortly. "You can't move those."

"No reason why not," said Kenneth.

"It's stonework?"

"Separation of virtues," said Kenneth. "It's the basic principle of wizardry, after all. Apply the principle of similarity to get out of a thing what is needed, and exclude all others. You can sever the stillness of a stone from its protection."

David stopped and stared at him.

"I—couldn't—find anything in the library," said Kenneth. David's gaze did not falter. The words inched out. "Nothing on the spell at all. So I devised it myself. Still, it's not that hard. Someone—someone else—must have—"

His words faltered into silence. David's gaze did not change.

After a minute, David said, quietly, "I'd like to see that spell."

"It's—it's a simple piece of stonework," said Kenneth. "I could teach it to the three of them. . . ."

David let his breath out. "That spell? The one you're changing?"

Kenneth nodded.

"It's common and widely used. *In the Order.*" He tilted his head and looked sideways at Kenneth. "Do you remember how many stoneworkers there are in the Order?"

Kenneth opened his mouth and shut it again. After a moment, he wondered why they had not recruited stoneworkers, when it was so crucial to protection.

"I'd like to see that spell," said David. "I—I suspect it's going to have some flaw you don't see at your age. It's unlikely that the masters of the Order would have missed something even without specializing in stonework. But I want to see it. I promise to wait until after to denounce it as folly."

A moment later, he turned into a raven and looked annoyed.

Kenneth's breath gushed out. "How long? Hours instead of days?"

The raven nodded.

Kenneth sighed. He supposed that he should not entirely neglect math and history for wizardry, leaving the castle would mean he would need his studies, and so it was good that the day had given him a chance to catch up.

"What would be folly?" called Jamie from the library doorway. Diamond looked over, and Kenneth went in, to explain briefly, drawing Rob from the shelves, and leaving all three in silence.

"That—that could work," said Rob with slow wonder.

"We can check your work," said Diamond, moving about with uncommon restlessness. "At least some. I could double check your mathematics." She hopped up. "And to think my parents were *so* disappointed when I went into stonework. If they had more stoneworkers—even one—" She grinned.

\#

"It won't work," said Diamond. In the room's darkness, the glow of the radiant stone cast sharp shadows over her face, and made her look the more weary and despairing. "The basic principle is sound, but it would like be trying to boil the sea with a burning coal. We don't have something strong enough."

Rob twitched her notes toward himself, but that was folly. Double-checking her work would not find some foolish error.

"What did you check?" said Kenneth.

"I started with granite—I knew not to begin with the easier ones, and by the time I was done, I was doing enchanted corner stones. And for cathedrals and colleges, not commonplace buildings. Not the strongest one could do what we need it to do."

Kenneth twitched. He would never had thought of enchanted cornerstones.

"It would," said Rob, not looking up from the calculations, "have to have a strength of legend. This does not call for an ordinary stone."

David moved, sharply. His eyes narrowed, and his lips moved, and when, a minute later, he blinked, he looked at them and seemed surprised at their attention.

"You have studied too long and need to walk about a bit." He stood. "And I need some time before I speak to you."

\#

Outside the sky was dark, touched by dozens of stars, and with more shining every moment. The curse had eaten up the day.

Kenneth glanced about the table. And David had insisted on the three being there.

David, looking haggard and determined, said, "There is a way to the Boneyard in Castle Rosarium."

They all brightened. He glared at them. Kenneth still felt his heart hammering harder in his chest.

"Don't go looking for it."

"Of course not," said Rob, as if insulted, and Kenneth nodded with the other two. David watched them with narrowed eyes.

"Tower of Stone," said Kenneth, dryly. "We are not in the habit of breaking laws to be silly. They do not want the people who build foundations to do that."

David blinked, looked relieved, and nodded before he went on.

"You do not have a stone strong enough to get you into the Boneyard and gad about in it unscathed. Especially since you will also need a scrying stone that will tell you that you approached the Eye of the World. I would cast it myself, but once in the Boneyard, I could not keep myself from turning into a raven—and so—" He grinned. "It's just as well that the Order has not lost this one."

He pushed an open book before them, showing a large jewel. Octagonal in shape, completely black, and flat as a table—Kenneth frowned, trying to remember—

"The Eightfold Stone," said Rob, brightly.

David rumpled his hair. Kenneth's eyebrows went up. He didn't remember it from history class, except that every now and again something would be described as being as secure as the Eightfold Stone could make it. David talked of their just using it—He swallowed.

"They'll let us have it?" said Diamond.

"Master Bonaventure arranged that *I* may have whatever is needed, as long as it is in the Order's possession and not in use to protect against a greater evil. It is, after all, to deal with the Web when we already know they are bent on death."

David sat back. "You three will have to master the scrying spell. By rote if necessary. Kenneth will do nothing except protect you with his spell, and I—" He scowled.

"Can you do anything to aid us?" said Kenneth. He could not spare the effort to shield him if it were not so, and he would have laughed were it not so bitter.

"I can warn you if your spell is fading," said David.

Kenneth grimaced, but that aid would definitely be wise to have with them.

"It's the next lesson," said Jamie

Kenneth blinked. "How far you have gotten?" He had watched their trials, but he had only noticed that the spells were, indeed, ones he had mastered.

Diamond cleared her throat. "I just learned it myself. I was going to ask for you to watch—" She looked between them.

Jamie snorted. "The spell you learned without someone looking over your shoulder."

"That," said David, "is allowed because Kenneth's old enough to see where things go wrong, not because he had gotten that far in his studies." He waved his hand at Kenneth. "Watch her. Then the two of you can watch the other of them. I think you have two days. I will have to make arrangements for you to travel."

Jamie winced, but said nothing. Kenneth closed his eyes for a moment. Young to have realized that there would be danger in it for David, but that doing nothing would also be dangerous.

"Then, whichever of you has mastered it best can do the task."

"Best to have all three of them," said Kenneth quietly.

Jamie grinned, with reckless enthusiasm, but it was still the way to go.

"Protecting all three will be little more than protecting only one, and if one falters, the next can take his place. They are all in danger without it."

After a minute spent looking from face to face, David grunted. "As long as you don't insist on Pearl."

"As long," said Diamond gloomily, "as they don't insist on sending her with us."

Chapter 14—Venture

Ahead of them on the path, Pearl displayed her spellcraft to Master Tidwald. The milk-white roses turned as blue as forget-me-nots beneath her hands.

Diamond turned aside. The other three went with her.

"Does she know we're leaving?" said Rob.

Diamond shook her head.

"Not unless you told her, Rob," said Kenneth, and for a moment, they laughed—a thin sound, quickly choked off.

Their path took them around the other side, to where David waited in the doorway.

He smiled. "Pack, all of you. Not to leave, but to spend two nights away. This time, we can leave after dinner and still arrive in the evening. Bring no books."

#

The stone underfoot was pale, with the faintest traces of color in it, like the mist that pressed in every side. The mists swathed the scene, so that within strides, nothing was visible. Even David was murky from walking at the back of their little company.

Kenneth did not look back often.

No plants grew. No streams flowed—not even only audibly, beyond sight. The trail formed nothing more than an indentation in the rock, but it was easy to obey David's injunction to not stray from it.

Steps appeared ahead. Chiseled in the hillside, they led up. Impossible to judge how far—but Kenneth's shoulders slumped as he slogged toward them.

"If we had left early," said Jamie, as he put his foot on the first, "we would have been fresher for the journey." His voice echoed oddly.

"If we had left earlier," said David, "we would have to spend longer at the place where you will sleep." His voice echoed even more oddly, sounding almost inhuman, and none of them spoke again.

The steps went up. And up. And up.

The first change was a darker shadow looming among the white mists. At first, it looked so vague that it might have been no more than a thicker stretch of mist. Slowly, it emerged into a shape: a rounded tower, with steps coiling about it, above and below them—coiling in a gap between the tower and the cliff that their path wound along. Kenneth, his feet aching, wondered why they could not take that stair instead. It did not come any door to the level that their path ended, but it had to be the building, not the floor, that mattered.

He thought. Who could be certain of anything in this monotonous mist?

At least they had gotten this far. They circled the cliff, and doors, as large as a cathedrals, stood before them. A tangled nest of sticks and straw perched at the top, to one side, but—Kenneth frowned—there was no visible way to open the doors, though a wooden bridge reached them, from the end of the path.

They could knock, thought Kenneth, and walked out. His footsteps resounded. With indignant squawking, two birds exploded from the nest. For a moment, they looked dingy black. Then they swooped toward him in fury, shrieking, and their wings flapped brilliantly in sapphire blue. He threw up his arms to defend his face, and saw flame-orange feathers from the corner of his eye.

"Hurry!"

The voice rose, and he risked a glance ahead. The doorway was open—and indeed showed no sign of the doors' existence—and a woman stood in the gap.

He ran. His footsteps thundered, with those of the others. The birds squawked more loudly, their feathers showing red and purple, but their plunges did nothing more than brush by all five of them, and they did not fly inside. Kenneth strode deeper in, opening space for the others—

No sooner had David run in than the woman pulled the doors shut—from the side. Bearing red and green sigils, they cut off the light from the outside, though the hall was not much dimmer for it. He looked about, trying to see what was glowing, and failed.

"My name," said the woman, "is Idaline. Be welcome to the House of Dreams."

She had light brown hair tumbling over a shapeless gray robes, but both the brown and the gray seemed to break into colors whenever glanced at sideways. Kenneth fought to keep from frowning in thought.

Diamond, breathing hard, straightened. "*My* house of dreams does not have a pair of birds attacking innocent travelers." Her mouth pursed. "More targeted, perhaps."

Idaline laughed, faintly. "We've tried to be rid of them, but nothing works."

"Spikes," said Jamie. "Spikes where they nest."

Idaline laughed again and shook her head. "As if those would work, any more than they would in dreams—come, your rooms are ready, and you will want to rise early tomorrow."

She led them back into the hall, and they followed—Jamie scowling. A low stone archway opened to a room full of book-laden shelves.

"You won't want the library," said Idaline.

With the most skeptical look on her face, Diamond said, "We won't?"

"Oh no," said Idaline. She pulled a book from the shelf—it bore no title—and opened it. Where the writing should have been, the page was a blur of strange forms, vaguely like letters, except that he could not focus on them long enough to be sure of that.

Rob's face lit up. "There was a wizard once who could read these books. While he was sleep-walking."

Idaline's eyebrows went up. "So true, o youthful scholar of history. So he said—or so they say about him. It was generations ago." She put the book back. "Any books you carry are safe as long as you do not take up residence here." She walked off between the shelves.

"You do without books here?" said Diamond, following but sounding dazed.

"There are precautions," said Idaline, without looking back, "but you five do not need them. You will be here at most two nights, and be gone between." She glanced over her shoulder toward David. "Is that not so?"

David nodded. "Much depends on how quickly we can find our stone in the Cabinet of Curiosities, but not whether it would be wise for them to sleep there."

Her nose wrinkled. "Of course not. And still less, you. She'll have you turned into a curio as soon as you turn into a raven."

"I did most of my running about today as a raven," said David. "I won't change there. Probably could not if I wanted to."

Idaline walked through an arched doorway. The pale walls beyond looked as if built of driftwood in their shades. The windows to the left looked out on the gray mist, no darker than before. Kenneth wondered whether it was dark by night here, any more than it was bright by day.

"I wonder," mused Idaline, "why they gave Marcia the cabinet."

"Because she's good at it," said David. "Her catalogues are the finest that the Order has seen in centuries, and certainly nothing's been lost—which is more than can be said for any of her predecessors for at least a century, maybe two or three. She's expanded it, too, though I grant you most of them do that."

Idaline looked sideways at him. A blood-red door appeared to her right. Kenneth blinked. He *thought* it was just the curve of the corridor that had hidden it.

"Here we are." Idaline opened the door to a small bedchamber. The bed was a niche in the wall, and on the wall, a curtain set with stars spread—big enough for a large window. "This is yours, Kenneth. Be careful with the window, though you can look out it."

He walked in.

"It will wake you in the morning. Don't come out into the hall, and don't above all else go anywhere until I come to fetch you."

Moments later, she was walking down the corridor. She told Diamond the next room was hers before he closed the door.

Perhaps she should not have talked up the window. Or perhaps it would be only prudent to see what needed care, since it was not forbidden. He pulled back the curtain, opened the window, and leaned out. The winding stairs could be seen clearly. They did not go near any window, let alone door. And he could see nothing of the cliff.

Moments later, directly below him, a window opened. Diamond leaned out.

"Diamond?" he said sharply.

Within a minute, all four of them leaned out—Jamie below and to the left of Diamond, Rob farther right and higher than Kenneth's. No sign of David—who knew of the House of Dreams, Kenneth conceded. But they quickly worked out that they had all gone into rooms on a level, with Jamie after Diamond, and Rob after Jamie.

"It's a good thing they brought us here only to sleep," said Rob.

"Are we awake?" said Diamond. "Or are we asleep and dreaming?" She peered at the mists and then pulled back with a shrug. "Well, you can wake up, and then a minute later, when you're already late, discover that you really dreamed you woke, so I suppose we can dream that we go to bed."

"And," said Kenneth, "we will have a long walk tomorrow."

Still, minutes later with the curtain closed, Kenneth lay abed in the darkness, and wondered whether the stairs could ever be reached, and what it was about the Cabinet of Curiosities that made sleeping here safer.

#

Bleary-eyed, Kenneth pushed the curtains aside. The light helped wake him—though the outside was still gray—but it could not drive away the dream fragments: of a radiant paragon of a bride, his bride, dressed in silver, and so vague in her person that he did not know her hair color, and how they planted roses or radishes or possibly both at once in a mechanica that was encrusted with verdigris so thickly that the red of the copper could not be seen beneath the green, and yet was still running.

Not that he could remember what it did, any more than what his bride looked like.

He dressed. And then he repacked. At the knock at the door, he picked up his pack and followed as Idaline collected the others. Past David's door, she opened another, violet door. There they went down three steps and found themselves in an octagonal cupola, where cast iron lattice work held glass in eight directions. A little of the house was distantly visible below. The glass door they came in by showed the mists—as did the one opposite, and to the right and left.

A table had a red-and-white checked tablecloth, with stacks of pancakes, and bowls of strawberries and blueberries.

Idaline pointed at the door opposite. "Leave that way when you are done. It will let you." Then she turned right and went out the door. With the door open, he made a glimpse of the corridor, but nothing more.

He walked over to the door of their departure, and left his pack by it. The others scrambled to join him.

"I wonder what's out the other doors," said Rob, wistfully.

Diamond and Jamie looked at him.

"Not enough to open one," he said, exasperated. "There might be books describing it. In other libraries, of course." His eyes unfocused in thought.

"Breakfast," said Kenneth, sitting down and handing out plates. He wondered whether to observe that this was the only building, ever, that he had seen that showed not the slightest trace of stonework in its construction.

"I had the *strangest* dream last night," said Diamond.

David started, and Rob and Jamie chorused agreement.

#

Downhill felt even odder than uphill.

Kenneth reminded himself that the forest had ended only a few strides before the mists, and how natural the outcropping had seemed then. The change might be subtle. . . .

A wooden walkway appeared before them—a railing with interspaced stairs and platforms. Kenneth hesitated.

David said, his voice measured though still echoing oddly, "There's morning mist. It may make it hard to tell where the dream mist leaves off."

Kenneth headed downward.

The building seemed to take form as his footsteps resounded on the wood: an enormous, intricate building. The mists muffled anything more than the general shapes of turrets and porches and outbuildings at first, but their steady approach brought more and more detail. Every eave and porch, almost every wall, was done up in intricately carved gingerbread, painted in shades brilliant, or pastel, or murky—some looked gilt. Gargoyles of astounding grotesqueness leaned over the roofs—far more than were needed as spouts for rainwater. Windows could not be made out too clearly, there being no lights behind any of them, but the lead formed patterns, and it seemed that no two of them were by the same artist, let alone showed the same pattern. Certainly none were plain sheets of colorless glass.

"Ah," said David. "They've added to it since last time. More than I heard, at that."

He pointed their way toward a door, one that might be called the front door. A garden spread to their right—at least, there were patches of earth like flower beds, and paths between them, though not so much as a leaf showed. It held statues, all jammed together: stern warriors, graceful maidens, hideous goblins, rotund frogs, stately kings and queens, leaping stags, outsized rabbits, resting fawns, and all of them gray.

"Good thing Pearl isn't with us," said Diamond, her voice sounding frail, and only David managed a snort. Kenneth wondered whether even Pearl could manage to be angered at the failure to plant flowers, here.

The door to the house was double, but no larger than that at his parents'. The two windows inset there were in so intricate a geometric pattern that between the lead and the slant of facetted though colorless glass, no one could see in or out.

The knocker consists of a confection of brass ribbons.

Kenneth knocked. The thud resounded. For minutes after, though he strained to hear, nothing else broke the silence.

Finally, one side of the doors opened. A face scowled at them: pasty pale, with a beak-like nose and deep-set eyes. She wore a conical hat, a sweeping dress, and a mantle over all, all of them in black. She opened the door no wider than she could fill the gap up. Nothing of the house could be seen past her.

Her glance moved from him to each of the other three students in turn, and finally to David. He hooked his hands in his belt and looked back.

Her thin mouth twisted. "Took you long enough."

"So you got the word."

"Got the word? Me? What gave you the notion? The way you reached the Cabinet instead of ending up—" Marcia smiled without humor or happiness. "Well, we shan't be so unpleasant as to discuss how you would have ended up if I had *not* got the word."

Marcia stepped back. And back again as Kenneth stepped in.

She had to. An enormous brass vase, taller than Kenneth and filled with peacock feathers, blocked off the other door. A corridor led back, and alongside it, a stairway went up. Its bannister was carved into the shape of ivy, and each of the steps had piles to one side, or the other, or both: branches, antlers, piles of cloth, heaps of rope. He thought he could climb it, in the bare gaps of the steps, but it would take grace as delicate as a mountain goat.

The corridor was no better. Just past the vase stood a stack, five deep, of frames, the first one showing a portrait of a ghost-pale woman in a garden. As soon as the corridor passed the stairs, it had boxes and baskets with boxes inside boxes and baskets inside baskets. He glimpsed of a mirror on the wall, so tarnished it barely reflected, and he thought the wall had golden-dun wallpaper, with a velvet pattern where it had not been rubbed off, but he could not have picked out the pattern.

A cloak chimed. Moments later, from other rooms, others followed. Some chimed high, some low, some in intricate melodies.

David pulled the door shut. "The Order of the Labyrinth has sent us here to collect the Eightfold Stone."

"So you said," said Marcia, coldly. "So Master Bonaventure said you might. If he said it of his own free will."

"He did it under no more constraints than time and tide brought," said David. "Needs must."

She snorted. "Don't philosophize at me."

She turned to the four of them. "Don't use your scry stone. It is one thing to know where it is, and another to know the right path to that place."

Kenneth nodded meekly, and the others with him—David as well. Marcia still eyed them again before she started off.

Behind the stairway was a door in a stygian shade of blue. Behind the door was a spiral stairway—leading up. In the walls around it, niches no bigger than his hand appeared at irregular positions. Some were no bigger than a child's hand. Each one held a stone figure—frog or horse or crow or any other beast or bird, squatting or standing or pirouetting, he saw no two alike—carved from stone of dark blue, or fiery green, or red with veins of gold through it.

He climbed after Marcia.

At the top, the doorway opened to a wilderness of clutter. The light was dim, falling in dusty rays from windows—all of which seemed to be stained glass, of roses, or armored knights kneeling before an enthroned queen, or geometric figures, or ugly random blocks of color. Some were so dark as to be useless as windows. One or two looked like stone, cut so thin that they let light through. And such light as the windows let in fell on—and cast shadows about—cabinets carved with the sun, the moon, and the stars; clocks elaborate with filigree in white enamel; shelves of tiny golden boxes and slim alabaster jars; fat jugs painted with cheerful faces, or grief-stricken ones, or furious; clockwork mice; ivory doves. . . .

David sneezed. Dust lay all about. In some place, it lay thickly enough to veil whatever lay below in undifferentiated gray.

Marcia led on, indifferent, and they followed, all of them sneezing now and again on the tortuous route, up dozens of stairs and down scores of hallways, all of them so stuffed with curiosities as to be dangerous to walk in. A brass pot held peacock feathers in gold and fiery red. Marcia swept them aside, and they swirled back as they walked after her.

They had not walked a path this long, or this twisted, in the Labyrinth of Thought.

A posy of bronze flowers in a clay pot stood before them, and behind it stacks of painting stood, with the visible ones being the stiff portrait of a woman in white, a still-life of unnaturally colored fruit, with purple apples and blue peaches, and a landscape of mountains, a masterwork of painting.

Kenneth shook his head. Very curious, very strange. Now and again, beautiful.

A heap of carpets had fringes of gold, or drab, or blue. A couple of corners showed patterns, some of perfect flowers, others of geometry. Kenneth glanced at the bare floor. Too precious to walk on, he deduced, and let his breath out slowly.

Marcia turned again, and his mouth tightened. How much of a labyrinth could one building be? Unless she deliberately led them on a route to waste their time and mislead them.

That thought was like a bucket of ice water. They knew the Order had a traitor, who could have been David's death. Kenneth forced his breath out. If David did not fear to come here, it would be folly to play the mother hen for him, when he had decided the risk was worth it.

Marcia walked down a narrow corridor. To either hand, a tapestry hung, solid black, with a pattern made in raised threads. Only now and again, in glancing light, could he make out a huntsman riding, or a bird in flight, or a fruit tree laden with ripe fruit.

"Well," said Marcia sourly, "here we are."

A tower room had eight sides. Every corner was jammed with stones of every color and shape, but Marcia walked to one corner, where one was as large as a platter, as thick as his hand was wide, and eight-sided. Black, opaque, and so finely grained that he could see no crystals—basalt, perhaps. The three were already pondering as they studied it.

"It's big," said Jamie.

Diamond rolled her eyes. "All the better to contain steadfastness. It has to be hard to move."

Marcia folded her arms and spoke sourly. "There it is. *I* am not carrying it out."

Kenneth pulled out his wand. They would need its strength without its staidness. If they could not move it now, they might as well leave it—and he could not let the younger students see him quail.

They drew their own wands, quickly enough that they had not watched what he did.

"It would be easier to lower it out the window," said Jamie.

"Never!" said Marcia.

"And safer, too."

Marcia sniffed and straightened. "I get everything *in* in safety. If you want it, you get this one *out* in safety."

Then she sneezed, ferociously, but Kenneth cast his memory back and conceded that in all the odd corners, there had not be so much as hint of damage or dents to anything. He spoke briskly.

"Jamie, cast protective spells about. The rest of us will carry it. Using the weaving spells to even out the effect."

Marcia muttered something about how they shouldn't have to *say* that, scholars who didn't know that without being told shouldn't be trusted with things like this, Master Bonaventure was a fool to force her hand. . . .

Kenneth glanced at David. "You can stop it before it falls."

David opened his mouth and shut it again. At least he knew he was the least practiced in stonework.

"I suppose," said Marcia, with slow begrudgement, "that I should let you down the grand stairs."

"Which," said David, "will only take us thrice as long."

"Twice at most," said Marcia. "I have no desire to let you linger."

Kenneth scowled, trying to reckon time. The clocks chimed. He blinked. It had taken them no more than two hours to reach here. It must, after all, have been shorter than the Labyrinth of Thought.

The stone sat before them. Four or six hours to carry it out. . . he fought down a sigh.

#

The stairs were broad and spread with drably brown carpet of the plainest sort. This would have helped more were the stairs not also arrayed with flowers—flowers of paper, brightly colored or sun-faded almost to beige, flowers of cloth, stitched or set to wires, flowers of porcelain and carved wood or copper—none real.

David slipped ahead. Flowers of paper and cloth—some of them—nodded as if real in his passing, and he opened the door, showing a glimpse of the porch and the ground outside. The morning mist had melted away. Kenneth reminded himself to not rush. They had trudged this far; they could trudge on, though the end stood in sight.

His heart still hammered when he led the way out onto another porch, and the heat of the day. The stone inched outward, with Rob, Diamond, and Jamie slipping out one by one, until they were all outside.

Jamie's foot was still moving from the threshold when Marcia slammed the door shut behind them, loudly enough to make him start. He forced his breath out. That was why they wove the spell—past and present and future evened out so that a moment's slip did not break the effect.

"Does she not care about the porches?" said Diamond, sourly. "This could fall through the floor."

"She saw you weave the spell," said David, with magisterial authority. "She knew that you could take it. For a time." He looked onward, and Kenneth started the stone down the stairs from the porch, into the heat of day.

"She must have strong spells," said Jamie, as sourly as Diamond. "To spend them on keeping it so evenly cool. It's melting out here."

"The curiosities need it," said Rob. "Some of them. Those that need heat or cold have their own chambers."

"And that we did not have to pass through them was just as well," said Kenneth.

"Onward," said David, and Kenneth looked about. Fields of grass and wildflower spread about them, but David already looked up the hill. "I wish I had used Master Bonaventure's leave to get others to carry this."

Jamie said, "Only if you knew that you could trust them. You could be betrayed again. All the more with this, where it could look like an accident."

"How did you know you could trust *her*?" said Kenneth. "She is in the Order, and we know there's a traitor."

All three of them paled, but David only blinked. "Marcia? Nothing means anything to her except the Cabinet. Nothing. We were lucky she didn't accuse us of trying to go down the stair in order to find a faster route through the Cabinet, so we could steal from it."

Jamie gave an indignant snort. After a moment, he laughed a little. "Bet you she think we did steal. We have the stone."

"And," said Rob, "we need to get it back."

"But at least we aren't going to the Boneyard quite yet," said Kenneth.

"Now that you have been made free of the House of Dreams," said David, "we can return now, and go on to Castle Rosarium. Since we made good time."

"I'm surprised," said Diamond. David raised an eyebrow. "That we didn't faint going out from that."

"It was never that bad," said David. "And now—she has improved the cataloguing. We didn't have to search—"

"She wanted us gone," said Jamie, still sourly.

Rob laughed and spread his free hand. "We have what we need. Let us not quibble about motives."

It was no time for distraction. "Let's go," said Kenneth, and inched onward. He glanced at the malcontent faces. Moving but in need of distraction. "At that, why is it the *Cabinet* of Curiosities?"

Rob laughed again. "There is a cabinet at the heart of it. We weren't allowed near it, but that was where they first kept the curiosities, and it sort of grew about that."

"Was it built in?" said Kenneth.

"The Masters of the Cabinet don't like it," said Diamond, primly, "when knowledge gets out." She lowered her voice. "They won't even let people record what the geometry in the windows means."

"What did you guess?" said Rob.

"The door was to impress the newcomer," she began. "A spell of grandeur."

Their path up the hill shifted past a hillock. Mists stood before them like a mass of pale porridge.

Diamond let her breath out. After a moment, she said, "The ones made from stone were all over the place." Her voice was thin as they inched on, and into the mists, and onward yet. "The stained glass was deliberately disordered, to prevent me from finding a pattern. Or anyone else."

By broad daylight, the mists looked stranger. Rays of sunlight illuminated them without any pattern that he could make out. When the house appeared before them, Kenneth let out his breath in relief. The door they had left by stood there, and David hurried to open it for them.

That did not reveal the short stairway up to the breakfast room, but a long and wide one, plunging downward, so ill-lit that the pale stone looked stygian.

"Don't try a luminous spell," said David. Kenneth set his shoulders and started down the stair. It was wide enough to hold them all, but the mere shadow of the other three, and the stone, darkened it.

"Do we have to close the door after us?" said Diamond. She did not quite manage to keep the quaver from her voice.

"Yes." After a moment, David added, "Things can be bad if something—blunders after us."

Diamond sighed. They went down another step, and Jamie pulled the door shut behind them. Its motion was silent, and the darkness after, great. Not complete. Not so utterly complete that they could not creep downward with the Eightfold Stone.

When he glanced about, Kenneth saw the light was enough to cast shadows on their faces. Except—the shadows cast looked as if the life came from different directions. It could not be the steps having different lights, because as Diamond moved from a step, she was still lit from above and to the left, and Rob, stepping on it, was still lit directly from the right.

Kenneth looked down at the stairs and tried to not even think about the light on him. It was the House of Dreams. He had dreamed of stranger things.

Step after step—he could not have said when the light had increased enough to see clearly by.

Nor when the way to the left melted into mist, so that they climbed down a stair winding about a tower.

Nor when the stone of wall and step turned into wood.

The oak door was clear enough, though. The stairs went on, but David opened the door to an eight-sided casting chamber, empty except for more doors.

"I wonder," said Jamie cheerfully—sounding only a little forced, "what would happen if we scried from here."

"You are too young for that," said David, heading for the door opposite. "Kenneth's too young for that. I'm too young." He pulled open the door. "Master Bonaventure is probably too young."

Outside stood the entrance hall. Kenneth kept his mouth firmly shut.

Idaline, standing by a window, looked over. "Did any of you know that you were in the same room you had been in before?"

"Only this one," said David.

"Good. You do not suit the House of Dreams. It is just as well that you can return to Castle Rosarium today."

"Well indeed," said Kenneth, already angling for the door.

Chapter 15—Casting

Sunlight shone greenly through the rose vines, into the windows and the room where the Eightfold Stone sat on the table with them gathered grimly around. David looked aghast.

"You can't possibly think to cast the spell tonight!"

"It isn't even sunset yet," said Jamie.

"After you lugged the Eightfold Stone about all day," said David. "If I had studied harder, I could have helped and not foisted all the work on you youngsters, but that was what we had to work with. I can not let you scry as well."

"We at least have to ready all the preparations," said Kenneth. "So that we can act promptly in the morning. Even if it would be wise to check this evening's work after a night's sleep."

His mouth set. Truly, David was not *thinking*. They had three days before it would have to be one of the three casting. That would make lugging about the stone look simple and easy.

"I suppose you'll be up at dawn," grumbled David.

"That's one advantage of the Lighthouse," said Diamond pertly. "Time and tide wait for no man, so they have the *best* timely spells."

#

It was still dark out, without the faintest glimmer of light to the east, and the stars still thick as daisies in a field.

Kenneth groaned and threw his arm over his eyes. He had never felt less like sleeping. Getting up would only rouse the others, who needed their sleep—before tomorrow's spell above all other things.

He should have used the prefect spell to master his sleep. But he hadn't. And perhaps even it would not suffice. . . .

Three days, and one had already started. He had no doubt that Jamie would leap to take his place if he learned that Kenneth had outgrown the age in which he could act, no longer slipped between man and boy. He rolled over. If David had thought of that, he would have leapt at the chance to cast the spell last night.

He heard motion. He lay still, and it came again, and then again, however softly. With a sigh, he stood, pulled on a robe, and walked as softly as he could toward the door.

Three guilty faces greeted him. Jamie and Rob said, at once, "We didn't mean to wake you."

"I couldn't sleep," said Diamond, almost over them.

Kenneth sighed. "Neither could I. Breakfast first—but that doesn't start until sunrise—and then the spells."

"We could start checking our work," said Rob, diffidently.

Kenneth shook his head. "That, we want to do by daylight."

#

The sky glowed like a fire opal, red and orange and fiery pink filling the clouds as if they glowed from within. The roses in the garden seemed more brilliant, and more blazing, than by daylight. The four of them sat, quietly, on the low stone fence of the pavement in one niche. The air was still cool with night.

Master Tidwell, passing by them on the porch, raised an eyebrow and walked on, toward the dew-laden grass. Pearl, her lip curled, followed Master Tidwell but muttered about fools about when they could still lie snugly abed.

"They must have to get that done before breakfast," said Diamond softly.

"Timing is all," said Rob.

Kenneth let his breath out slowly. The sky eased, toward peach and pink, and he said, "That sort of sunrise means rain later."

"Probably," said David from the doorway. He looked the four of them up and down, and his mouth pursed.

Kenneth pushed off the fence to stand. "Breakfast?"

#

The kitchen lay in stillness, and was even cooler than the outside air. No one else was there, and none of them spoke. Kenneth was glad when they laid aside their bowls and spoons to head out—and even more glad when he heard the voices that showed that Master Tidwell and Pearl had ended their morning work, but not soon enough to catch them.

Minutes later, they reached the casting room, to check their work twice and three times by the growing daylight. Kenneth checked the work that would trace their path four times—he could imagine ways that would be larger and more tortuous than all the labyrinths he had ever been in, combined. But they still, before the hour was out, gathered the things up, traipsed out the door, and followed David down a different set of stairs, one that needed a luminous spell as soon as they set foot on it.

By its light, they descended three flights of stairs, switching back and forth, lit only by their luminous spell, and with their shadows stark on the walls. Then a coiling stair led up again before turning into tunnel that led smoothly but slowly downward.

Kenneth looked at the stone—the same stone as the castle—and fought down a groan as foolish discouragement of the younger ones.

"I didn't know they had a labyrinth in the Castle," said Jamie, sourly, his voice echoing. "Protection is one thing, but I would have thought that you had to make the walls of roses to make the magics mix."

"They don't," said Diamond. "That's the purpose of this—structure. It's not a protective spell. It's a ensnaring spell. To prevent anything leaking out. They must have inordinate need to seal off the magic."

"More than Quiet Valley?" said Rob in disbelief.

"Perhaps they just thought they might need it," said Jamie, sounding more thoughtful. "If this was one of the first, perhaps."

"No," said Rob, definitely. "Castle Rosarium got its door to the Boneyard as one of the last places."

"Perhaps—they realized it was really needed," said Jamie, and scowled. "But they would have gone back to rebuild the others if it were. . . ."

"It's the sleepers," said David, his voice deep. "To the best of our knowledge, they all lie in mere enchanted sleep. No one wants them to sleep with kings and conquerors if it can be helped."

That silenced them. Their footsteps echoed, their shadows loomed, and Kenneth found that David's words had summoned up the perils ahead, and he could not lay the thoughts again. They could sleep with kings and conquerors—

Whether they went on or went back and put a childish trust in the Order's protection, he reminded himself.

The tunnel opened into familiar flagstones, and his shoulders slumped in relief. Even if it meant being in the Boneyard, work would distract him from those.

They walked out, and into it, and lowered the Eightfold Stone to the floor, just outside the Boneyard. All four of them turned to face him in silence, their faces catching the light from the spell. He let out his breath. If he worked quickly enough, and failed ignominiously, they could still retreat in safety. He would just look like a fool.

With care, he held out his wand to center the spell, and began it. Moments later, a black but translucent sphere surrounded them.

The three pulled out their crystals with brisk confidence, as if they had never dreamed he could fail, and scried. Three repeated images of the Eye of the World appeared, and Jamie led off. David and Kenneth brought up the end, watching, as they picked out a path.

Their journey, this time, had far more stones along it. Opals ablaze with more colors than rainbows; coarse-grained granite carved in vague animal shapes, with edges being too sharp for being weathered into vagueness; thin pieces of slate with writing on them; marble sliced even finer, fit for a window—he watched it go by until his fingers itched. So much had been learned and lost.

David did not turn into a raven, or even look strained as he walked along. They passed shelves filled with pebbles. Some were wave-worn glass, but others showed no sign of anything extraordinary, not even a vein running through the rock or an odd color. Jewelry tumbled on the next shelves, and it did not even all hold gemstones.

Diamond gasped. Kenneth blinked—they certainly had not walked as far as at the Cabinet of Curiosities—and looked. The Eye of the World. There was no mistaking it for any other, not at that size, and with all those colors blazing through it. Jamie and Rob pocketed their stones and pressed the edge of the sphere until it encompassed the Eye. Their arms went about the stone, to take it up from the shelf.

Diamond scowled at her scry stone. "It's *changing*. The path back is—" She spread her free hand.

"Much?" said Kenneth sharply.

"No, but if it increases—"

"It will," said David, surveying the shelves about them. "It's not the path to the shelf, but to the Eye. You two—" He pointed at Jamie and Rob. "—walk behind her." When Jamie scowled, he added, "You already broke your scrying spells by putting away your stones."

Kenneth walked back, slowly, to ensure the shield remained up about them all as they trudged on. When he knelt before the stairs to take up the Eightfold Stone, he felt light-headed with relief.

They weren't done yet, he reminded himself as they ascended. First they had to return, and then they had to scry something, and something of use that they could recognize. Then they had to persuade the master wizards of the prudence and wisdom of using that knowledge. Then they had to actually attack—and triumph—against the Web, which was not weak. Their enemies had triumphed at the Fittons.

The stair turned.

No, all of that except the return came second. The first thing after the stairs was securing the Eightfold Stone.

On the other hand, perhaps only scrying was protected against when a grown man tried it. Attacking might prove much easier for the Order.

Through the stairs, up into the corridor. Kenneth let out a long, gushing breath, and wondered if the route protected them.

"I suppose," said David, his voice hollow and melancholy, "that there is no hope of persuading you to wait till the morrow for your spellcraft."

The three's laughter was more child-like than anything he had heard from them since—before they had arrived for the term. They had sounded that young the term before. They hurried for the stairs.

David turned to Kenneth. "You know you can not shoo them from the room. You have no reason to believe that doing no more than being in the room will leave them immune."

"Nevertheless." Kenneth surprised himself with how harsh his voice was, and followed the three up the stairs. David followed him.

"And," said David, on the landing, "at some point tomorrow, you may discover that you have fished, and fished, and fished, and can fish no more. You may have let one of them do it."

"I hope not," caroled Jamie from the room. "That means it would take longer."

"Enough," said Kenneth. "I will start looking for the latest mechanica that they have made."

David followed him into the room, joined them around the table, and quenched the light.

Moments later, the image of gleaming metal loomed in the stone. A larger mechanica than before, it was complete except for the gap awaiting the stone. A large stone, Kenneth noted. He looked past it, at the walls, for any sign where it was. The stone looked like that behind the rose in the scrying stone—

The floor trembled, and the air *twisted* about them. Kenneth grabbed the Eye of the World, but felt no stone affecting it. For a sickening moment, he wished he had not put away the Eightfold Stone.

Then he hurtled through the air. Darkness surged about him, sometimes touched with gray, purple, brown, or blue, and with nothing, and no one, visible, he hoped that the others had escaped.

His path twisted and turned, and with a wrench, stopped. His feet found stone under them—flagstones no larger than his foot. Gloom lay all about, and he could not tell where what light there was came from. His heart hammered, his breath came harshly, and a frightened whimper came from behind him, making him feel icy cold. He turned. Jamie, Rob, and Diamond stood behind him, their faces like ghosts in the gloom. A flap of the wings showed where David perched.

He forced his breath in and out. With David a raven, he had to act.

Walls stood to either side, built of small stones mortared together. Between that and the flagstones, this was not the Labyrinth of Thought.

Then, they had not known that labyrinth as soon as they arrived.

"You stopped us, didn't you?" he said to the raven.

David nodded with as much solemnity as a bird could muster, more than Kenneth would have thought possible. Kenneth sighed.

"We can hope that the wizard did not intend to bring us here, that David disrupted the spell that thoroughly, but the door at Graytowers did not bring me and Jamie to the wizards, only to the Labyrinth. And—" His gaze moved over the three of them. "That spell was set to catch youths and maidens. Do *not* trust to their missing that gap in any other spell, either."

Jamie nodded, sharply. "Put the Eye of the World away. A shame to lose it now, but—it's not useful."

"I have a bag," said Diamond, and moments later, she was knotting up the draw string and saying, "We don't know if catching both of you in the opening spell affected where you landed." She scowled, looking up. "I suppose it does not matter until we are free to analyze the spellcraft."

Rob drew a deep breath and looked at the way. His voice was firm. "Wands out."

"And curse at once," said Diamond. "As you two did at the Labyrinth of Thought." She looked down as she drew her wand. "I—I could use the spell to find a way to a doorway. Perhaps."

"I *could* use it to find roses," said Rob. "This is the place with them, from the crystal. Whether it leads to the outside, or to the heart of this place—where we might foil them—it has to be better than blindly blundering."

Diamond scowled, and nodded. "It could lead to both—a doorway *and* the roses."

"Good," said Jamie. "David escapes to the open air, and we foil their plans."

They all looked at him.

"There's no point in forgetting that things can go well. We have to keep our eyes open to seize our chances as they arrive." Jamie flourished his wand. "That's how Kenneth and I escaped the Labyrinth of Thought, and that's how we'll escape this one, too."

David cawed.

"Wands out," said Kenneth. "Curse first, question after. And walk. The longer we wait, the more time we give them to prepare for us."

"I will watch the path," said Diamond. "To see if there is a pattern to it."

"Wise," said Kenneth, and turned to Rob.

After a moment, Rob pointed down the way they had faced as they arrived. Kenneth felt a misgiving. If they faced it, perhaps it was the way the spell had carried them, and they walked on their own feet to the fate their enemies intended.

And perhaps it was not, he told himself.

#

The corridor twisted and turned, and forked over and over, with nothing to tell one way from the next, but Rob's spell never faltered. Neither the light, nor the stony smell, nor the width of the corridor shifted. The stones used did, some, but so subtly that only someone knowledgeable in stonework could tell—shifts in the grain, and finer differences.

David flew, or walked, or perched on one shoulder or another. Kenneth glanced at him, remembered how there was never any sign that he would turn, whether to bird or to man, and kept his attention on the way. If this maze ever showed any signs of its magic, he could pick those out.

Diamond said nothing about their path, and they must have walked far, far, far long than in the Cabinet.

Where time had fooled him, he reminded himself.

"I wonder if we can tell the time," mused Jamie.

"I have a timely spell in order," said Diamond, looking at a side passage. "It's after noon. An hour and a half."

His feet ached as if realizing the time had brought the pain. He walked on. No one asked for the time again, as hours built up.

Finally, a door appeared ahead, as blockish as the corridor, iron-bound, with no lock that they could see. Rob pointed to it in silence.

David flew ahead, briefly stood a man, cast a spell, faced them, said, "It's open," and was a raven again.

Kenneth let out his breath. Perhaps they would need David to take a man's form again in order to escape. Perhaps David would be able, if the need arose.

But Rob could not go first, not when he held the spell. Kenneth went to open the door.

Sweetness gushed in. A courtyard of black stone held bushes with snow-white roses, the flowers so thick they all but hid the greenery. Overhead the sky flamed in scarlet, peach, and flame across the thin clouds.

Most of the courtyard was hidden by roses, but it was not a thicket. Paved paths wound between the bushes. Kenneth inched outside. David walked along, just behind him, silent as his head shifted from side to side, and his dark eyes picked out this and that. The three almost, despite the path's narrowness, managed to walk side by side as they inched out and peered about.

Nothing moved in the garden, not even so much as a leaf nodding in a breeze, but he, too, had to look for a doorway out. They should return quickly if they found none, and head the other way.

Color swirled ahead, more vivid and brilliant than the sunset, like a cloud that formed an oval gemstone. Kenneth vaguely heard the spells hurled by the others as he tried to entangle the thing, but the spell passed through it as if it had no form. In the moment when he, dismayed, caught his breath and wondered whether a spell could imprison cloud, the color took on new form. A wizard appeared before them, wearing robes like a fire opal, squarely built, his short hair and beard as white as the roses about him.

Jamie started another spell, but their voices were all raised in a jumble of spells of binding and confinement.

With a contemptuous laugh, the wizard waved his wand. Roses surged out and seized them. Thorns prickled with startling pain. Kenneth cried out, and felt the blood trickling on his hands.

Rob began another spell, and the wizard, scowling, pointed his hand. Other branches grabbed Rob with blinding speed, and the others. Thrashing only drew blood. Kenneth turned his head, and a branch lashed across his face. For a moment, he feared it would blind him. He froze, and the branches wove about, holding him in place.

David leapt upward, flapping his wings, flying as close to straight up as he could. Shoots sprang up and snagged him, pulling him down. David straggled frantically, cawing at the wizard. Blood appeared on the black feathers, and several feathers floated down. Kenneth tried to collect his breath, and managed to wonder whether David knew the wizard, or just was enraged by their capture, but —his changing would only kill him.

He might not be able to stop it, came a cold thought. And the roses about David were turning red.

The roses about the others were turning red as well. Three or four about Diamond, seven or so about Rob, dozens about Jamie, and out of the corner of his eye, he could see red petals fluttering about him. The thorns were sharp.

The wizard laughed again. "Neither man nor woman, *youth nor maiden*, boy nor girl, will hinder my plans—and certainly, no crow!" He looked them all over. "Struggle all you like. I prefer the blossoms to be white, but I will not begrudge you."

Kenneth let his breath out. Even Jamie, he thought, had ceased his fight.

The wizard turned away. Kenneth blinked. The man had not, after all, come out to see his captives, or if he had, he wished to do another mission as well. He looked at—it was hard to see about him, all the more in the sunset light, but Kenneth thought he looked over a mechanica. Then the wizard moved about it, and their view was clear. Diamond groaned. It was the mechanica, perfectly, entirely built, lacking only the stone.

The wizard inspected every inch. Then he turned and walked out. A door snicked shut.

Time passed. Nothing stirred. He let out his breath. Leaves shifted, a little, about his mouth.

It felt like, though it could not have been, minutes when Jamie said, "What? He just left us here with the mechanica they—or he—put so much into? Without bothering to start it?"

"Time's not right," said Diamond, wearily. Her head hung a little, and she winced and jerked it back up. "It's liminal magic. After all his work, he wants the magic to be as strong as it can be. It seems that sunset does not suffice."

Silence reigned. Not so much as a breeze moved in the rose leaves to make a sound. Nothing came from beyond the walls, whether it was silent outside, or the maze they came through was thick enough to muffle the sound of waves, or lowing cattle, or a monastery's bells.

It would need magic to muffle the last, but —the wizard would want to keep this place silent. Making a mechanica would be loud enough that he would want to keep the noise inside.

Kenneth sighed. He would also want it far away from everywhere else, lest it be noticed merely as a vast labyrinth. There would be wilds outside.

A sound came from Jamie, as if he were thinking, and though the sunset grew less light and more dark, Kenneth saw Jamie moving among the branches—slowly, very slowly.

After a moment, Jamie stopped. His voice pain-filled, he said, "It can tell when you move, even slowly."

Rob said, his voice dull, "It has to wear off. It's based on a plant, and not even a tree, let alone an oak or a fir. Living and dying is intrinsic to them. It would be a master wizard indeed who could split off that from its other virtues."

"Roses last for weeks," said Kenneth. "At least the flowers. The leaves, all summer. The bushes, for years, sometimes."

Rob sighed. "You heard of the spell, back at Castle Rosarium. It tears people to pieces and drinks their blood. I have never heard of a a wizard who used it to imprison people for long."

"Then," said Diamond, "we should escape and add to the knowledge of that spell."

Kenneth closed his eyes. Wearing off might prove faster. Test every hour, he told himself. Watch the sky to measure. It was not as if he would get—if any of them would get—any sleep.

The sunset had turned to crimson and violet. The sky overhead was still blue, but carried a single star. He wished he could still bring himself to wish on one. He eyed the three, who had slumped as best they could in their roses; he would not see them again until morning.

He opened his mouth to warn them against bleeding themselves dry, when David cawed—and then again, and a third time. In the silence after, Kenneth strained his ears.

Voices, however faint. He could not make out what they said. Jamie looked up, sharply, and winced.

His heartbeat marked the moments. Finally, the voices came clear, abruptly, as if they had come about a corner.

"That was the whole agreement. I would never have consented to help you otherwise. You have nothing else I want."

The second voice was of the wizard who had trapped them. "You are too impatient. Timeliness is all."

A snort and then—"It's not patience that I lack. It is the folly to trust *you*. You've already bungled this once."

The wizard sighed. "Very well, very well—you will never excel in any study if you expect tasks always to prosper the first time you attempt them—but since you have insisted, we shall do it now."

Two dim shapes appeared in the doorway. For a moment, Kenneth thought that they had given themselves the vision of cats, or even true seeing in the dark. Then a small light flared up and cast a bluish glow. The wizard looked uncanny by it. The weasel-faced man next to him glanced about the garden as if fearing attack.

David cawed. Kenneth had not realized how bitter it could sound.

The weasel-faced man stopped. "Wait a moment. We need it."

"So we do," said the wizard. He walked up to a bush.

"You didn't just leave it here?" The voice rang with astonishment.

The wizard's voice continued tranquil. "The Fittons were no fools. Nor were they known for the weakness of their spells. It would protect against rain."

Jamie tensed so much that even by the bluish light, Kenneth saw the roses darkening about him. They looked black, not red. Diamond and Rob looked aghast. Kenneth felt a fool. He had asked whether anything had been stolen from the Fittons.

The wizard moved through the spell, the same one he had seen Rob cast. The leaves rustled—sullenly, not as if a breeze were blowing them—and the branches move aside, far more slowly than they had for Rob's spellcraft.

The thorns pricked at Kenneth. He forced his breath in and out and watched the bush as the branches revealed what lay within.

Two skeletons hung there. Kenneth swallowed. Neither the wizard nor the weasel looked at the bones. Beneath the weasel's avid gaze, the wizard knelt to take up the box.

Kenneth closed his eyes. There was no doubt left, then.

He forced his eyes open again. The wizard already lugged the box toward Jamie.

"You're a fool," said the weasel. "He'll be worse than his parents. You shouldn't have shown him the bones."

"*I*," said the wizard, "learn from experience."

The rose branches swung up to take the box from his hands, and others twined about Jamie's arm. He fought. He fought so hard that the roses for feet around turned that deceptive black, and David, with a caw, threw himself against the vines, trying to break free, but the branches pressed on Jamie's hand and forced it on the latch.

The click sounded, quiet though it was. The branches slumped. Jamie collapsed. Tears glittered on his face.

With a flourish, the wizard lowered the box onto the path, before the weasel. The weasel pulled it open, and took out another box. Balancing it on his lip and using his free hand let him shut the first, to serve as a table. The light over it cast shadows and made the carved sides impossible to make out.

The weasel slowly, with a smile of anticipation, opened the box. The latch clicked, and he lifted the lid. And then his face froze into a mask of horror.

"What is it?" said the wizard sharply. When only silence answered, his voice grew sharper. "What is wrong? What is so horrible? It didn't turn you to stone, or kill you between one breath and the next."

A moment later, he said, "I suppose it could have stolen your voice."

"Be quiet," snarled the weasel. He reached in and pulled out—a box. It gleamed like mother-of-pearl.

"A box," he snarled. "A thrice-accurst *box*!"

The wizard looked appalled. Moving slowly, like an ancient man, he walked over. Then he scowled in thought.

"That's—that's a Dombrey box." Slowly, he turned to look at Diamond. With a sudden, savage look of hope on his face, the weasel looked as well.

"What fools you are," said Diamond, her voice cool and contemptuous. "Even from here, even by this light, I can see the patterns: the sun, the moon, stars, a clock. Even for a Dombrey, that box will open when the time is ripe, and no sooner." She shifted a little. "And no later, either."

For a moment, the weasel's face was blank. Then it contorted to a mask of rage. He whirled on the wizard, who seemed almost composed. Kenneth blinked.

"This—Is—ALL—YOUR—FAULT!" He stepped toward him, and made a fist.

The wizard's face set like granite.

"You and your dilly-dallying! If you had done that with the father instead of the son! It may never open now—I may have missed the only time—"

Words seemed to choke him.

"I did as I pledged," said the wizard. "You have no grounds for complaint."

The weasel raised his fists. The nearest roses leapt out to seize him. Kenneth squeezed his eyes shut, but he could not close his ears.

The screams were mercifully brief. When, minutes later, he opened his eyes, the roses stood as calm as before, and he could only suspect that the new body hung as the old skeletons had.

The wizard was gone. The sky was pure black, ablaze with stars. The pale Milky Way ran through it. In the starlit garden, everything was vague shapes in black and gray and white. Enough that he could make out where the others were.

He managed to make his mouth move. "Jamie," he said, and a thought struck him. "David. I am so sorry."

After a moment, as if remembering that they had just learned of the deaths, Diamond and Rob echoed his words.

David cawed softly.

"Thank you," said Jamie, his voice wooden.

None of them struggled against the roses. For a moment, Kenneth pondered telling them to. To let the roses drain them dry. When the wizard could have torn them apart as easily as he had the weasel-faced man, he had to keep them alive for some purpose, and Kenneth could not imagine a good one. Struggling might thwart him, and it was not as if they had many ways to even try. The Fittons, two grown and practiced wizards, had trained as much as anyone could to face these evils, and failed.

Rob's voice was dull. "I might be able to move the roses. If only they did not move so swiftly—"

"Something to bear in mind," said Diamond, wearily. "We might yet see an opening."

"Rest," said Kenneth and wondered how he sounded. "Whatever the wizard intends for us, we will have a better chance, if any, if we rest." After a minute of silence, he said, "He may work on the mechanica and give us an opening."

Jamie snorted. "We can slip between the cracks."

Kenneth said nothing. Neither did anyone else. He wished he could cast the prefect spell, but he closed his eyes.

He woke, shivering. The thorns did not seem to prick so sharply, but the branches were like little ropes. Bloody red light glared from the east, where the half moon loomed over the wall. Just risen—and therefore just before midnight.

Happy birthday, he told himself. Many happy returns of the day. He glanced about. The others slept, and he did not want to disturb them.

He tugged at his arm. Thorns bit. He wished he had had the wit to use his left arm for the test.

Not that it was likely to make a difference—Heaven help them all.

Sleep, he told himself, and shivered again. The others slept, he had slept himself for all the cold, and he would not find a way to escape at this hour.

Unless the wizard's time came at night.

He sighed and studied the moon. Half full—it would reach zenith near dawn. The moon was always changing to full from new, to new from full, and he had no notion how it might affect the spell-craft. If he had studied liminality more closely—

He would have had to forgo his other studies. He would never have scried this, and never have tripped the trap to be brought here. And neither would any of the others. David would still be a raven, but safe. Jamie would be ignorant of what had befallen his parents, but safe.

The moon inched higher, and shrank in size, and grew paler, almost golden, and then to a pearl in the sky, though it still left the scene in grayish shades.

He did not even know whether the time the wizard awaited had anything to do with the sky, or anything else in common with the rest of the world. If he knew liminal magic, no doubt he could use his own birthday—his coming of age at that—if, that was, he could use any spellcraft at all.

He looked toward his hands. He could not see them properly. He was amazed he could still feel them after hanging so long.

A cold breeze made him shiver again. He yanked on his left arm. It came free.

For a blank moment, he felt certain that he dreamed, but the knowledge did not rouse him further. He blinked and tried to move his other arm and then his legs.

Whatever had stilled the motion of the branches had not removed their thorns. Stab after stab, many times hard enough to draw blood—when he freed his right arm, he thought of his wand and spellcraft. He could not risk it. Not when a gesture, blocked by a rose, could set all awry. He was their only hope, uncertain though he was.

He inched his way out. Thorns drew more blood, and roses turned darker than they had when he was captive.

His escape and the noises had not woken the others. He drew a deep breath and moved his arms, wincing from the thorn wounds, but disentangling from the roses would be easier with outside help.

He snorted. Though easier still with spellcraft.

He eased over to Rob. The flowers and leaves almost hid the boy from view.

"Rob," he said, his voice low. "Rob." He looked in the branches and wondered how much blood it would draw if he reached in to poke him. Shaking was obviously impossible. "*Rob.*"

Jamie moaned. Then he said, sharply, "*Kenneth?*"

"Shush!" said Kenneth—realizing after a moment that he had been louder than Jamie. Diamond and Rob, from the noises they made, were rousing, and David eyed him, with moonlight glittering from the eye.

He heard nothing else.

"What happened?" whispered Diamond.

"I woke. And then, after an hour or two, I pulled loose. No, I don't know why it weakened, but it bled me on the way out. So—Rob next."

David cawed.

Diamond said, "After all he did, it seems strange that he let that great a flaw in."

"It may be a trap," said Kenneth. "We have to risk it. He did, after all, leave the gap that let me scry in the first place."

Rob nodded, and the leaves rustled about his head. "How—how hard did you have to pull?"

"Not very." Kenneth leaned into the bush. The branches let him move them aside, until his fingers hit one actually holding Rob. Then he could no more move it than he could move a mountain. He wrestled with it, stuck himself with many thorns, and got Rob not one whit freer.

"Kenneth," said Diamond, her voice low.

Kenneth, breathing hard, fell back from the roses. They were so close, so close, there had to be a way—

"It's your birthday, isn't it?"

Kenneth blinked. Then he scowled, but he said, "Yes."

Her voice turned singsong. "The spell holds boys and girls, youths and maidens, men and women. But this is the day when you leave off being a youth and become a man."

Silence fell. The thoughts fell into order with appalling swiftness—an order so neat and obvious he wondered he did not see it when first he realized he could win free, and leaving him no hope.

"You—"

Only from the direction could Kenneth knew who spoke. Jamie's voice was not recognizable.

"Kenneth. You have to escape if you can. Save your life at least. Bring back news of this evil."

For a moment, Kenneth stood in silence, and felt mulish.

"If you hadn't come with me through that door, you would never have been caught up in this, or been in peril of your life."

Kenneth did not move.

In the silence, David cawed, faintly.

"We're not that far gone yet." Kenneth glanced at the moon. "There's still the mechanica and damaging it past repair."

The metal glinted.

"Did you learn impairing spells?" said Jamie.

Kenneth winced. Stonework built, it did not destroy. Even scholars who continued after the regular course had to specialize for that. He had no useful spells.

He wished that speaking spells were easier, but he walked over to look. Jamming something into the gears, perhaps, but the metal was strong enough to shred cloth, and fine enough that trying to jam a shoe in would get nowhere.

Branches from the rosebushes? The though made him shudder.

There the gap stood, awaiting the stone. For a moment, he thought, pointlessly, that they must have found a fine opal, the gap was quite large. Then his thoughts moved, and his heart started to hammer.

"Diamond, where do you have the Eye of the World?"

"Huh?" said Rob, but Kenneth already walked toward her.

"It's not a liminal machine until it has its opal. It will not be a liminal machine with the Eye of the World in it."

He dragged in a deep breath. It was tantamount to suicide, it would enrage the wizard, and it would preclude any chance at escape—as if they had any. At least his motives were pure.

"She—she put it away," said Jamie faintly.

"In a bag," said Kenneth.

"On my right," she barely murmured.

Where the branches had shifted together into a particularly tight weave. He bent over, forced down a sigh, and tried to reach through the tangles.

He moved too swiftly, and a branch clawed at his face, sending blood dripping warmly down his face. He jerked back—other thorns caught at him, causing more blood to spurt—and he tried to wipe it from his forehead.

"Don't!" Jamie leaned forward—Kenneth could see the roses darkening—and said, "This isn't some kind of tale. There isn't a lovely maiden in a tower who can weep into your eyes and restore your sight if you put them out."

Kenneth tried to staunch the bleeding again. They were only scratches from thorns, he had not bled that much when escaping, but the blood kept coming. Sweat carried it into his eyes, and he blinked; he could do nothing blind, and it looked very like he could not save his sight from its flow.

"Use your sleeve," said Rob. "It's not going to survive, even if we do."

It took longer to tear it off than he had realized, and then to bind it on—but the bandage did what his fingers had failed, and he could not feel the blood dripping.

"Now," said Jamie, "*go*. Bring news back. Give the Order a chance to stop him and avenge us."

"How?" said Kenneth. "Scry my path with the Eye of the World? And we already know he can move that mechanica, even if I could escape alone."

After a silence, Rob said, diffidently, "He might lose his chance to start it, with motion," but his voice held little hope.

The sky was starting to gray, in the east. Still a deep charcoal gray, but not black. Kenneth drew a deep breath and went back to kneel down by Diamond. He peered through the branches, and looked at the bag. That bag caught in the branches.

"Diamond," he said slowly. "Lean the bag into the branches."

She was silent but after a minute, he could see the tears in the cloth. The stone could just barely be seen, and it was not falling.

He stared at it as if his glare could speed it. Then he snorted and reached out. The most basic spell of stonework, though he would have to lay the spell on lightly.

Diamond gasped. The Eye of the World ripped open the bag and smashed into the branches. Kenneth cut the spell, and it fell into his hand with its ordinary lightness.

"That was so heavy!" said Diamond.

"A weighty spell," said Kenneth. "The one you learned in the first week—and learned to apply to feathers. A stone was simple."

He stood with the Eye of the World in hand for a moment. Odd that having to do the deed reminded him that he was only foiling the wizard's plot, not saving their lives. He strode over the mechanica, his heart beating harder with every step, before he could dream that he could dream up some plan to escape using the stone, and lowered it inside.

For a moment, nothing happened. His heartbeat sank back down to normality. Perhaps—perhaps he could flee, and bring back news—

Then, the mechanica began to hum, deep inside. The sound grew. Gears turned, meshes interlocked, and delicate arms reached out to hold the Eye in place, like a jewel on a giant's ring.

The colors shifted in the Eye, as in an opal, but here they took on form, showing—showing his father's house, and his father with his oldest brother, both looking smug. Kenneth forced his breath in and out.

Then the visions started to float out of the Eye.

Kenneth took a step backward as a falcon flew into him, but it did him no harm, only flew over the vast cliff the vision also showed. Others appeared around him: wild rose bushes, their white bloom looking like vast sheep in a meadow, the Lighthouse casting its last beams over the sea as day dawned, the wizard pothering over his papers.

The mechanica was intended to extend the virtues of the stone. And it had controls—he hurried to look at the knobs. Drawing a deep breath, he summoned up a new vision, to show the land about them. The labyrinthine path made him wince, but he could make out the surroundings. Paths led from the labyrinth, but he had no time to escape. He reached to adjust where they appeared, as other visions flickered about, flowing out from the mechanica or appearing far away.

One showed the wizard glanced up as one vision flitted through his room. Kenneth's mouth set. He did not have much time, then.

He tested a lever. One specific vision appeared, and his breath gushed out. Rob had been right: a map of the land, allowing him to control where the visions flew. And he could focus in on places there.

He set the visions to fly off like falcons, toward the Castle Rosarium, Quiet Valley, the Lighthouse—and in all of the places, to where master wizards could see. After a moment, with care, he sent one to Graytowers, into Master Bonaventure's study.

The sound of footsteps jerked him away. He could not concentrate while the wizard blasted him, and he could try to shield the others. He stepped from the mechanica, stood between the doorway and the rose bushes where the others were captive, and reminded himself that he and Jamie had taken down master wizards.

He drew a deep breath, trying to steady himself.

The wizard appeared in the doorway. Kenneth hurled a spell to bind him.

The wizard's eyes flashed, leaving Kenneth blinded for a moment, and blinking away tears for more.

"Do you think we did not *at once* protect ourselves from such petty mischief as the greatest fool among the scholars might learn?" His lip curled. "Not that I would have been troubled. You caught only some slight and foolish wizards with your spellcraft."

His robe roiled with color, Kenneth realized.

"There is nothing you can do to stop me." He raised his wand.

Stop, thought Kenneth. Stop—

He cast David's spell. The arm stopped in motion. Kenneth felt drained more than any spell had ever left him before. No wonder David had turned into a raven and stayed so for so long.

Moments later, the wand started to move again, slowly but without hesitation.

David, Kenneth reminded himself fiercely, had stopped all five of them, and more motion. He could not stint, any more than David had—when he would not even turn into a raven for it. He cast the spell again. The wand wavered. There was never a spell that required only a simple sweep of the wand, Kenneth reminded himself, and cast it again. And again. Cold though it was, he sweated, watching the arm moving slowly but endlessly.

The wizard spat out the words. "You. Can't. Do. It. For—ever."

"Don't have to!" said Kenneth. His breath came harshly. He might need to longer than he could. He cast the spell again.

Another spell sounded, a wizard shouted behind him, and he could not so much as turn to see who their new attacker was.

Roses surged out to seize his foe. Master Tidwald, his drab hair and beard untidy even for him, strode past him.

Kenneth lowered his wand and fought for breath. He had held out. He had held out, long enough—

Moments later, he felt the hands seizing him. Gently, they lowered him to the ground. He did not even try to stir. He listened to the sounds about him, but saw David, and the three, as they walked into his field of vision—tattered, bloodied, but all of them walking. He smiled. And David a man again, and not a raven at all.

"Leave him there," said Master Tidwald "We shall have to ensure that it is safe to leave."

David sat by him, and the three, all of them quiet as the master wizards moved about the garden. The Eye of the the World still sent up visions here and there, until Master Bonaventure sat its controls for a minute or two, twisting, turning, and gauging. Earnest, low-voiced discussions ensued, loud enough that Kenneth could hear that they could not remove the Eye.

Coffins were borne in, and Jamie looked away. Diamond grabbed his hand, and Rob the other, as the Fittons' bodies were laid in them—and a third coffin for the other wizard of the Web. Kenneth felt surprised to see that his hair was russet-red. A master wizard followed on the heels of the coffins' closing to scold them for letting injured children wait. And in the morning cold as well.

"We can't put the blood back," he said ominously. "They need rest and curative spells. And above all else, they need to rest somewhere warmer than this."

He waved a hand at the bushes. Kenneth glanced over, and winced at the vivid reds there. He had bled the most, or perhaps Jamie had, but none of them had bled little.

"All the more reason to not move them lightly," said Master Bonaventure. "Any attack would be harder on them. Therefore, the prudent thing is warming spells."

"Conjuring spells!" said one thin woman, poking her head through the doorway. "Conjure up blankets, and let them rest. But after the posset! To ensure that this does not give them bad dreams for the rest of their lives."

Someone muttered that they needed a triple strength posset for that.

Minutes later, wrapped up in a red blanket, with wizards still bustling about, Diamond whispered, "I don't think I'm going to sleep quite yet."

David smiled. "Just rest. You will have days to sleep. If I have to get your parents to pull you from Graytowers for the term."

#

It was noon, and growing quite warm, when some said, "She's a Dombrey. Let her try to open the box."

"It's set to open only at some condition," said Diamond wearily.

"All the more reason," said Mistress—Gloria, lifting it up. "It might open this hour, and not in another."

"Might have opened at dawn, and not now," grumbled Diamond.

"Besides, I have heard your sister boast of them. Pearl claimed that they had the great magical property of appearing in a timely manner."

Diamond rolled her eyes. "Just stories. Never met anyone who had actually had that happen—"

When Mistress Gloria put the box down beside her, she reached out her hand. It clicked open.

How much the garden had bustled, moments earlier, became clear, for it all stopped. Every gaze turned silently toward Diamond.

She swallowed and pushed the lid back. After a moment, she started to laugh, however hollowly. It took her a minute to master herself.

"It's a box," she said. "It's a—" She looked again, and her face froze. It took her a minute to say, distinctly, "It's a Mornington box."

The words sank in slowly, and made no sense even then.

"What could be more natural?" said a man walking across the garden. A dark-haired, fair-skinned man—Diamond's father, Kenneth realized. "The most common use of those boxes was to deliver an inheritance. With a Kenneth Mornington here—" He spread his hands.

"If—" said Jamie. "If he had forced her to try it last night—"

"Let us avoid such unpleasant conjunctures," said Corwin Dombrey. "Let us rather rejoice that we have escaped what could have come to pass, and can contemplate, instead, what was the purpose of your ancestor in sealing it up." He bent to take it up. "Which we can do better, young Master Kenneth, if you reveal what its contents are. And this is not a conditional box."

"It's very old," said Mistress Gloria. "In that style."

"So was the Dombrey one," said Master Corwin. "And the Flint one, at that." He put the box before Kenneth, who looked at the ruddy wood—cherry wood, he guessed—and slowly reached out.

It clicked open. With lay a book—a spellbook—and several gemstones. Master Corwin's eyebrows went up, but he said nothing.

Kenneth's breath flowed out, and he drew in back in again. Then he closed the box. "It will travel better so."

He did not listen with care to the whispered questions of how long ago there had been a Mornington wizard.

#

Despite the heat and the ruckus, Jamie, Rob, and Diamond all slept. He had nodded off once or twice himself, and so could not swear that David's unmoving awareness had been as constant as it seemed.

A mousy man, whose gray robes shimmered with colors, pronounced as if at a trial, "Gregory and William were those involved in this, and they had no allies. Simon, Lucinda, and Piers were recruited to assist and—" He cleared his throat. "William killed them all for ingratitude."

Someone snorted, somewhere in the garden.

"No one else has reasons to strike the children for their part. And there are no spells to prevent their escape."

"David," said Corwin Dombrey. "It was the talk of the Order. David Servant had been betrayed. Someone talked."

The mousy wizard cleared his throat again. "The truth of that matter is—someone gave William a spell to detect a particular bird. It would work on one that was a bespellment. And the spell was given years ago, long before anyone had any reason to suspect it would be a danger to David Servant. Perhaps even William."

In the quiet after, Kenneth thought that there was little they could do about that.

"Very well," said Master Bonaventure, sounding content indeed. "Back to Graytowers. The infirmary is best suited to deal with their injuries, and they will need to be tested before term to see what tutoring they will need."

I did my best for our studies, thought Kenneth, resentfully. With no help from the Order—except David.

"I hope there's a bed for me," said David. "Unless there's another infirmary that's more fit?"

Master Bonaventure shook his head.

Chapter 16—Conclusions

Birds whirled about the tower in the bright afternoon. Occasionally, the sound of voices reached the windows, but not even the tone, to guess whether they speculated brightly about the invalids in the tower, or groused over their studies.

Magic, Kenneth knew. They wanted the ill to have peace and quiet.

For all that, Master Bonaventure stood as if the room were a lecture hall with class about to begin. Then, Kenneth thought, he could not complain to Master Bonaventure that any of them were too ill for class. They had taken the tests of spellcraft, and David had even left.

He wondered whether they could attend as soon as term began.

"I read up on history while you were tested," said Master Bonaventure, tranquilly. "There was a Master Maximilian—who did stonework—who was a Mornington. Came from a merchant family and married a daughter of another. His children all turned merchants. So Master Maximilian commissioned boxes—his own, the Dombrey one—that a worthy heir might receive it.

"And there was a Master Edgar Flint who resented that, though the history does not say whether there was bad blood between them, or Master Edgar thought he had rights to what Master Maximilian stored there. But he stole it and sealed it away."

"To no avail," said Diamond, judiciously.

Master Bonaventure nodded. "Now we are done with the past and must speak of the future." He sat and spread out some papers. "You did not study evenly. Rob, you will need tutoring to even out in mathematics. Jamie, you will need the same in history."

The boys nodded gravely. Kenneth realized, startled, that they must have kept up in everything else. He wondered how much he would need.

"And then—Diamond, you are advanced for the fifth year course for stonework, but you are not ready for the sixth year. It will do you good to get in more practice on some of what you learned so—irregularly."

Kenneth blinked. They had not studied for longer than they studied at school. And they had taken days to get the books for it. How could she have blasted through four and a half years of study?

Master Bonaventure drew a deep breath. "Jamie, Rob, you are not quite ready for fifth year studies in stonework, but you are so close that we concluded that tutoring you would be wiser than making you repeat all of the fourth year. You were—spotty in your studies, even outside the history and mathematics. You will be ahead in a few respects even, but protection, and history and plants, are too narrow for your studies. You will need to generalize more." He sighed. "Some of your work is sixth year, Jamie, even in advance of Diamond's. And some is even seventh year. Using those books, we suspect you studied what you wished to study and did not dutifully follow along. It does not make a good foundation."

Jamie looked sullen.

"One would think that a master of stonework would be, of all wizards, the most knowledgeable about the need for a strong foundation."

Kenneth swallowed. He hadn't pushed them that hard to study. Indeed, all three of them stared at Master Bonaventure as if what he said made no sense. And not the rebukes for the specializing.

"Past that, Diamond, you have placed out of mathematics entirely. You can use the library or ask for aid, but you have mastered seventh year mathematics and must study on your own to continue. Rob, you have done the same in history. And, Kenneth, you have placed out of stonework."

For a minute, the words made no sense.

"You have the library, if you wish to advance," said Master Bonaventure. "You have Master Maximilian's book as well."

"I've used the library for the last two terms," said Kenneth. "I had hoped to stop studying by guesswork." He waved his hand at Rob and Jamie. "If I had known they were being patchy in their studies, I would have pounced like a hawk on a mouse to make them study more consistently."

Jamie snorted.

Rob said, seriously, "He would have."

"I'd do no more than keep my hand in—but who would hire me for any ordinary sort of building after I defeated the evil sorcerer William?"

"He wasn't a sorcerer," said Master Bonaventure.

"He is by now. For purposes of my finding employment."

The door opened. David stood there with a letter in hand.

Kenneth fought down a twinge of envy. Rob had received a flood of letters from parents and siblings. Diamond's mother had wrote as well—

"It's for you," said David, holding it out to Kenneth. He blinked, and took it.

A minute later, Rob said, "What is it?"

"It's from my parents." He felt astounded at how clear his voice was. He hoped it did not sound too hollow. "I asked for some spending money—to buy black clothes for—"

They knew that. Diamond was frowning.

"And they say that they won't, and also, that they will be on a journey when the fall term ends, and so I had best make arrangements for, and pay for, that. As I am grown."

His thoughts refused to fix. His tuition was paid for all seven years, but he did not know whether he could stay. He had more to pay for than his tuition.

David cleared his throat. "You were a minor still when you devised that spell, the globe that moves. I took the liberty of registering it on your behalf."

"It is a valuable spell," said Master Bonaventure. "Already wizards were asking for its use, and willing to pay the fee, as soon as they heard of it."

"They were indeed willing," said David. "There are already fees paid for the use of it. There will be more."

"Besides," said Rob, "you have no choice about where you will go then. Since you can not go home, my parents will insist on your coming to stay with us. After all, you saved my life. It's little enough."

Jamie laughed. "And they will try to recruit you for the Order."

"Good," said David. "If one thing is clear, it is that the Order is gravely lacking by having no wizards who are masters of stonework."

#

The day for the funeral was gray. How suitable.

Kenneth sighed, turning back to the room that had not had time to feel familiar after his spring arrival. Being sent back to the tower had not felt like settling in. The mischief of the opening of the fall term had glanced off like water from a duck, and he had noticed little more than that the gargoyles were once again few and generally silent. Now he had other matters.

He looked at the clothes. The most sober set he could muster. At least he had dark colors.

"Good morning," said Elgiva, radiantly gold in the doorway. She visibly smoothed out her smile as he looked over, and there was black cloth draped over her arm. "Gaius and Magdalena gave me leave to look at your clothes after they were laundered." She hesitated. "The story about the black got about, and I knew a spell to do it."

Kenneth blinked, stared, and collected his wits enough to take them and thank her for her thoughtfulness.

"Fortunate that classes do not start until after the funeral. Even if we are peevish because we wanted you to study with us—" She smiled. "I shall master my childishness. The three who are joining us can help with the spells. And it is good for you, this great advance."

#

By the gravesite, the clouds had turned to charcoal gray. They did not rain, or rumble thunder even in the distance, and they did not diminish the crowds.

Jamie, next to his uncle, received condolences gravely, with his red hair and black clothes making him look even paler. Half the mourners seemed awkward about David. Perhaps, thought Kenneth wryly, they thought he might turn into a raven, not knowing he had stayed in raven form for the days to master it and stay human now.

Kenneth stood awkwardly with Rob and Diamond. They garnered many glances, too.

Master Corwin came across the graveyard, with a woman his own age, and four people a generation older. Diamond introduced her mother and grandparents.

"Such a pity that Pearl could not make it," said Mistress Rosa, in a low voice, "but her studies are delicate. They were disrupted after all." Her voice went still lower. "Can you believe it? She can't go back to Quiet Valley."

"They are deeply concerned about the disruption," said Master Corwin. "All the more in what we have found in Master William's works—" He shook his head. "You have added to the places that the Order must guard, with that labyrinth and that garden."

Rob looked past them. Moments later, he was introducing Kenneth to his parents and a passel of siblings.

#

At Graytowers, on the first day of class, with the other fifth year scholars heading off to stonework class, a brightly blue bird flew up to Kenneth and hovered in midair.

"The top room on the third tower," it called, and vanished.

Some students hooted with laughter, and one said, "Foolish as leaping through that gate!"

Kenneth tried to smile, and headed off on the correct path, which few scholars traveled on. He climbed the stairs alone. Birds flitted by the windows as he passed them. Finally, he reached the floor. The room held no one else. It was obviously a classroom, with few desks, and a display case of stones. Some of which he could recognize from what he had read of Master Mortimer's work.

His heart started to beat not so much faster as harder. He only stood, looking about.

A door opposite opened. Behind was a room that could not fit in the tower, but a man in wizard's robes, with granite-gray hair and beard, swept in. He looked severely at Kenneth.

"You would be Kenneth Mornington. For this honors class."

"Yes, sir," said Kenneth, dry mouthed

He sniffed. "At least you are prompt. I must observe that several of Master Maximilian's spells have never been duplicated. I trust you will allow me to ensure that they do no harm."

Kenneth smiled. "Of course."

There was a scramble of claws and black feathers at the window, and the master wizard opened it. Moments later, David stood on the floor.

"And you would be David Servant. Not entirely prompt."

"Yes, Master Owen," said David.

"Since the students have deigned to arrive, class will begin. It will be prompt."

David grinned at Kenneth. Moments later, no longer grinning, they scribbled notes frantically.

#

Kenneth looked at the Mornington box.

Diamond worked, earnestly and happily, on resetting the conditions on hers, and Jamie had put his away in case some grandchild of his had need of one, and could bear to use it, but he—he supposed he could learn what he could. For now it would hold the book.

Master Owen would be disappointed if he did not. Despite the dangers.

He closed the box and stood. He could, he supposed, taking his running up those stairs and down again as his walk for the day. He ran a hand through his hair. That was one thing that had been easier in all the places they had been hidden.

"Good evening," said Diamond from the doorway, brightly. Others clumped behind her—Jamie and Rob, but Elgiva and others, as well. "The rumors insist that a special, advanced, honors class was set up just for you alone, but I thought it wise to check."

"You were wise," said Kenneth. "It is not true." He turned to face them. "David Servant is also taking the class."

Jamie chortled, and all the others started to laugh merrily.

"You," said Jamie, "are going to end up building a grand place to hold the Eye of the World and its mechanica. All by yourself."

"Not I alone," said Kenneth. "Diamond will do the mathematics for it, Rob will choose the best site, and I will design much of it. But *you* will be the one building it, to make the protections as strong as they can be."

"You left out building the homes near it," said Elgiva. "Near enough to keep watch, and use the Eye, but far enough off for your children to play freely. You will do that building."

Kenneth laughed. "You know me too well."

Elgiva smiled radiantly. Who knew? Kenneth thought. Perhaps he would live in one.

Also by Mary Catelli

Curses And Wonders
Dragon Slayer
Eyes of the Sorceress
Fever and Snow
Mermaids' Song
Sword and Shadow
The Book of Bone
Witch-Prince Ways
Dragonfire and Time
Enchantments And Dragons
Jewel of the Tiger
Over the Sea, To Me
The Dragon's Cottage
The Maze, the Manor, and the Unicorn
The White Menagerie
A Diabolical Bargain
Madeleine and the Mists
Magic And Secrets
The Lion and the Library
The Princess Goes Into The Forest
The Wolf and the Ward
The Witch-Child and the Scarlet Fleet
Treachery And Spells
Winter's Curse
Crow Curse

About the Author

Mary Catelli is an avid reader of fantasy, science fiction, history, fairy tales, philosophy, folklore and a lot of other things. (Including the backs of cereal boxes.) Which, in due course, overflowed into writing fantasy (and some science fiction).

www.ingramcontent.com/pod-product-compliance
Lightning Source LLC
Chambersburg PA
CBHW071144170626
46809CB00002B/761